THE GOLD CHIP

DOUGLAS HIRT

WOLFPACK
PUBLISHING
— EST 2013 —

The Gold Chip
Paperback Edition
Copyright © 2023 Douglas Hirt

Wolfpack Publishing
9850 S. Maryland Parkway, Suite A-5 #323
Las Vegas, Nevada 89183

wolfpackpublishing.com

Paperback ISBN 978-1-63977-997-0
eBook ISBN 978-1-63977-597-2
LCCN 2023936788

SOMERVILLE TOWN MAP

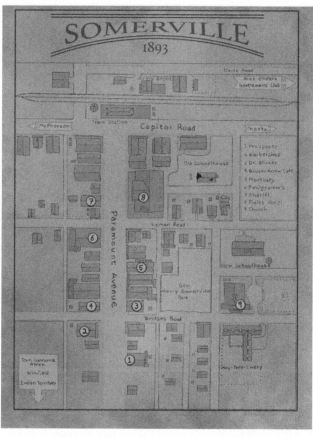

A special thank you to my son, Derick, for his work on the Somerville town map.

For Virg and Karen

THE GOLD CHIP

THE GOLD CUP

DAY ONE
MONDAY

An instant before Libby's gloved hand connected with the cold doorknob of Wilson's Barbershop, the door sprang open and an icy gust of howling blizzard whooshed her inside.

"Whoop!"

The five men gathered there turned at her abrupt appearance, eyes narrowing.

Mr. Tappermounty, who had seen her arrival and opened the door, closed it now cutting off the swirl of snow that whipped the hem of her skirt. He wore his usual black coat, black vest, and black tie; his face, austere and wan. Had it ever worn a smile? Not in the seventeen years Libby had known him. She often wondered what sort of melancholy, little boy he might have been.

Libby composed herself. Toasty air filled her lungs. The barbershop was strangely quiet, six pairs of male eyes staring at her as if she had left something unbuttoned. "I declare," she smiled brushing the snow from the sleeves of her coat, "this will be another three-dog night."

Dr. Blinker had alerted her that the town council

would be meeting here tonight—Mr. Wilson, Mr. Tappermounty, and...she looked around. Where was Dr. Blinker?

Sheriff Bainbridge frowned from his comfortable perch upon Mr. Wilson's red velvet Berninghause barber chair. The day the chair had arrived from Cincinnati, Ohio Mr. Wilson had invited the entire town to admire its fancy wood cravings, the rich upholstery, and shiny footrest. She'd written a nice article about the event for the *Independent*, earning her father two free haircuts.

Jimmy warmed his hands at the stove, his sleeves bound up in garters as if he'd just come from sorting mail. He grinned at her. She appreciated a friendly face. She and Jimmy were the same age, had gone to school together in the old one-room soddy east of town. Now a bright, new two-story brick schoolhouse stood at the end of Lyman Road where the mail-order houses were built.

To Libby's surprise, Lieutenant Danforth was numbered amongst the gathering. Grasping the bowl of his pipe as though to warm his fingers with it, he leaned casually on the counter, the elbow of his blue uniform blouse nestled recklessly amongst bottles of perfumed toilet water. His blue eyes sparked in the lamplight. "This is a pleasant surprise, Miss Barrett." The lieutenant's measured Southern drawl was as easy on the ears as was his face on the eyes.

"Thank you, Lieutenant." His presence at the town council meeting puzzled her. Jimmy, being the town's bookkeeper, had a legitimate reason to be here, but the commander of the tiny army depot alongside the railroad tracks?

Danny Wilson, perched on a chair and swinging his feet, grinned at her. "Hi-ya, Miss Barrett." He stuck a peppermint twist into his mouth and drew it slow through puckered lips.

"Hi-ya, Danny." She sought again for Dr. Blinker.

"Why are you here, Miss Barrett?" Mr. Tappermounty's deep voice was a somber monotone usually reserved for the bereaved.

"Well, I'm pleased to see you, too, Mr. Tappermounty." They acted as if they had not expected her?

"I invited Miss Libby, gentlemen." Dr. Blinker emerged from the deeper shadows at the rear of the barbershop into the yellow glow of the lamps mounted to the walls.

Her spirits lifted. In spite of Dr. Blinker's annoying habit of thrusting stilted prose upon her, his was a friendly face she trusted.

"You invited her?" Sheriff Bainbridge transferred his scowl from Libby to the stout dentist.

Dr. Blinker hadn't told them? Hmm. That was even more curious than Lieutenant Danforth's presence amongst the town's prominent members.

Mr. Tappermounty turned to the dark window and peered out at the wind-whipped snow filling Paramount Avenue. The bleak and cold seemed to fit the undertaker's chilled soul.

Dr. Blinker was a portly man of about fifty. His receding gray hairline reminded Libby of her father. He looked around at the men there and drew in a breath, the large gold chain across his vest straining. "I was certain I'd mentioned it, gentlemen," he said innocently, pinching his neatly trimmed beard. Smile lines deepened at his eyes. "I assumed this meeting ought to have an esteemed member of the press present." He turned toward Lieutenant Danforth. "Don't you agree?"

"Miss Barrett is always welcome far as Ah'm concerned." Lieutenant Danforth's diction hinted at aristocracy. He hailed from Georgia, but that was about all she knew of the army officer. She dare not appear too inquisitive at the risk of encouraging his attentions. The Lieutenant needed no assistance in that area.

"I think we are all in agreement with the Lieutenant on that." Dr. Blinker's view traveled around the room, lingering on Sheriff Bainbridge. "The citizens of Somerville have a right to know what we discuss here tonight. I certainly intended to mention having invited Miss Barrett. Must have, ahem, slipped my mind." He crossed to the stove and turned his palms to it sending a conspiratorial wink her way.

The doctor was a crafty fellow, even if his grinding prose read like winter molasses. Libby felt a frown threaten and quickly erased it. *Frowns do not compliment a lady. They return to haunt one's face when one is more mature,* Miss Penelope had warned repetitiously.

"Gentlemen." She handed Danny her notebook, untied the maroon, silk ribbon of her bonnet and hung the gray, wool overcoat with the other coats on the clothes tree by the door. "Your clandestine meeting here has me wondering what might be so important that you have not gathered at Plains's Hotel dining room, as is customary." She removed her doeskin gloves and placed them upon the small table holding a stack of magazines and the latest edition of the *Somerville Independent*.

Sheriff Bainbridge, taller and broader than either Mr. Wilson or Dr. Blinker, and about ten years their elder, shifted uneasily on the barber chair. "Clandestine?" He snorted. "There's nothing secret about it, Miss Barrett. We merely wanted to hash out the details with Danforth before taking it to the people for a vote." He'd empha-sized the last word, re-crossing his feet upon the polished nickel footrest. His dark brows lowered over smoky gray eyes and hitched darkly toward Dr. Blinker.

Slouched in a chair along the wall, still wearing his barber apron, Mr. Wilson was a slender man with slicked down salt and pepper hair and an impressive handlebar mustache—both perfectly groomed. The pleasant smell of shaving cream and toilet water seemed to always hover about the man. Mr. Wilson struck a match and put it to the ashy end of a half-smoked cigar. "We're here because we have a little room to spread out with no interruptions. Nothing more treacherous than that, Miss Barrett."

"And a new stove." Jimmy declared, backing off a few steps from the ferociously radiating iron firebox valiantly holding the icy whistler to the other side of the chattering windowpanes.

Mr. Wilson flung the match into a brass spittoon, stood and offered her the chair.

"Thank you, Mr. Wilson." She took the seat and straightened her spine Miss-Penelope's-finishing-school-erect. Danny handed her the notebook. She flipped to a blank page, placed the notebook upon the brown jersey of her skirt and touched the point of a pencil to her tongue. "Well, the press is here. Let the meeting begin."

"It already has begun," Sheriff Bainbridge said, working his jaw like he wanted to spit, but not sure he ought to with a lady present.

She looked to Mr. Tappermounty scowling out into the night at the rampaging snow monster flailing the town, and then to Mr. Wilson who dragged a three-legged stool across the floor and straddled it. Only Dr. Blinker, Jimmy Winchell, Danny, and of course moon-eyed Lieutenant Danforth seemed pleased that she was here. Maybe the story behind this meeting was bigger than Sheriff Bainbridge and Mr. Wilson wanted to let on? She'd have to listen between the lines to get the true account of the matter. Not the smallest detail or the subtlest insinuation would get past L. A. Barrett, Ace reporter for the *Somerville Independent*! A warm tingle made her smile. L.A. was so much more professional sounding than Elizabeth Ann. In spite of how Mother had hoped and prayed, had fussed and primped, she never really was the Elizabeth sort—*frilly petticoats and ringlets that get in the way.*

"In that case, what did I miss?"

"We only just got started, Miss Libby." Dr. Blinker cleared his throat, grasped the lapels of his vest, and with a nod, deferred to the sheriff.

Sheriff Bainbridge leaned forward in the red velvet chair. "We were discussing the possibility of a new building program."

She scribbled *building program* at the top of her page. "Excellent. Somerville is a growing little place." That wasn't exactly true, but it was, she knew, the fervent desire of most of Somerville's two hundred and forty citizens.

The sheriff gave a short laugh. "Oak trees grow faster." His narrow view scorched Dr. Blinker, Mr. Wilson, and Mr. Tappermounty—the three representatives of the Somerville town council. "Nothing grows round here, especially my salary."

Dr. Blinker rolled his eyes. "We've been through that before, Walt. The town is practically broke..." They all looked accusingly at Libby. "...now."

She winced. It was no secret some of those two hundred and forty residents blamed her for the town's financial shortfall.

The Sheriff stiffened slightly in the ornate chair. "We don't have the tax base to do much of anything, and that ain't likely to change so long as we hold onto nineteenth century thinking. A new century will be on us in another seven years, gentlemen. Regrettably, I have to wonder if there will be anyone left in Somerville to send up a bottle rocket to celebrate it."

Libby noted his comment with the single word *Progress.* "And you've met here because of-?"

Tappermounty turned from the bleak window; a bleak man with a bleak face. "Because if we don't do something, this town is going to die like so many other wide-spots-in-the-road out here in the West." He sighed. "Just like my business is doing."

Jimmy chuckled. "That's a good one, Woodrow. A dying business. Ha, ha!"

Even Danny laughed.

Mr. Tappermounty didn't see the humor, but then, he never saw the humor in anything. Libby felt sorry for him.

"I assume the town council has come up with a plan to improve Somerville's misfortunes?" It must have been so, otherwise why this meeting?

"Indeed, we have, Miss Libby." Dr. Blinker turned toward the lieutenant. "And we may have found exactly the help we need."

She looked at the handsome army officer. *Lieutenant Danforth?* A wrinkle creased her forehead. She quickly removed it before it could do permanent harm. "How might Lieutenant Danforth help?"

"Not Ah, Miss Libby, but the United States Treasury Department. Ahem, Ah do have certain political connections."

"Treasury Department? Please explain that, Lieutenant." Although she didn't understand, she did like what she was hearing. This could be big—really big!

The young lieutenant looking confident and dashing —she tried not to think of that—stepped away from the counter without upending any of the bottles there. The brass buttons of his uniform blouse caught the lamplight in golden flashes. "As you know, the trackside army depot is where we hold supplies in transit. Munitions, materiel, medical supplies. Some of it is transferred to military trains, and some of it is loaded onto supply wagons to be moved to camps far from the railroad."

"And other items, too," Jimmy said, raising his eyebrows as though it was a secret only those here shared.

She took his cue. "You're speaking of the government payroll presently being held there?"

Lieutenant Danforth drew thoughtfully on his pipe and blew sweet smoke at the ceiling. "Someday the railway will connect all our far-flung outposts, Miss Libby, but until that day comes, we remain at the mercy of mules, wagons…and the weather. As you well know, the weather has been a fickle mistress of late."

"The weather a fickle mistress. I like that," Dr. Blinker declared. He pulled a slim notebook from an inside pocket and uncapped his Waterman Ideal Fountain Pen. He'd recently purchased the pen by mail-order, and flourished it about whenever an opportunity arose. "I might use it someday."

Lieutenant Danforth bowed in playful deference to the older man. "Be my guest, Doctor."

Libby's impatient pencil tapped a tarantella on the paper pad. "So, gentlemen, how exactly is the United States Treasury Department going to save Somerville?"

Sheriff Bainbridge shifted in the chair. The army has over ten thousand dollars stored in the depot awaiting weather that won't freeze the tail off an army mule or mire a government wagon in three feet of gumbo. It might be spring before Lieutenant Danforth and his men can deliver that money. Frankly, Miss Barrett, that makes me a little nervous. And this ain't the first time. Same thing happened two years ago. Remember? All that money sat there for months. Every stranger who came to town was looked upon as having evil intents."

Mr. Wilson rolled his cigar between his lips, it's stench a curious antiphony to Lieutenant Danforth's pipe. "Yep, every stranger—both of 'em."

Jimmy roared, and snorted to catch his breath.

Sheriff Bainbridge scowled. "Laugh if you want, James, but first time this town gets shot up and that depot razed, you better hope your window is shuttered tight. Over at Fort Hays, there was a daylight robbery of a government gold shipment right under the noses of a battalion of soldiers. I don't want that happening in *my* town."

Dr. Blinker grinned, "Afraid you'll have to start earning some of that fat salary we town council members pay you?"

"Funny." Sheriff Bainbridge aimed a brown stream of tobacco juice at the spittoon. He'd apparently come to terms with his objection to spitting in the presence of a lady.

The lieutenant was about to speak when the door slammed open. A gale of snow swirled through the barbershop and a big man in a shaggy buffalo coat filled the doorway like a grizzly bear.

Libby lurched. "Mr. Gannon!"

Tom Gannon looked to be in a bad way.

"Tom!" Both Mr. Wilson and Dr. Blinker exclaimed at the same time.

The old rancher staggered, his big hat tugged down over his awful red eyes, his coat caked in snow. A Winchester rifle was tucked under his arm and a whiskey bottle grasped by the neck. Mr. Gannon appeared dazed by the light and started to sway in the icy wind as the room went frigid, the raw air tinged with the odor of stale whiskey.

"Doc," Mr. Gannon groaned. He took a step toward Dr. Blinker, tottered and collapsed.

———

Libby sprang to catch Mr. Gannon; his weight almost too much for her as he struggled to regain his balance. She had never seen him in such a sad state, never known him too drunk to stand.

Tom steadied himself and gave her an intoxicated grin. "Shank you, Mish Libby. Hold this, Danny." He thrust the rifle into the lad's hands and staggered toward Sheriff Bainbridge, grabbing him by the shirt front and hauling him out of the Berninghaus as if it had been little Danny sitting there—and the sheriff wasn't a small man.

Tom collapsed into the chair and waved for Dr. Blinker.

Mr. Tappermounty shouldered the door shut against the gale and cast a perplexed look at the others.

Dr. Blinker swallowed hard. "Wh-what's wrong, Tom?"

Tom opened his mouth and shoved a finger into it. "My 'ooth 's killin' me, Doc. Three days now."

Dr. Blinker inched closer as though poor Mr. Gannon with his head cranked back and his finger jammed into his mouth might at that moment have been endowed with the spirit of a grizzly bear. Libby's thoughts halted on that idea. There might be a story angle buried in it somewhere.

Dr. Blinker cast a glance at Mr. Tappermounty. The scowling undertaker returned a brief nod. Libby would have missed the exchange entirely had she not been looking at Mr. Tappermounty at precisely that moment.

Dr. Blinker's lips tightened. "Tom, we're not in my dental surgery."

"Don't matter, Doc." He moaned.

"See to it, Matthew," the sheriff growled, shifting his

view briefly to Mr. Tappermounty. Was he upset at being evicted from the chair? Libby found that hard to believe.

Dr. Blinker pried the bottle of whiskey from Mr. Gannon's hand. "How long have you been hitting the juice, Tom?"

"Two day...maybe three. Don't 'member."

"Whiskey didn't cure the pain, I presume?"

"Cut it some in beginnin'. Now it 'urts like sin."

Libby frowned. Did Mr. Gannon really believe a bottle of whiskey and intestinal fortitude could solve a medical problem?

"All right, all right. Let me just take a look." Dr. Blinker extracted Mr. Gannon's finger and peered inside." He lurched back almost at once, rolled his eyes and fanned the air. "Whew! You're about three-quarters pickled."

Mr. Gannon moaned, rolling his head side to side, working the wide hat off his head. It hit the floor with a soft thump.

Libby picked it up and moved behind the barber chair. *Poor Mr. Gannon.* She gently stroked his thin, gray hair. "We'll take care of you, Mr. Gannon."

"You sure enough have a bad tooth, Tom. Cracked right down the middle." Dr. Blinker appeared quite bewildered. "But there ain't much I can do for you here."

She bent for a look. The odor of whiskey and the stench of decay wrinkled her nose.

"Ahem. Miss Libby. Some room please."

"Oh. Sorry, Doctor." She did sometimes tend to let professional curiosity get in the way.

The sheriff began pacing. "Just pull the blasted thing and be done with it, Matthew."

Why was he so impatient?

"Pull it with what, Walt? My fingers?"

Mr. Tappermounty shifted his scowl toward Mr. Wilson, "If you have a pair of pliers, get them."

Mr. Wilson gave a small start at what was as near to an order as Libby had ever heard come from the taciturn undertaker. Frowning, he shuffled to the back of the building and returned a few seconds later with a grimy pair of rusty pliers, working the handles to loosen them up. "Will these do?"

"Those are dirty!" Libby said, appalled at the notion of using them in a medical procedure. "Filth breeds bacteria, and bacteria cause infections. Dr. Lister proved that years ago."

"Indeed they are, Miss Libby." Dr. Blinker examined them briefly and grinned. "We may have the makings of an exciting drama here."

"Drama? Good heavens, Mr. Gannon is in pain." Dr. Blinker, a frustrated writer, seemed to be always scouting for a "story". And whenever he found one, she inevitably became the first reader to be victimized by his pedantic prose, mixed metaphors, and showy similes.

"No fear. We'll wash them. Howard, put some soap and hot water on these."

Mr. Wilson glowered. "You might add a please to that. This is *my* barbershop."

Libby rolled her eyes. *Now was not the time to be petty.*

Mr. Tappermounty unwrapped a square of spruce chewing gum, and then turned back to the window and the snarling winter beast clawing at the icy panes.

Libby eyed the rusty pliers suspiciously. Would Dr. Blinker actually attempt an extraction here, in Mr. Wilson's new barber chair? What if there was blood? "Maybe we should help Mr. Gannon over to your office where you have the proper tools?"

"Just do it Doc," the old rancher mumbled. "Can't 'urt no more than it already 'urts."

"All right, all right. Mr. Wilson, will you wash the surgical instrument...*please*...you cantankerous goat," he grumbled under his breath.

Mr. Wilson snorted and filled a basin with water from a pitcher. Hands trembling from either anger or nerves, he lathered-up the pliers good and foamy as if he intended to shave them. He rinsed them in clear water and gave them to the doctor who baptized them with a generous splash from Mr. Gannon's whiskey bottle and dried them in a clean towel leaving a rusty smear. Mr. Wilson would have a hard time getting *that* stain out.

"Now you just hold still, Tom. I'll have that tooth out of there in no time." He filled Mr. Gannon's mouth with fingers and pliers, half crawling onto his lap to attack the tooth from an advantageous angle.

"Murb, thert groub lut."

"No, no—won't hurt but for a moment, Tom."

Certainly not so! But Libby didn't think it was the sort of prevarication the Lord would hold against him.

Dr. Blinker grabbed hold of the tooth, grunted, and gave a sharp twist that nearly launched the old rancher out of the Berninghaus.

She winced, pressing a sympathetic hand to her own jaw.

Sheriff Bainbridge and Lieutenant Danforth sprang into action, holding Mr. Gannon in place while Jimmy Winchell steadied Dr. Blinker's precarious perch upon Mr. Gannon's knees.

Her reporter's curiosity drew her closer to the pile of men. The gagging odor of overripe decay stilled her breath. With a hand cupped over her nose, she bent for a closer look.

A muffled crack emanated from Mr. Gannon's mouth. The old rancher gave a wail and well-nigh burst free of his restraints.

"Eureka!" Dr. Blinker cried, holding up a bloody, three-pronged cocklebur in the pliers' jaws. "Wilson, get me a something to soak up this blood—*please*."

Roused from his trance, Mr. Wilson fumbled for the bowl of cotton balls and another clean towel. The doctor tamped cotton into Mr. Gannon's mouth and wiped blood from the rancher's chin. *Another ruined towel.*

"There you go, Tom. You'll be good as new in a couple days, soon as the bleeding stops. Course, your blood being practically hundred proof John Barleycorn, it may go on seeping for days."

The sheriff and the lieutenant let up on the big man and Jimmy helped Dr. Blinker to the floor in a more or less dignified manner.

Mr. Gannon clutched the towel to his mouth. "Shanks, Doc." The cotton balls garbled his voice. "Feels better already."

Libby grabbed up her tablet and scribbled, *Dental surgery in Barber Wilson's new Berninghaus barber chair.* She'd refine the headline later.

Mr. Tappermounty began pacing, hands locked behind his back and his face scrunched together like a bolt of rough corduroy. "Glad that's over."

"You're glad?" Mr. Gannon muttered, his rummy eyes taking them all in. A crooked grin appearing amongst the folds of the towel when his view settled on her. "Mish Libby. I do apologize for my rude behavior, bustin' in here and all." The whiskey slurred his words and cotton balls muddled them. He attempted to remove his hat, surprised to discover it missing, and even more surprised to spy it in her hands.

"No apologies necessary, Mr. Gannon. You were in horrible pain."

"It'll ease some now that 'ooth is out." His grin was kind of cute, and shy. His view moved on to the sheriff.

"Guess I owe 'ou one for tossing 'ou out of the chair like I done."

The sheriff waved it off.

Mr. Gannon took his jaw in hand and tenderly worked it sideways, stared at the blood-soaked towel, then at Dr. Blinker. "Shanks, Doc. I owe 'ou, too."

"Stop by the office when you get a chance." He peered at his hands, and washed them in the soapy water on the counter.

Libby said, "Are you all right, Mr. Gannon? You should stay there in the chair for a little while."

His pale blue eyes glinted in the lamplight. "Been 'urt a lot worse." His hand moved to his left shoulder, fingers gently probing as though remembering an ancient ache.

Lieutenant Danforth grinned. "You are a powerful man to hold down, Mr. Gannon."

"Well, Lieutenant, I suspect 'ou might be, too, if the circumstances be reversed." He attempted to stand, reeled and grabbed the chair for support. "Whoa-Nellie. Reckon I better get back t' the house while I'm still able."

Libby said, "You're in no condition to ride, Mr. Gannon. Especially with this storm roaring through the eves. I think you should remain here. You might freeze to death before you get back to your place."

He staggered a few steps and gave her a lopsided grin that stretched his unshaven cheeks. "Don't worry 'bout this old trooper, Mish Libby. One time me 'n Captain Benteen chased Red Cloud clears ups into the Ba-kota badlands in a January howler that makes tonight look like Too-saon on the fourth of Joo-lie."

She frowned. Why did some men wear suffering like a badge of honor? "You were a much younger man back then, Mr. Gannon."

He smiled, his eyes brightening a bit, remembering. "Aye, that I was, Mish Libby. I appreciate the concern, but

Cochise'll be wondering what happened t' me." He retrieved his rifle from Danny. "Shanks scout fer keeping an eye on dis."

"Did ya ever kill any Injuns with that rifle, Mr. Gannon?"

For a moment Tom Gannon was someplace else, and that place was not pleasant. Then he shook himself and grinned at the boy. "Naw, not a one 'less you count the four Commanches that raided my chicken coop last week. This here '92 is just a tike, like 'ou, Danny. But I shent more 'an a few of 'em on to their ancestors with my old army Shpringfield, and dat's a fact." He took his hat from Libby, pulled it down on his head and staggered toward the door."

The undertaker opened it for him and a gale of snow whirled through the barbershop.

Shank you, Mr. Tappermounty." He tipped his hat to the undertaker and reeled out into the storm with Mr. Wilson's towel pressed to his mouth, his voice lifting in a drunken garbled ditty, *"An' the hostiles come t' get 'our scalp just empty 'our canteen, and put 'our pistol t' 'our head and go t' Fiddler's Green."*

Mr. Tappermounty shut the door, looking mildly amused. They crowded at the window to watch Tom reeled out into the jaws of the winter beast. He tottered off the sidewalk to the road, attempted to slide the rifle into the saddle scabbard, succeeded on the third try. His is boot searched for the stirrup, found it by trial and error, and heaved him up on his horse's back...and right over, off the other side.

———

Libby flinched at the snow-muffled thump.

The sheriff and Mr. Tappermounty rushed out to

help Mr. Gannon up from the street, brushed him off, and hoisted him safely upon his saddle. As he rode off into the swirling snow, she whispered a prayer for a safe journey home. In spite of all the violence he'd seen in his life, Mr. Gannon had a good heart and a gentle nature.

She remembered the funeral when Mr. Gannon laid Cassie to rest beside their three children, under the mulberry tree. The barren plot behind the small house he and Cassie had built already held three crude head markers. During the funeral Mr. Gannon never shed a tear, only stared at that dark hole in the black Kansas earth. He seemed to stop breathing for so long, Libby had worried he might keel over and join Cassie.

He didn't talk much for a long time after Cassie's death. Then one day a face from his past showed up in town. Cochise moved onto the ranch and Mr. Gannon seemed to perk up with the companionship. The old Apache warrior was a mystery. Everyone knew that Cochise wasn't his real name. He had an Apache name, an American name, and a Mexican name, but Mr. Gannon simply called him Cochise, and the Indian never corrected him on the matter.

Libby said, "Shouldn't someone go with him? He's likely to freeze to death in this blizzard." Was that a spark of interest in Tappermounty's eyes? She refused to believe he'd think such a thing.

"Freeze to death?" Sheriff Bainbridge scoffed. "Not Tom Gannon. Tom Gannon's too ornery to die. The Apaches tried. Rattlesnakes and General Grant tried. They all failed. What chance does a little Kansas blizzard have? So long as he stays in the saddle he'll be all right. Nothing between Somerville and his place but a long straight road. Not a farmhouse, nor a single turnoff. Just six bleak miles of Kansas prairie." Having put that notion to rest, Sheriff Bainbridge cleared his throat and said, "Now, where were we?"

Libby forced her thoughts back onto business. It wasn't easy. She consulted her notepad. "Army payroll... robbery at Fort Hays...not on your watch."

"Oh yes, I remember. Okay, here's the deal. Somerville needs to grow, but it ain't going to do that unless people have faith in our town. Now I ask you, Miss Barrett, what builds solid faith? What would make folks look at Somerville and say, 'Now, here's a place I want to live.'?"

That was easy. "Hire a second school mistress, and help raise money for another church? Baptist?"

Mr. Tappermounty cast an accusatory scowl her way, "We can't afford the schoolmarm we have now."

Her eyes narrowed slightly at his abrupt interruption. It was no secret the Council were still angry that she had inspired the town to build the new schoolhouse.

Sheriff Bainbridge continued, "A bank."

"But we have a bank."

The sheriff huffed. "We have a tinderbox with a tin-bucket safe any ten-year-old could open. No, Miss Barrett, Somerville requires a solid brick bank with a powerful vault."

"I suppose..." She scribbled *brick bank*, but was unconvinced. "How will another bank attract folks to Somerville when the one we already have hasn't?"

Dr. Blinker gripped his lapels and said, "Nearest *real* bank hereabouts is over at Albert City. Too far for the people of Somerville to take their money. 'specially in the dead of winter."

Libby conceded that maybe the town did need a proper bank, but still didn't see how that would attract more families than another church might. "So, what role does the army play in this, Dr. Blinker?" She glanced at Lieutenant Danforth.

Sheriff Bainbridge took over again. "In spite of Lieutenant Danforth's most excellent troops, you have to admit a wooden shack alongside the Santa Fe right of way is not the safest place to secure a government payroll."

The lieutenant flashed a pleasant row of straight, white teeth, his blue eyes twinkling a humorous glint. "Although you have to admit, sheriff, there is little danger here in Somerville. Ah dare say, we can go off and leave the door unlocked and the government's money would be safer than most big-city banks made of brick."

A low chuckle moved about the barbershop.

Libby saw through the charade now. "What you're really saying is, we ought to build a bank to protect the army's money?"

"Not *we*, Miss Barrett," Mr. Tappermounty droned, "the United States Government. The Treasury Department, to be exact. If we can convince them that Somerville would be the best location for a new Federal Bank, it will put us on the map."

"In a big way," Jimmy Winchell added. "You remember the spurt of growth we had when we installed a post office in Pealgramm's general store."

Spurt of growth? Libby's mouth dropped. Was Jimmy talking about the same Somerville? "Two old drovers setting up a tent outside town hardly qualifies as a growth spurt, Jimmy." Her view traveled to each of them. "If you gentlemen think the government will foot the bill to build a bank, then what is the purpose of this meeting?" It didn't appear to be the big issue they were making of it. "This business could have been conducted in the dining room of the Plains Hotel as easily as here."

Mr. Wilson, straddling his three-legged stool listening to all this, straightened up suddenly and removed the cigar from his lips. "The problem is, although the government *might* build the bank, with Lieutenant Danforth's recommendation, there still isn't any real incentive for them to do so. You see, the Lieutenant is correct in suggesting that Somerville is a sleepy way-station. Hardly anyone knows we exist, let alone that there's a ten-thousand-dollar payroll waiting for a spring thaw to be moved. But if we-"

"If we were to sweeten the pot," Mr. Tappermounty broke in, glancing away from the blizzard whistling through the window sash, "with say, a prime piece of Main Street real estate, they might be more inclined to look at the proposal."

Prime piece of real estate? Did she hear him correctly? Did such a creature even reside within the city limits of Somerville? None of this made any sense...and then she understood. "So the question becomes, *whose* prime piece of Somerville real estate are you to sacrifice to the government." Her eyes narrowed at their poker faces. "I see now why you might want to play this close to the vest, gentlemen...and out of sight of those businessmen whose property might be imperiled."

"No, no, Miss Libby." Dr. Blinker released his lapels and stepped forward. "It ain't like that at all."

"Isn't it?" She touched her pencil to her tongue and wrote, *The Great Somerville Land Grab.* She still couldn't think of any single piece of valuable property in Somerville ...except...

Her eyebrows hitched up and she gave them a sly smile. "It seems to me the most prime piece of real estate on Main Street might very well belong to the Plains Hotel. No wonder you moved your regular meeting place to here. Very clever, gentlemen." She noted by their startled faces that she'd rightly divined their motives.

"Now, now, Miss Barrett. It's not that way." Sheriff Bainbridge squirmed in the barber chair.

Dr. Blinker stiffened and grabbed his lapels again. "That reporter's nose of yours is sniffing up the wrong creek, Miss Libby."

A pinched literary nerve made her grimace. "I may be sniffing a cold *trail* and *paddling* up a wrong creek, but I'm at least on the right tributary. Look at yourselves, shrinking like little boys caught with their hands in the cookie jar."

"Is this true?" Mr. Wilson's suddenly concerned look cast at Dr. Blinker. "Matthew?"

"Course not, Howard."

Mr. Tappermounty gave a lurch and pressed his nose near the frosted window. "Say...what's this?"

"What is what, Woodrow?" Jimmy asked.

They moved to the window. Libby shouldered her way in amongst them, her breath clouding the pane as she peered out. The evening glow was long gone from the sky, the whirling snow reflecting the light from a few windows in town.

Mr. Tappermounty scrubbed the steam from a pane with his hand and pointed. "There. In the street."

She spied him then. Her first thought was that Mr. Gannon had fallen from his horse and was staggering back into town. But no, this was a smaller man, bundled in a horse blanket. As he came into the spill of light from the barbershop window, he stopped, whirled around in a swoon and collapsed.

"My goodness." She looked at Sheriff Bainbridge. "He's fainted."

———

Sheriff Bainbridge and Mr. Tappermounty plunged into the blizzard, hoisted the stricken man between them, and carried him in from the cold. They laid the shivering man on the floor, his two, long gray braids nearly frozen stiff. Eyes closed, cheeks gaunt, lips thin and pale, teeth chattering castanets, he trembled as if with the palsy.

"Is he sick?" Danny asked, joining in the press of bodies. Libby took his arm and held him back. Dr. Blinker knelt beside the man. Lieutenant Danforth peered over the doctor's shoulder. "Why, that's an Indian."

"Sure 'nough," Jimmy Winchell said, craning his neck for a better look.

Dr. Blinker pried the man's rigid fingers apart and opened the frozen horse blanket. It crackled as it parted in the warm building. "The poor man is nearly frozen."

"He must have been out in the storm a long time." Libby grabbed her notebook and made a new entry. *Half frozen Red Man stumbles into Somerville in the midst of the worst blizzard of the decade.*

"What's wrong with him?" Mr. Wilson asked.

"The poor fellow appears to be ill." Dr. Blinker pressed a palm to the Indian's forehead. "He's feverish in spite of the cold."

The Indian's eyelids fluttered, dark eyes staring at the ceiling a moment, then rounding to the faces peering over him. "*Kim-at-o-kit! Kim-at-o-kit!*" he said in a voice barely louder than a breath.

"What did he say?" Mr. Wilson asked.

Sheriff Bainbridge edged closer. "Don't know. It's Injun talk."

Lieutenant Danforth looked up at the sheriff. "Sounds Sioux,"

Libby glanced from her notepad. "Sioux? Here in Kansas?"

The fellow began to shake as if with the ague.

"Maybe Mr. Gannon would understand his words," Libby suggested.

Dr. Blinker said, "I don't think this old-timer's going to last long enough to find out, Miss Libby."

Mr. Tappermounty looked him up and down. "Five-six, maybe seven. Hmm?" His face took on a contemplative demeanor.

"Mr. Tappermounty!" Libby scolded. "He's not even dead."

Jimmy said, "Can you do anything for him, Matthew?"

Dr. Blinker shook his head. "Keep him warm is all." Worry-lines deepened across the doctor's forehead. "I think this fellow's got the *fever*." The gravity Dr. Blinker placed on that final word struck Libby.

Sheriff Bainbridge hunkered down at the Indian's side. "Can you talk English?"

The sick man's dark eyes slid slowly toward him. "Water."

Without even waiting for a please, Mr. Wilson sprang to his feet and grabbed up a pitcher and a white china cup. Pitcher and cup clinked nervously. Dr. Blinker lifted the poor fellow's head and helped him with a few sips. Mr. Wilson hurried off for a blanket to tuck about the Indian's thin, shivering frame.

Libby couldn't remember the last time she'd seen an Indian other than Cochise. There hadn't been one in or around Somerville in years. "Where could he have come from?"

"No telling," Sheriff Bainbridge said. "Likely a loner. Lots of 'em just wander about these days."

The Indian grabbed Dr. Blinker's arm and struggled to pull himself up. "White buffalo."

"What is that?" Dr. Blinker bent an ear closer.

"White buffalo." His dark eyes grew large, casting about, staring finally at something none of them could see. "Out there."

The fervor in his voice sent an electric current up Libby's spine. She shivered in spite of the heat radiating off the Ben Franklin Stove and scribbled the sick man's words on her pad.

"What white buffalo?" Sheriff Bainbridge asked.

The Indian mumbled something in his native tongue, then went into the most awful ague she'd ever seen. When he finally settled down, he managed to say, "Buffalo…make gold chips."

They looked at each other, mystified.

She must have misunderstood his broken English. "What does he mean, 'gold chips'?"

The Indian's fevered eyes locked onto hers with a wild urgency. "Gold buffalo chip. Great White Buffalo make." He fumbled under his threadbare vest, too weak to retrieve whatever it was his trembling hand sought.

"Let me help you," Dr. Blinker said.

The Indian fell back in what Libby thought was a swoon, but it wasn't. "Got to tell. Before too late."

Dr. Blinker reached inside the grimy vest. "Found something here." He extracted an object about the size of a diner plate, wrapped in a piece of animal hide and bound up with a leather thong. Blinker grunted lifting it, and set it on the floor with a heavy clunk. "My word, no wonder he was staggering!"

"What is it?" Mr. Tappermounty asked. They drew closer over the sick Indian trembling on the floor in an expanding puddle of melted snow. Dr. Blinker worked the knot loose and peeled back the stiff leather wrapper. The thing was a dull golden color, roundish and flattish, with concentric ridges and what looked like bits of dried grass stuck to it. Dr. Blinker lifted it to the light so they could better see. It definitely looked gold…and something else, too. She didn't make the connection right away. When she did, she gasped. Her brain reeled, refusing to accept what her eyes were telling her. The others around her seemed to be coming to the same conclusion.

Jimmy was first to voice what was now obvious to them all. "Why, that's a buffalo chip! A golden buffalo chip."

"White buffalo," the Indian muttered, his unsteady finger lifting toward the wall of Mr. Wilson's barbershop. "Make gold. Me catch. Break corral. Run away." His arm fell back to his chest, his eyes closing, his breathing shallow. "Chase…three day…No strong no more. Circle walk…and…and me…me here."

"Where is the buffalo now?" Mr. Tappermounty asked.

The rattling windowpanes and whistling doorjamb seemed to diminish in Libby's ears. She could almost hear her own heart beating as she held her breath, waiting for the Indian's next words.

The poor man entered a few moments of trembling delirium. As his palsy stilled his black eyes opened and found her face with a pleading hopeless that reached deep inside her and grabbed her heart. He spoke again and this time he seemed to be talking to her, and her alone. "Two day…where sun sleeps." Another spasm tossed the old Indian like a rabbit in the jaws of a wolf. When it passed the poor soul lay still, eyes closed, his chest stilled.

Libby gulped. "Is he…dead?"

Dr. Blinker put a finger to the man's neck and narrowed his eyes in concentration. "Yep. This Injun is a good Injun."

"Dr. Blinker!" she scolded. "Crudeness is uncalled for. A poor soul has just passed into eternity."

He gave a crooked smile and shrugged. "One day we must all put off these mortal coils, Miss Libby."

Her mouth dropped.

Mr. Wilson crossed himself.

Some of them "tsked" while others shook their heads.

There was a moment of somber silence, and then they gasped. The Indian bolted upright and glared like Reverend Overmier giving one of his fire & brimstone sermons. "Alas, I shed this ragged tent and across yon Jordan flee." His eyes rolled up in his head and he fell back on the floor.

"My word." Heart hammering her ribs, Libby swallowed down a lump that constricted her throat.

Dr. Blinker, looking flustered, felt the Indian's neck a good long time, then put an ear to his chest. "Dead...I think."

She glanced at the others. The cigar in Mr. Wilson's mouth was dead, too—as dead as the man on the floor of his barbershop. Jimmy and Lieutenant Danforth stared without uttering a word. Danny, eyes big as nickels, looked as if he might be sick. Sheriff Bainbridge scowled. Undertaker Tappermounty looked unhappy, which Libby thought odd since his business had just taken a turn for the better. Maybe he was thinking the burial would be a charity job seeing as the city coffers were too meager to pay for his services. Somerville didn't have a potter's field to bury indigents.

Libby remembered her first calling and put pencil to paper. "What was it he said? Across yon river?"

"Obviously delirious," the sheriff barked, dismissing it with wave of his hand.

"Dr. Blinker, can you tell the press what this poor soul died of?" Although by the book only a dentist, Dr. Blinker was the closest authority Somerville had on medical matters. The nearest genuine physician was Dr. Brownlee over at McPherson.

He cleared the phlegm from his throat and grasped

the lapels of his vest. "An educated guess—err, I mean my learned diagnoses would be Aboriginal Hemorrhagic Fever."

"Aboriginal Hemorrhagic Fever." The words whispered amongst them in awe-struck solemnity. Libby had never heard of the disease, just the same, Dr. Blinker might as well have announced the Black Plague, or that the Apocalypse had come, for the effect it had on all of them.

Jimmy gulped. "Is it…contagious?"

"Highly contagious. We ought to get this fellow planted right away."

"The ground is frozen three feet deep." Lieutenant Danforth reminded them, a hand covering his mouth and nose as he bent for a closer look. "Are you certain the fellow is dead?"

"You should not get too close." Dr. Blinker took the lieutenant's arm and drew him back a few paces while the sheriff respectfully spread the blanket over the Indian.

"Ah thought Ah saw movement." Lieutenant Danforth stretched to peer over Doc. Blinker's shoulder.

"A fading spark fleeing muscles and nerves, Lieutenant. It happens all the time."

Mr. Tappermounty said, "We can carry him over to my place. Got an extra coffin in my wagon shed. The lieutenant is correct; ground's too hard for a proper burial. I'll nail him shut and he should keep until spring.

"Let's have a closer look at this." Dr. Blinker plopped the golden object onto a cabinet, rattling the bottles of toilet water behind the curved glass doors.

Libby squeezed into the gathering for a better view of the object. Gold colored and more-or-less saucer-shaped, it did, for all the world, look like a buffalo chip. "It can't be," she said, denying what her eyes were telling her.

"Preposterous!" Mr. Wilson declared.

Dr. Blinker turned it over and examined the backside, tugging bits of dry grass from the folds. "It's sure enough gold all right. Stake my reputation on it."

And he should know, having made gold teeth for several of the citizens of Somerville, including Father and the sheriff. But Libby still refused to believe it.

Jimmy prodded the golden manure with a forefinger. "What are we going to do with it?"

"If we had a proper bank, we could keep it there," Sheriff Bainbridge said, sounding smug, as though here was another reason to finagle the government into supplying Somerville with one.

Mr. Wilson touched it next, and each of them followed suit.

The buffalo chip was rough and cold.

"It *can't* be genuine." Libby's intellect rebelled at the very idea in spite of the evidence to the contrary. She looked back to the poor soul on the floor beneath the blanket.

"What if it is real?" The sheriff's gray eyes took on a far-away look. "The owner of such an animal would be rich beyond imagining."

Mr. Wilson stared at him, and threw up his arms in exasperation. "The cold's addled your brain, Walt. There ain't no such animal and you know it. This is the stuff of fables."

"Fables?" Dr. Blinker stroked his beard. "I wonder?"

Surely Dr. Blinker wasn't falling for this!

"You can keep it at the depot if you like. Ah'll see that it is locked in our safe."

Sheriff Bainbridge said, "Thank you, Lieutenant, but I will lock it up in the safe in the office."

Libby's view fixed upon the object. *A golden buffalo chip.* An outrageous notion...yet?

Mr. Tappermounty blew a long breath and shook his head. "Reckon we can call this meeting to an end."

Everyone agreed circumstances had inextricably altered the course of this night's agenda. Dr. Blinker suggested they keep what happened here quiet until the sheriff and town council could get to the bottom of it.

"News has been made, gentlemen," Libby said. "I will be publishing the story in Friday's edition."

"Must you?" Dr. Blinker asked. "Perhaps we ought to wait until we know more of his ailment before alerting the town?"

"Let her write her story, Matthew," Sheriff Bainbridge said. "What can it hurt?"

Mr. Tappermounty said, "A couple of you gentlemen help me haul this fellow over to the parlor."

They bundled the Indian in a blanket-sling and carried him out into the stinging blizzard.

Watching through the frosted pane, Libby sighed. The wealth of kings in his pocket, and what good did it do him? Her lips tightened, dragging her eyebrows together in a Miss Penelope unapproved scowl. Reverend Overmier could take that idea and run with it for a month of Sundays. She decided to keep the insight to herself.

News had been made. A story needed to be written. She drew on her woolen coat. This had to be the most exciting event in Somerville's recent history.

Sheriff Bainbridge retrieved her gloves off the floor where they had landed during the excitement. "Your hands will be cold."

"Thank you, Sheriff."

Dr. Blinker stepped up behind her. "Miss Libby?"

She turned, adjusting the muffler about her face.

"If you find a moment tomorrow, could you please stop by my surgery?" His beaming smile sent warning-hair tingles all along her arms. She'd seen that needy-hopeful smirk before. "I, ah, I've been working on a new yarn."

A lump as weighty as the heavy gold buffalo chip on the toilet-water cabinet congealed in her stomach.

"I, ah, I'd like to have your professional opinion."

She hid a frown behind the woolen scarf. The thought of wading through Dr. Blinker's wearisome prose pushed the Indian's golden chip momentarily from her consciousness. "I'll see if I can make it."

He grinned. "Thank you."

Libby rushed head-bent into the icy fangs of the blizzard, slanting her steps toward the lighted window of the *Somerville Independent* building across the street.

———

Howard Wilson gathered the soiled towels and placed them in the laundry basket in the back room. Past the small window above the wash tub he watched his son filling the coal bucket from the bin in the alley behind the building and then carry it double-handed back into the warm room. Danny hadn't said two words since the meeting had come to an end.

"This has been some kind of night," Howard said, hoping to draw his Danny out from the stoic boy who'd suddenly become a quiet stranger.

Danny only nodded. He cracked open the stove and put a scoopful of coal into the firebox. Howard frowned. Danny had grown a bit tonight; glimpsed the hard edge of life. "Throw in an extra scoop and tighten the draft so's it'll burn all night and won't be too cold in here come morning."

Bundled against the blizzard, the two walked home, which was only a block down and a block over on Lyman Road. Howard placed a hand on Danny's shoulder. "I know what you're thinking, son. Tonight you've seen death close up. Life...death...that's the way of things."

"I wasn't thinking about that," Danny said thoughtfully. "I know that people and animals die. Mister White Paw died last spring. And Emma Anderson's pony died when it broke a leg, remember?"

"I remember." The silence lingered.

Danny said, "That Indian. Do you—do you think he's in heaven right now?"

So, this was the weighty question that pressed upon Danny. Howard pondered it, and couldn't find a proper response. "Well, I don't know the answer to that, but I'm pretty sure that wherever the Indian is right now, he's with his fathers—with all his ancestors who've gone on before him. And he's probably happy for that." It was a weak answer, but it seemed to suffice and lift Danny's mood some.

Inside the vestibule father and son removed their rubber overshoes—wellies, Keavy called them—and slipped through the parlor door. Keavy smiled wanly from the chair where she sat, her basket on the floor, her fancywork upon her lap. "Ah, my men have come home to me," she said.

Howard said, "How do you feel?" When he'd left her after lunch, she'd been cramping.

"Well enough to have a dinner ready fer ye two. I'll just be settin' out the table fer us." She set her needlework aside and started to rise, giving a wince.

"You *just* stay where you are, Keavy," Howard's firm tone was not to be argued with. "Danny and I will set the table." For some women, this time passed with hardly a missed beat. It had never been so with Keavy. Over the years Howard had taken upon himself the role of housekeeper and cook—when he was able—during these the few days when his wife endured the monthly curse of womanhood.

The table cloth was old, but lovingly mended, the plates chipped and cracked. The silver plating had worn off the inherited utensils that Keavy's mother had brought over from Ireland when Keavy had been a little girl. Howard could have bought her a new set, but there was history in these pieces, and there wasn't much extra money coming out of the barbershop. What little of it there was both he and Keavy agreed ought to be tucked away in the cracked gravy boat, secreted up in a corner on the top shelf.

Keavy had set a chicken carcass to boiling yesterday morning, and now the soup was rich and tasty with lots of soft vegetables amongst delicious yellow globules of fat.

"Did it go well tonight, Howard?" Keavy asked as soon as grace had been said.

"Hmmm."

Keavy glanced up. "What happened?" Her view shifted toward Danny. "And ye lad? Ye've been moping about like a tinker wi'hout a wagon."

Howard said, "The meeting broke early as a result of a couple interruptions."

Danny blurted, "An Indian died on pa's floor, right there next to the stove!"

Keavy's eyes widened toward her husband. "Is it true?"

"Afraid so. The fellow stumbled into town mostly frozen to death. He didn't last long after we carried him inside out of the cold. Tappermounty took the body to his place."

"Poor man. 'Tis a bad omen." Keavy crossed herself twice. "We must have Father Henley sprinkle the barbershop next time he's t'rough town."

Danny said, "The Indian had gold on him."

"Gold? Praise, what is an Indian doin' with gold, now I ask?"

Howard cleared his throat. "It wasn't just gold, dear. It was…" He paused to choose the proper words. "It was a buffalo patty, like what used to cover this land before settlers moved in. It only appeared to be made of gold."

"Dr. Blinker said it was gold," Danny countered, eyes opening wide with awe.

Howard frowned at being corrected by his twelve-year-old son. Over the next few minutes he laid out the evening's adventures, and when he finished, Keavy sat staring, her mouth agape and dinner forgotten. She said, "Howard, with such a beast, we'd be livin' on a pig's back."

"It can't be true, Keavy? It's a fable or something."

Keavy gave a short laugh. "Ye don't believe in the little people eit'er, but t'ey are real. Ye've seen the faery rings. Now how to explain t'at?"

"I can't explain that any more than I can't explain a buffalo dropping golden buffalo chips." It amazed him sometimes how much of the Old World superstitions remained in his wife. He'd learned long ago not to argue it with her.

"What do ye plan to do, Howard?"

"Do? What's there to do?"

She flung a hand toward the wall. "T'ere's a golden treasury somewhere out t'ere. Ye ought to be t'inkin' of findin' that beast and makin' it ye'r own."

"I don't have school tomorrow," Danny informed hopefully.

"Not you, too?" Howard shoved his fingers through his hair in frustration. "Listen you two. I'm a practical man. A businessman. I'm not going to go traipsing across a frozen prairie looking for a mythical beast. There may be faeries, leprechauns, and unicorns in Ireland, Keavy, but they don't live in Kansas. And neither do gold-pooping buffaloes."

———

Libby slammed the door shut snipping off the icy claws that had chased her across the street. The amputated appendage struggled across the room, flickered the lamp on Father's cluttered desk, and died at Father's feet. She leaned against the door as if her slight weight could keep the winter leviathan from bursting through.

Father looked up from his work. "Meeting over all ready?" His gray eyebrows hitched above the spectacles that had slid to their comfortable position at the tip of his nose so that his brown eyes easily peered over their gold rims. He wore a knit cap on his balding head and held a pen near the inkwell in knit-gloved hands, the fingers of which had been cut off at the knuckles.

She unwrapped the scarf and let out a long breath. "The meeting came to an abrupt and unexpected end."

Father dipped the pen, tapped the nib to the edge of the well, and turned back the copy he'd been editing. "Mr. Gannon interrupt it?"

Libby crossed the small room, draped the scarf over a hook and hung the coat. "How do you know about that?"

"I was at the window contemplating whether to clutter my editorial with a messy adjective, or rely on a simple verb, when he came into town all hunched down in his shaggy coat looking like he was riding that proverbial Pale Horse."

"Use the verb. Poor man was in awful pain." She turned her palms to the small Franklin. "May I add more coal?"

"Go ahead."

"He came looking for Dr. Blinker. Bad tooth. He'd been dulling the pain with whiskey for days. The good doctor extracted it right there in Mr. Wilson's shop with a pair of *rusty* pliers."

"Hah. Well, there's a filler for page three."

"I tried to tell them the operation was ill advised and that Mr. Gannon might come down with infected blood."

"Did Blinker listen to you."

"No, the stubborn man." She exhaled sharply. "People die all the time from infected blood."

"Some people. Not Tom Gannon. He's too ornery to die."

She looked at her father, surprised. "That's what Sheriff Bainbridge said."

He rotated his head over his shoulder at her. "What did Bainbridge say?"

Libby moved from the coal bucket and pushed father's eyeglasses up the bridge of his nose to their proper location. "That Mr. Gannon was too ornery to die. What does that mean?"

Father went back to scratching the foolscap. "It means Tom Gannon has avoided the services of Mr. Tappermounty so many times, that old shade Mr. Death finally gave up trying to collect him."

"No one is immune to the Grim Reaper." Libby didn't understand how men could treat things like blood poisoning in such a cavalier fashion. "But someone did die tonight," she added cryptically, and went quiet.

Father took the bait and looked over again. "Leading off with a teaser?"

"A writer never gives away the plot all at once."

"Who died?"

"An Indian."

"Here? In Somerville?"

"In Mr. Wilson's barbershop."

Father set the pen down and rotated his chair. "Yeesss?" he prodded when she went quiet again.

Libby rolled her chair around, leaned forward in it and proceeded to tell everything that had happened, never once referring to the notes she'd taken. "It all sounds absurd to me."

Father's face remained unrevealing, but she knew his keen mind was teasing apart what she'd told him, his skeptical, news-hound brain lifting the pieces of her story to peer at their dark undersides for a clue. All at once his lips tightened, his eyebrows lowered, and he fetched his desk calendar from under a pile of discarded papers and riffled through what was left of February. Most of March disappeared between a pinch of pages, and that left only a finger-lick and a swipe to bring him to April first. "Month and a half. Hmm," he said as if to himself, but Libby knew better.

She leaned back, the chair giving a dry-hinge creak. "I thought so, too, but what's the point? I saw their faces. If it was a fool's joke, they pulled it off slick as ice on a rail." The words conjured a fleeting memory of a young girl skating down frozen AT&SF railroad tracks, and a mother's pinched disapproval.

"Where is this treasure of manure now?"

"Still in the barbershop when I left. Sheriff Bainbridge said he would lock it in the safe in his office."

Father took up a pencil, tapping the point of it upon the scarred oak desktop as he thought over what she'd told him. "Dr. Blinker verified it genuine?"

"He did indeed. I touched it. We all did. The poop still had threads of dried grass sticking out of it!" She felt a little uneasy speaking of it this way, and if it had been anyone else but Father…

"Dr. Blinker ought to know," Father conceded. "He

made these." Father stuck a finger behind his cheek where two golden crowns caught the lamplight.

"But it's all so impossible!" She shot out of the chair and stalked to the window watching horizontal snow pelt the panes. "This is…this is…infuriating."

"The Indian?" Father asked.

"Lieutenant Danforth thought he might be Sioux." She turned. "We don't have any Sioux here in Kansas, do we?"

"Not generally this far south. Some used to drift down from Pine Ridge, but not many anymore. I suspect Mr. Tappermounty has him safely nailed into a coffin by now?"

"I should hope so. Dr. Blinker thought the poor soul died from a contagious fever." She rubbed the goose flesh from her arms and moved from the window, closer to the stove.

"Who all was at the meeting?" he asked her.

She exhaled, ready to leave the gold chip behind and proceed to something she could be sure about. "The Town Council and Jimmy were there, also Sheriff Bainbridge, Lieutenant Danforth, little Danny, and of course Mr. Gannon for a little while."

"Danforth. Now that is interesting." Father's forehead furrowed. "Why invite an officer of the military to a meeting involving town business?"

"I thought it strange, too. From what little was discussed, it appears that Dr. Blinker, Mr. Wilson, and Mr. Tappermounty have connived a scheme to persuade the Treasury Department of the United States Government to build Somerville a big brick bank."

"Is that so?" Father pondered a moment. "A real bank would be a welcomed addition to our little community."

"So they claim. Sheriff Bainbridge thought it a safer place for the army to secure its gold than their depot. He wished we had a bank to keep that golden...chip," it was hard to even speak of it as a genuine article, "secure until they could get to the bottom of the mystery." She stopped, thought, frowned. "Coincidence?"

Father frowned. "Coincidence is a rare bird, daughter. Should you catch one, hold onto it tight." Father resumed tapping the pencil. "There may be more of a story here than you first imagined."

"Hmm." Libby rolled her chair back to her desk and stood a moment in narrow contemplation. *Had there been one coincidence or two?* Her scowl deepened risking future disfigurement of the sort Miss Penelope had warned about. "Once this weather breaks, I do believe a visit with Mr. Cochise is in order."

"Mr. Gannon's Cochise? Whatever do you have cooking in that reporter's brain?"

"What's cooking is, if there is an Indian legend about a white buffalo that...that...well, you know...then maybe he's heard about it?"

"Need I remind you Cochise is Apache, not Sioux."

She breezed that aside with a flick of her wrist. "Minor detail."

"To you, perhaps."

Libby gave a conspiring smile. "And it will give me an opportunity to check in on Mr. Gannon. He was in a bad way when he left town."

DAY TWO

TUESDAY

F *rigid breath…* No, no, that's not right.
Cold fists… No, not right either.
Icy claws… Hmm. That might work.

Icy claws slashed the prairie all night. Come morning, Kansas had proved itself an indefatigable opponent. Exhausted, the snow-beast drew back, sliding a frigid dome over Somerville while crouched in the surrounding flint hills, playing a waiting game. But if the Garden State of the West had proven too formidable an opponent for the hippogriff of ice and wind, the iron-spine Kansan Jayhawkers were even more tenacious.

"Hmm. Still not right." Bundled and scarved, booted and gloved, making her careful way along the slippery sidewalk, Libby Barrett, wordsmith—so *The New-York Times* was calling journalists these days—massaged metaphor and simile, shaping them to fit the article she intended to write for next Friday's edition.

Though it offered little heat, the pale morning sun was a welcomed sight in the hazy sky. Walking on the south side of Paramount Avenue toward Pealgramm's General Store, Libby accepted what warmth it could give. This side of the street offered yet another benefit. It was the opposite side from Dr. Blinker's Dental Surgery. If she managed to escape detection, she might avoid his latest efforts to mangle the English language.

Her destination was three shops ahead when, "You-hoo, Libby," a chirpy voice called out.

Past the fog of her breath Libby spied little Hazel Overmier, dressed in black and draped in a natty beaver cloak leaning out of the grocer's doorway and waving. Placing a cautious shoe upon the icy boardwalk, Hazel tiny-stepped her way over, carrying a colorful Mexican grass sack and beaming a bright smile.

"Did you think it would ever end?"

Libby laughed. "I was pretty certain by July the blizzard would have broken."

Hazel te-hee'd. "Where're you going?"

"Just to Pealgramm's to collect the mail," which was only half true; to Hazel Overmier, less said the better. Now that everyone who'd been at last night's meeting had had time to ponder the event, Libby was ready to search out facts and insights into the dead Indian's claims of a white buffalo and a gold chip. She'd planned to start with Jimmy, who she knew better than anyone else who'd been there.

"I'm going there, too! We can walk together."

They stepped delicately through snow and over ice, arm in arm under the theory that four limbs were more sure-footed than two.

Hazel said, "I heard you were there last night."

"There?" Libby asked innocently.

"You know. The raving Indian and his…" she lowered her voice, "…special little secret."

Libby's gaze pinched in a gentle, Miss Penelope-approved, frown. *A secret the whole town would soon know about now that Hazel Overmier had learned of it.* Libby had hoped to break the story in Friday's edition of the *Inde-*

pendent. "Oh, that silly secret. Nothing more than the ramblings of a poor, sick man knocking at death's door."

"Mr. Tappermounty doesn't think it's silly."

Mr. Tappermounty had spoken of it to Hazel? "How would you know that?"

"I asked him, of course. I visited the Parlor second thing this morning hoping for little a glimpse of the Indian, but Mr. Tappermounty had already secured him inside a box." As if to explain her interest in the matter, Hazel added, "I wanted to pray over the dear fellow, you know. Maybe put in good word for him." She jabbed a finger heavenward. "Give him a little boost."

"Did Reverend Overmier suggest it?"

"Tsk-tsk. Dear no. He'd never approve. He says I'm too inquisitive for my own good."

Inquisitive was a milder word than Libby would have chosen. Busybody better fit Hazel Overmier. "It was wise of Mr. Tappermounty to seal the coffin. Dr. Blinker thinks the poor man died of a horrible fever." Libby caught herself. Had she inadvertently given too much information to Hazel?

But it was old information to Hazel. "Aboriginal Hemorrhagic Fever."

They had arrived at Pealgramm's front door. "Where did you hear that?"

"Why, Dr. Blinker told me, of course."

"You've spoken with Dr. Blinker, too?"

"First thing this morning." She smiled cleverly.

Hazel had been a busy lady. What had put her onto the trail? Who else knew about the Indian, the white buffalo, and the gold chip?

As if possessing a talent for reading thoughts, Hazel said, "I was on my way to Saunders's," she lifted the grocery sack, "when Dr. Blinker called to me from the door of his surgery. He said if anyone would be interested in what happened last night, he knew I would."

"Did he now?" Dr. Blinker had given Libby the distinct impression he had wanted to keep the incident quiet until more was known. Had he mentioned the hoped-for bank, too, or Mr. Gannon's infected tooth?

"But I think it was only an excuse," Hazel went on hardly pausing.

"How so?"

"Well, after he tells me about the Indian, quick as a patent-medicine man picks your pocket, he shoves a stack of paper at me and asks if I wanted to read his latest story."

Ah, it was beginning to make sense. Obviously she wasn't always his first reader. Libby felt a smirk come to her lips. "What did you think of the story."

They entered Pealgramm's and shut the door behind them. The round stove in the middle of the floor filled the general store with a comfortable warmth. At the counter Mr. Pealgramm was weighing out a measure of rice for Betty Heelcroft. Over against the back wall, Jimmy Winchell clung precariously to a ladder, stretching for a box on a high shelf. On either side of the store, curved-glass display cases teased the eye with ivory combs, gold watches, and nickel plated revolvers. A small pharmacy in one corner displayed a mesmerizing assortment of small, fancy bottles filled with sparkling elixirs—green, red, honey amber. Packages of quinine, cathartic pills, stomach bitters, plasters, and various female remedies beckoned from the shelves. In another corner, a tiny cubby bore the official seal of the United States Post Office. Here Jimmy would sort the mailbags that arrived every few days by postal coach attached to the AT&SF.

Hazel said, "Oh, I couldn't read his story right then. Too much on my mind. The Indian, the gold buffalo manure, Mr. Tappermounty, my grocery shopping, and the spool of green thread I need to finish my Easter Service dress.

"Hi, Libby," Jimmy waved from his tippy position upon the ladder, caught himself, and scurried down.

"Hi, Jimmy." They'd known each other so long, formalities never intruded into their greetings.

"Come for your mail?" he asked, making his way along the tight aisle behind the curved-glass displays.

Hazel took off in the direction of cloth bolts and thread spools.

Jimmy slipped into the tiny post office room and his head popped up in the rectangular window, now wearing an official postal clerk hat with a green visor. "Looks like your regular delivery of newspapers." He stacked the counter with the *Denver Post*, *The New York Times*, the *Springfield Republican*, the *Chicago Daily Tribune*, and the *Kansas City Times*. "Got some letters here for you, too." Jimmy swiveled his stool and peered at a wall of little rectangular mail slots, picking letters from one of them.

"Jimmy," she said in a quiet voice, "have you ever heard any Indian legends about a white buffalo?"

He glanced over and grinned. "Don't tell me you believe it, too?"

She stiffened. "Of course I don't. My job requires I discover the truth." She glanced about and lowered her voice again. "What do you mean, '*too*'?"

"Mr. Tappermounty was by earlier. He's convinced it's all true. Said the Indian had three more nuggets of gold buttoned into a shirt pocket."

"Where had he found gold on a Kansas prairie? No one has ever found gold in Kansas...except years ago when Colorado had been part of the Kansas Territory."

"Makes you almost want to believe." Jimmy gathered

the letters, dropping them into a paper sack one-by-one. All these look like bills. Paper company. Sterling Ink Company. One from someplace called Acme Lead Typeface, Inc. Oh! Here's one addressed to you, Libby. From the Desk of the Editor, *Chicago Daily Tribune*."

"Me?" She snatched the envelope from his fingers. It was indeed from the *Tribune*. What might...? She quieted her excitement and assumed a refined, Miss Penelope-approved professional expression. "I'll open it when I get back to the office." She slipped the envelope into the paper sack with the rest of the *Independent's* mail.

The bell above the door jangled. Mrs. Wilson and Danny came in, bundled and stomping.

"Hi-ya, Miss Barrett." Danny waved. Keavy Wilson managed a wan smile and headed for the pharmacy corner where the female remedies were kept.

"Hi-ya, Danny. Why aren't you in school?"

"Golly, haven't you seen Lyman Road? School's closed on account of the all the snow."

Libby laughed. "School never closed for snow when I was going."

"Even when it stood eight feet deep," Jimmy added.

"Awe, it never snows eight feet here, Mr. Winchell." Danny waved and went to his mother's side.

Libby lowered her voice again. "Should you hear anything about last night's incident, will you tell me?"

A smile pushed at Jimmy's pale, freckled cheeks. "Shucks, you know I would."

Libby gathered the bag into her arms. Over by the sewing counter where Hazel was counting out pennies, Mr. Pealgramm's voice cracked like a tiny whip, "*Nein, nein*, impossible *Frau* Overmier." Pealgramm shook his head. "White buffalo. Gold *scheisse*! No, no. Foolishness it is."

"What if it's true?" Hazel came back. "If you were to possess such an animal, you'd be a rich man."

"Only foolishness. Good day, *Frau* Overmier." Shaking his head, Warner Pealgramm toddled over to assist Mrs. Wilson.

Clutching her bag of rice, her head cocked just so, Betty Heelcroft appeared to have found a curious trinket to detain her.

Libby and Hazel met at the door. "That man has no imagination," Hazel said.

"Or he has good common sense."

Hazel squinted in a manner Miss Penelope would not have approved. "Isn't the press supposed to be fair-minded, or something?"

"I will be fair-minded when I pen my story, but there's wisdom in exercising a healthy dose of skepticism in matters such as these."

Out on the boardwalk, Hazel's eyes burned with sudden mischief. "I'm going to the army depot to ask the Lieutenant about last night, Libby. Come along with me."

And fend off Lieutenant Danforth's moon-eye advances? She wasn't quite prepared to cross swords with the lieutenant just yet. "I'd love to, but I must get back to the office." Libby lowered her voice to a just-between-you-and-me level. "Do inform me of what Lieutenant Danforth has to say about this mystery. For the newspaper, you understand." Libby intended to interview the lieutenant later, but Hazel's nosiness offered a unique opportunity. People more often confided openly when no newspaper reporter was asking sagacious questions.

"I will."

"May I come, too?" Unseen, Betty Heelcroft had slipped out the shop with them.

"Why of course." Hazel offered an elbow and Betty latched on. As she and Betty went carefully down the boardwalk toward the railroad tracks, Hazel sent Libby a conspiratorial wink over her shoulder.

Hazel was on a mission. Official *newspaper* business. Libby smirked and said softly, "Let's see if you discover anything."

Turning back toward the *Independent's* office, a far-off trail of smoke threading thinly into the sky caught her eye. Who, she wondered, would be camping in the flint hills this time of the year?

Just as quickly as the thought entered her head, it tiptoed through her busy brain to nestle down in a cozy corner somewhere in her subconscious.

———

Thank you Mr. Wind.

Last night's gale had conveniently swept clean a patch of frozen mud between two snow drifts. Libby stepped off the boardwalk onto the cleared bit, working her way across Paramount Avenue toward the newspaper office. She was puzzled. Hazel seemed willing enough to believe the story of a magical white buffalo, which wouldn't have surprised anyone, but austere Mr. Tappermounty? She glanced at the undertaker's drab gray building tucked between the bank and the music hall, a couple doors down from Dr. Blinker's surgery. What had convinced the man who never smiled?

Libby changed directions and a minute later poked her head through the undertaker's doorway. "Hello? Mr. Tappermounty?" She closed the door behind her and stood in the little parlor—dark maroon brocade settee, two matching chairs, a little table holding a Bible, a large painting of golden stairs emerging from billowing clouds, climbing toward pearly-white gates within a golden archway. The scent of spruce lingered in the air. Black curtains hung in front of a passageway. She shivered. Grim workings happened back there.

"Hello?"

Footsteps. The curtain's parted and Mr. Tappermounty stepped through, dressed exactly as he had been the night before. Exactly as he dressed every day, as if he owned only one suit of clothes. "Miss Barrett?" He frowned. "I was expecting you...sooner or later."

"I've a story to write," she smiled, "and it appears I've already been scooped."

"Scooped?"

"Someone beat me to the story."

"Ah. Newspaper jargon." He sighed, lifted his gaze to the pressed tin ceiling, and nodded. "You've spoken with Mrs. Overmier. She poked her head in here before I'd finished my morning coffee."

"Sounds to me she believes the fable."

"Fable?"

"It must be. Surely you—"

"The older I get, the more I learn of this world, the less dogmatic I become. Anything is possible, Miss Barrett."

"Jimmy Winchell says it was new evidence that convinced you. What might that be?"

Mr. Tappermounty's view sharpened and he crooked a finger, beckoning her through the black curtains into the ominous temple where he performed his dark rituals. She was relieved to see no dead people. The dull metal bleeding table held only pasteboard boxes. The blood buckets on the floor were empty. Gum rubber hoses hung from wall hooks alongside knives and twine, and colored waxes of different hues. Sealed bottles lined a shelf and a small crate stenciled *embalming fluids* stood in a corner. A faint odor of formaldehyde hung in the air.

He saw her staring at the crate. "I don't use that

often," Mr. Tappermounty droned. "Only when a loved one must be sent by coach to a distant town." He cleared his throat. "Over here."

She followed, her view still on that ominous crate. "Did you embalm the Indian?"

"I did not. He is very likely frozen through and through by now. He is in the shed behind the parlor. Do you wish to see the coffin?"

"No," she answered too quickly. Then in a more controlled voice, "Maybe at another time." What could she learn from a sealed coffin anyway?

Mr. Tappermounty gave a rare, thin smile and withdrew a cigar box from a bank of cubbyholes. It was labeled simply: Indian. "His possessions. Not much here. A pocket knife, string of glass beads, silver belt buckle, and these." He plucked out three pebbles. They appeared to be pieces broken from the golden buffalo chip.

"Are they real?"

"Dr. Blinker says they are of the same substance as the larger piece the Indian had been carrying."

Libby looked at him, bewildered. "Mr. Tappermounty, how is something like this even possible?"

His shoulders gave a small roll. "That, my dear young reporter-lady, is a question best asked of men of science. I suspect the famous Mr. Darwin could have provided an explanation."

"You really believe it's true? This whole affair is beginning to sound like something out of a Grimm's fairy story."

He pondered, a corner of his lip caught in his teeth. "I don't know if I believe it or not, but at the moment I find myself, err, between customers. Therefore, I have decided to spend a day or two poking about the hills. What hurt can come of it?"

———

The sun had climbed higher, the cold had eased its grip, and now faintly from the north came the long, wavering wail of the 11:10. The siren call of an Atchison, Topeka & Santa Fe locomotive never failed to stir Libby's imagination. She hesitated on the boardwalk in front of the mortuary torn between two directions—the *Independent's* office one way, the railroad depot the other. Somerville was only a wide spot on the AT&SF right-of-way, a place for long drinks of water into boiler tanks, a mail stop, a rare visitor, or a Montgomery Ward delivery of city goods. The line's real destinations were the big towns further south and west—Albuquerque in that New Mexican land of mystery and enchantment, Los Angeles at its terminus.

Her feet made the decision. Hugging her bundle of mail, she headed for the railroad station.

A railroad flung open doors to the world! Adventure lay in either direction along those tracks; westward all the way to California, and eastward to Chicago. Chicago was going to host a World's Fair this year. The *World's Columbian Exposition*, they were calling it. It was declared to be a showcase to the newest technologies. Libby longed to attend, to be a part of the bustle and excitement, but alas, here she was. A city-at-heart girl trapped in Nowheresville, Kansas.

As Libby eased down the slippery steps to cross over Lyman Road, a little green and black bundle waved a gloved hand and picked up her pace through knee-deep snow. Ava Pickering's crooked trail of footsteps ran back past the row of mail-order houses right up to the front door of the brand-new two story brick schoolhouse at the end of the Lyman Road.

The Somerville Public School had started as an extravagant dream that nearly ended as most lavish visions end. The project failed to win the tight-fisted Town Council's approval. Rising to the challenge, pen-sword in hand, Libby wrote an epic monograph on the importance of education, and praising Somerville's determination to forge headlong into the soon-to-arrive twentieth century. The *Independent* published *A Monument to the Future* in six installments that inspired an outpouring of civic pride. The Council dug in its heels. The People petitioned a vote. When the dust settled, a sturdy, enduring Monument to the Future had come into being.

Libby waited for Miss Pickering to slog her way over. "What are you doing out and about on this cold, cold morning? I heard school had been closed?"

"School is closed but I still have to tend the stove or the building will be too cold for the children in the morning." Ava eyes widened. "Is what I hear true?"

Libby's jaw clenched. The story was spreading like a prairie fire in August. She blanked her expression and asked innocently, "What is it that you've heard?"

"About the Indian who died last night in Mr. Wilson's barber chair, and his treasure, and the bison that—well, you know."

"Oh, that silly story." Libby dismissed the importance of last night's excitement with a wave of a hand. "Well, first of all, the Indian didn't die in the chair. He died on the floor. And as for the rest of it, would you believe such a fanciful yarn, Ava?"

"Silly nonsense, I agree." She paused, holding back a bubbling excitement. "But, you were there Libby. Mrs. Balin said so. And Mr. Holmberg said he'd heard, too."

Winifred Balin knew—and the telegrapher! This was getting out of hand. "When did you speak with Winnie?"

"This morning. Down at the depot. She was sending a telegram to her brother in Cripple Creek. He works at the

Portland Gold Mine, you know. I was at the depot sending Mother a missive telling her of the horrible weather we are having here. I'd have put it in a letter, but by time a letter would have made its way down to Tyler, it would be spring." Ava giggled.

If this kept up, Somerville's population was certain to grow. "You and I both know there can be no truth in it. You're an educated woman, Ava. Now you tell me, how is such a thing possible?"

Ava's smile faltered under the weight of logic. "I know, Libby." She sighed. "But wouldn't it be wonderful if true? Mercy, I wouldn't know what to do with such found wealth." She glanced down Lyman Road at the schoolhouse and then back. "I only earn thirteen dollars and fifty cents a month. If it wasn't for the room and board Somerville's citizens generously provide, I couldn't bring ends together."

Libby placed a gentle hand upon Ava's shoulder. "I know it's difficult. I've spoken to the Town Council about hiring a second teacher to help you. Their steadfast answer is, there isn't enough money in the town's coffers to hire a second school mistress."

"If anyone can sway the Council, it's you." Ava paused and her lips twitched ever so briefly downward. "I know the Council blames you for the town's financial struggles, but that was such a wonderful story you wrote in the *Independent*. How could they have denied Somerville a proper schoolhouse, even if its second story is only used for storage at present?"

"That will change. Somerville is going to grow," she said hopefully, but secretly she wondered…? The town had acquired two new families in the year since the school had opened. Hardly what one would call a population explosion. Maybe a big, solid bank would be the boon they needed after all? There is a feel of permanence when a town builds with stone and brick. Her view flicked briefly to the new schoolhouse.

She considered mentioning the Council's scheme, but decided against it, at least until she knew more details. The discussion about a bank had been tipped off the rails by a frozen Indian and a golden buffalo chip before she'd learned anything definite. When she did tell anyone, it would be the whole town in a front page story below a banner headline!

Ava said wistfully, "What a big difference it would make if there really was a white bison. Why, Somerville would become a boomtown overnight."

Libby felt a scowl pinch her face—one ponderous enough to give Miss Penelope conniptions. "Don't believe it for a moment, Ava. You are a logical woman… unlike some others in town." A vision of Hazel Overmier flitted through her brain.

"Oh, I know that, Libby." Ava giggled. "Silly nonsense is all it is." Ava's words said one thing…the wily tone in her voice told Libby something else entirely.

———

The whistle of the approaching train was much louder now as Libby ascended the platform of the AT&SF Depot. Mr. Holmberg—station master, telegrapher, and baggage clerk—had shoveled the snow off of most of the platform in anticipation of the 11:10's arrival. For the moment she was alone.

Eastward, a mile down the track, a big, black exclamation mark punctuated the sky. She might have pursued the metaphor a bit further were not her thoughts still back with Ava Pickering. Libby felt uneasy, and not able to put a finger on why. *Boomtown*, Ava had declared. Was that it? Was boomtown the cocklebur sticking in her brain?

The great iron behemoth drew nearer, but today the stirrings of impending adventure did not thrill Libby as it normally would have. Lately, the notion of far-off adventures had lost their magnetic draw. Was watching trains a form of self-flagellation? She shivered in the cold morning. Instead of waiting for adventure to find her, she ought to return to the office and get to work on the white buffalo story, or confront the Council members for more information about their scheme to bring a bank to town.

"Hey Libby. Meeting someone?" Jimmy came up the ramp pulling his little mail cart.

She sighed. "No. No one."

He grinned and nodded at the approaching train. "Hoping one day the AT&SF will sweep you off the platform and carry you away to Paris or Timbuktu?"

Libby laughed. How well Jimmy knew her. "Even St. Louis would be exotic compared to Somerville."

The steam whistle shrilled and the boards beneath her feet began to pulse. She and Jimmy stepped back as the massive black engine rumbled closer, bell clanging, relief valves hissing steam, pistons slowing, drivers clacking across rail joints. Puffing, sweating, hot iron creaking, couplers clanking; the engine rolled to a crawl, gave a small, dying shudder and a final gush of steam that condensed almost at once into ice crystals.

Three passenger cars, two freight cars, a flatbed hauling a big lump under canvas, a postal car, a stock car, and finally the caboose. A conductor emerged from the rearmost passenger car and set a step stool in place. Further down, an iron latch clattered and a door rumbled open. Jimmy pulled his cart over to it. He and a man from within had a short friendly chat while exchanging postal sacks.

A man emerged from one of the passenger cars, looked around, and stepped down to the platform. Grip in hand, he moved off a few paces and watched the door he'd just come from. It was a rare occurrence indeed when a stranger disembarked in Somerville. He appeared in his mid-years, alert eyes, full face, thick body, baggy black suit, bowler hat. He carried a threadbare overcoat over one arm. His dark beard was flecked with gray.

Jimmy finished his business at the postal car and wheeled the mail sack back to her. He was about to say something when a second man stuck his head out another door, looked around, and then came warily down the steps. Two strangers? They glanced at each other. Something unspoken passed between them. The first man strolled off toward the stock car where a ramp had been lowered and two horses were being off-loaded.

The second fellow waited a while and then casually followed. He was young, tall, and mustachioed. He paused at the depot window to inspect the reflection looking back at him. The way he moved made Libby think of a cat ready to pounce. He wore a long, gray coat, the grip of a revolver in a cross-draw holster showing beneath the unbuttoned flap. His dark eyes shifted as he passed her, giving her a bold, appraising stare, a leer almost. His lips parted in a thin smile, and then he moved on down the ramp toward the stock car where the second horse waited, the first having already departed eastward along Capital Road with its rider.

"Did you see the look he gave you? What was that about?" Jimmy asked.

She frowned. "He was telling me what he had in mind."

It took a moment, then Jimmy's head snapped around. "The cad!" His eyes scrunched and glared at the man mounting the horse and moving slowly down the street.

"Who can they be?" Libby wondered aloud.

Jimmy said, "Two strangers in one day. This ties the record."

"They're traveling together."

Jimmy glanced toward the Plains Hotel where the younger one had tied his horse to the rail and was just going inside. "How do you know? Woman's intuition?"

"Reporter's observation."

———

Father was bent over the setting table patiently plucking letters from the type case and fitting them into a composing stick. He glanced over when she came in from the cold, then went back to the tedious task of setting type. "Did your news-nose sniff out anything of interest?"

"It's exasperating." Libby dropped the bag of mail onto the little table by his desk and removed her hat and gloves adding them to the pile. Beyond the open door to the back room, Mother's shadow moved about. The strong smell of lampblack being mixed into boiled linseed oil hovered in the air. "I think our little town has gone mad."

"How so?" Father asked, examining a lead letter grasped in the tips of his tweezers.

"Hazel knows all about last night, and guess who she heard it from? None other than Dr. Blinker."

He laughed quietly. "If Hazel knows, all of Somerville will soon know. People like Hazel Overmier make newspapers like the *Somerville Independent* superfluous."

"That's not all. Dour Mr. Tappermounty is actually

going to attempt to find that silly white buffalo. Can you believe it!"

He glanced at her over the rim of his spectacles, his gray eyebrows hitching up. "Interesting."

"Ava Pickering thinks such a creature would be a wonderful asset to the town. Hazel is convinced it's real. Winifred Balin telegraphed the news to her brother in Cripple Creek—he works for one of the gold mines there. Mad, I say, except for Jimmy and Mr. Pealgramm."

"I'm sure there remains a few sane individuals in Somerville." He plucked a letter from the bin, examined it frowningly, tossed it into the melt pot and selected another, which passed his inspection and went into the stick. "Howard Wilson, for instance?"

"I haven't interviewed Mr. Wilson yet, but he's on my list."

"Lieutenant Danforth?"

"*Nor* the lieutenant." She tried, but failed to keep her tone neutral.

Father favored her with a grin. "He is very much the gentleman."

She knew where this was going. "Perhaps, however, he's not *my* gentleman."

He chuckled and went back to composing his backward sentences. Father was treading old ground and she did not want to go there again. "Don't say it."

He spoke without looking up from his work. "Plainly I don't have to. When we sent you down to Winfield College, both your mother and I had hoped…"

Libby crossed her arms. "Two strangers got off the 11:10 this morning," she said forcing a change of subject.

Father took the hint, plainly miffed at her tactless diversion. "No one at the depot to meet them?"

"I'm certain they weren't visiting friends or relations.

They were traveling together but didn't want it to appear so."

"Oh? That may be newsworthy."

"I thought so. One was middle age, cheap suit and overcoat, alert. The second younger, vain, wearing a revolver and looking as though he knew how to use it." Her skin chilled as she recalled the bawdy leer he'd given her, and she backed a step closer to the stove. "The younger one left by one direction and went into the Plains Hotel. The older man rode out of town. East. Toward Topeka."

Mother poked her head out the doorway, rubber-gloved fingers pointing ceilingward, wet ink glistening blackly. "Listen to your father, Elizabeth Ann. Lieutenant Danforth would make a fine catch, and he's shown interest in the bait. Better set your hook before he gets away. At twenty-two, you really ought to be thinking about the rest of your life, you know."

"Mother!"

Father winced.

"I am thinking about the rest of my life!" Libby spun on her heels and crashed into her desk chair, scowling in a manner that would have given Miss Penelope conniptions. She snatched up pen and paper, dashed off a few notes from her brief meeting with Mr. Tappermounty—penmanship be damned—and then bundling herself into coat and scarf, plunged back into the Kansas icebox, rattling window glass on her way out.

———

By early afternoon the blizzard was in full retreat and folks began to venture away from their stoves and down comforters, and emerge from their warm rooms. As they did so, news of the dead Indian and a white buffalo crackled like prairie lightening through Somerville, Kansas. Soon most every one of the two hundred and forty residents had heard the tale, and at least two hundred and twenty of them had formed an opinion on the matter.

Because opinions are difficult to fetter—it's just their nature—they quickly began to be shared, and just as quickly something akin to a sectional divide began to form. Although the opinions varied in detail, they generally fell into two broad camps: The "what if it's true camp" on one end, and the "it's impossible camp" on the other end. Libby had definitely pitched her tent in the later.

The afternoon lengthened as Libby prowled Somerville wearing her reporter's cap, bending a stealthy ear toward the conversations that were frequent, loud, and often animated. More often than not, what she heard made her teeth grind. She forced herself to exercise restraint. She was, after all, a representative of the press. In spite of her personal beliefs, she had to at least pretend to present a neutral front.

How anyone could believe the white buffalo story baffled Libby. She'd almost convinced herself someone was playing a grand joke on the folks of Somerville... except a man had died. She'd seen him dead with her own eyes, and Mr. Tappermounty had nailed his poor, pale, nearly-frozen body securely inside a casket.

In only an hour Libby had overheard at least seven heated debates, and naturally as soon as her presence was discovered, the debaters pummeled her with questions she could not answer. One thing, however, was becoming perfectly clear. Any story she might write for Friday's edition would already be old news.

With that now obvious, how might she give her story a twist, a unique angle? Perhaps something slanted toward the mythology of white buffaloes? Cochise might be able to help her with that. Or maybe a story on the psychology of fables? Libby was familiar with the new science of psychology, having once read an article on the topic in *The Popular Science Monthly* magazine. Over in Europe, a man named Wundt was making quite an enterprise of it.

Neither idea inspired her and she put the problem temporarily aside to simmer a while.

Walking back to the newspaper office, she hoped Mother and Father were too busy setting up for the next print run to resume meddling into her romantic life. *Romantic life?* Libby sighed. Romance really wasn't in her future—at least near future. She had a career to think about. An exciting adventure lay ahead of her...somewhere. All she had to do was find that right locomotive to hitch her dream to. She sighed again. And really, other than Jimmy and the persistent Lieutenant Danforth, who else was there in Nowheresville, Kansas for her?

"Hello, Cupcake."

His voice brought Libby to a halt. The stranger who'd passed her and Jimmy on the depot boarding platform earlier that day slouched in the doorway against the display window of Hibbner's Department Store. "Going my way?

"I beg your pardon," she said, a note of indignation in her voice. His comment had been brash, and they hadn't even been properly introduced.

He straightened from his slouch and stepped out onto the boardwalk, looking her up and down in the same brazen manner he had earlier. "Well, well. This dreary borough does indeed hide a jewel." His words carried a faint accent; one she'd heard before, but just then couldn't place. "A bright trinket like you would look real fancy on my sleeve." He crooked an arm.

She gave it a leprous glare. "I am not a trinket, and jewels often attract pirates." His cocksureness was a trait Libby rarely encountered here in Somerville, except perhaps for Mr. Gannon. Mr. Gannon's self-confidence came from years lived on the wild frontier; quiet and restrained, with none of this stranger's barefaced suggestiveness.

The stranger gave a short laugh, the corner of his mouth creeping up in crooked grin that, under different circumstances, Libby might have found kind of cute. He said, "I think you and me, we ought to take a little stroll. Maybe make a memory or two."

The very idea sent a chill through her. "I think not, sir." And then she remembered where she'd heard that accent before. Doctor Ernest Dowling, her economics professor at Winfield College, had spoken with just the same inflections. She said, "New York or New Jersey?"

His eyes narrowed and his jaw tightened ever so slightly. "You're pretty keen for a girl. Joisey, if it makes a difference. As if anyone out here in the haystacks would care."

"Oh? You'd be surprised. We seeds *out here in the haystacks* care about a lot of things." Libby crossed her arms. "And accompanying brash strangers on walks is not one of them." She turned sharply and strode away, her spine and shoulders tense, but the man didn't try to stop her. Instead, his words trailed after her, low and challenging. "We'll see about that, Cupcake."

Libby felt her heart racing. Her reaction, she decided, was silly. The man had been impertinent, and displayed a suggestive arrogance that was anything but gentlemanly, but they had only exchanged words. Nothing had happened...or had there been something...? His cute grin lingered in her mind. Had she not been flattered by his attention—just a little? She recoiled at the thought, her face warming. Absolutely not! How could such a notion enter her head?

She forced her pace to slow and put aside the emotions of the moment. The proper thing to do was to reason through what *had* happened. A reporter dealt with facts not feelings, so, what were the facts? Two strangers had arrived on the morning train. One of them from the east coast, and presumably both, seeing as they traveled together. The *Joisey* stranger obviously didn't want to be here *in the haystacks*...but he had made it clear he wouldn't mind playing amongst them with one of their *jewels*. Jimmy had been right. The man was a cad!

What had brought him...them...to Somerville? Certainly not the scenery, or the weather. Land speculators? Unlikely. Especially this time of the year. Might it be the army payroll held in the depot along the tracks? Libby didn't think so. The payroll was well guarded by Lieutenant Danforth's troops, and if need be, Sheriff Bainbridge and every able-bodied man in town who could shoulder a rifle. Two men would hardly attempt to take on all that. They'd need an army of their own.

The gold buffalo chip then? She pondered that idea and rejected it. The delirious Indian had stumbled into town only last night. There had been insufficient time for word of it to have drawn strangers to Somerville.

Criminals running from the law, seeking a place to hide out? The younger one definitely looked the lawless type.

Traveling salesmen? She shook her head. No trinket cases.

There was still the curious fact that they didn't want to be seen together. What was their game? Highbinders bent on fraud? Intriguing thought, that. It was a puzzle.

Libby enjoyed puzzles...especially when she set her mind to solving them.

———

A line of dull red coach cars the color of the bleak Arizona landscape shimmered on the lonely spur line; an ill omen to the somber collection of burnt people encompassed by a blue wall. Women, babies, young children, and old men huddled beneath the hot sky while tired soldiers moved them along, urging them into lines, impatient that regimentation was such a foreign concept to the people gathered there.

He stood in the heat, atop a little rise of land watching. He did not want to be there. A voice at his side said, "They're frightened."

"I would be, too, Corporal."

And now he drifted amongst dusty blue uniforms, through desultory laughter, past gaunt faces of wax, slowly melting beneath the relentless sun. Buckles rattled, boots scuffed. Words drifted in and out of his consciousness.

They won't like it.

They'll get used to it.

Florida will crush their spirit.

The burnt people watched warily as he passed by; large eyes as black as the hair that framed them. The line move timidly, climb the steps, enter the hot rail cars. Too many women and children, too few defeated young men. The remnants of shattered families.

As the crowd shuffled past him one defiant warrior hovered protectively over a woman and young boy. The man's deep-etched face looked familiar. He limped from an old wound. Drawing near, the Apache came to a stop, recognition widening his eyes. He voice was a ghost from the past. "Tom Gannon."

Tom inhaled sharply, chilled air filling his lungs.

"Tom Gannon," the voice repeated, "let the spirits of the past sleep," it said, speaking Spanish.

Tom's eyes opened to needles of daylight, his mouth dry as the desert he'd left behind. The jaws of a vise crushed his head and he groaned.

Cochise sat in the straight-back chair grinding a pestle in a mortar, watching from across the table. Tom shut his eyes against the painful light pouring through the window and tried to work moisture into his mouth. "Time?" he managed to croak.

"Day much gone," Cochise replied in Spanish.

Tom was becoming aware of the ache in his jaw, but that was not as bad as the throbbing in his head. "Colby?"

Cochise switched from Spanish to English. "Him in barn. I put the horse away after I put you to bed."

Tom well enough knew the Apache's manner of speech, but his inclination to switch back and forth between languages, sometimes in the middle of a sentence, was still a little jarring. Giving a small groan, he pushed himself up and leaned back against the wall. "Might I trouble you for a glass of water?" His words sounded muddled. He explored his mouth with a careful finger and dug out a wad of blood-soaked cotton, tasting fresh blood.

Cochise set his grinding task aside and filled a glass from the pitcher on the sideboard, then checked the tea kettle that had begun to trail a thread of gray steam on his way over. "Bad dream?"

"The usual."

"Hmm."

Tom rinsed his mouth, spit blood into a porcelain wash basin, and then drank until the glass was empty.

Cochise returned to the table and his grinding.

"What's it you're concocting there?"

"Medicine for hangover."

"I didn't think the Apache knew about hangovers until they discovered the white man's whiskey."

He grinned. "We learn *muy rapido*."

Tom tried to recall his trip to Somerville. Much of it was a blur. He remembered searching for Dr. Blinker, remembered the barbershop and that there'd been a lot of people there—Sheriff Bainbridge, the army lieutenant, and a few others…Miss Libby one of them. He wondered briefly what she was doing there, but it was all just a jumble of images now that the whiskey had worked its way out of him. "That was some devil of a storm," he mumbled, eyes closed again.

"You passed out when Colby bring you home."

"Good horse, Colby. He's seen me home more 'an once. I don't remember a blessed thing much after leaving town. I was asleep in the saddle, you say?"

"I said passed out."

Tom heard Cochise rise from his chair and move haltingly to the stove. He parted an eye watching the Indian spill the contents of the mortar into the iron tea pot and clank a spoon in it with the intent to beat the tar out of the concoction. He poured the "medicine" into a coffee cup and started back with it, pausing a long moment at the window to stare at something outside. The limp was conspicuous today. It's always worse when the weather turns cold.

"Reckon you're right. Passed out is more like it"

Cochise handed Tom the steaming cup. "Drink."

Tom took a cautious sip. Instantly his face wrinkled and he shuddered involuntarily. The concoction was gawd-awful bitter, smelling of skunkweed and boiled cow hooves. "What's in this?"

"You no want to know. Drink it *muy rapido*. Taste goes away. Not long."

Tom steeled himself, tossed back the concoction, and then howled for more water to cut the bitterness. "I'm not so sure your remedy isn't worse than the disease,"

Cochise hobbled back to the sideboard, deposited the coffee cup in the copper wash bowl and refilled the water glass, pausing again at the window to study something beyond the glass.

Tom grabbed the glass like a drowning man a life preserver, drained it as quickly as he had the first time and said, "What's going on out there?"

He seemed to have caught Cochise in a moment of contemplation. The old Indian came out of it, took the glass from Tom and said, "Campfire in hills."

Tom groaned to his feet and groped his way to the window where the stinging light momentarily blinded him. He saw only painfully white snow, smooth as a bowl of cream, bottom-rail-of-the-corral deep. "Where?"

Cochise pointed toward the thin, gray filament climbing from the hills, rising arrow-straight into the cold air.

Tom squinted into the distance. "Who'd be camping in this weather?"

Cochise shrugged. "Maybe tomorrow I go look, Tom Gannon."

Never one to be accused of being long-winded, Cochise hobbled to the stove, chucked a log into the firebox and then sat on his sleeping pallet in the corner and began mending an old pair of moccasins that had split at the seam.

Tom peered at the far-off smoke, wondering.

Probably a hunter.

————

Quis, quid, qua…qua…quaaaan…

Libby made a face that would have been thoroughly discouraged by dear, sweet, acerbic Miss Penelope.

Quan…quando! Yes, that's it. *Quando!*

*Quando, ubi, cur, quem ad modum, quibus admi…admin…*Hmmm. *Admini-n-i.* She felt her forehead furrow again and tried to put Miss Penelope out of mind. *Admini-c-u…u…ulis!*

Got it! *Quis, quid, quando, ubi, cur, quem ad modum, quibus adminiculis.* She growled a quiet rumble deep in her throat. Why on God's green earth had Blankenship insist she learn it in Latin? Wouldn't plain English have sufficed? *Who, what, when, where, why, in what way, by what means.* Every journalism school taught the fundamental rules of proper reporting, but only at Winfield College under the tutelage of Professor Erwin Blankenship must one have to learn it in a language dead to all but Linnaeanists and Catholics!

"Don't frown, dear," mother scolded.

"It is a fine piece of writing, Libby," Father said, sawing at the steak on his plate. The street beyond the Plains Hotel window was already dark and they were the lone guests in the small dining room. Setting up for a print run always made for a tiring day. Seldom was there any time left at the end of it for Mother to prepare supper.

"It's trite and uninspired," Libby objected. "I managed the who, what, when, and where, but stumbled over the rest of it. What is the *quem ad modum?*"

Father said, "You did your best with what you had to work with. In this business not every article is going to rate four columns in *The Picayune*. Sometimes simply filling a quarter column with black ink in the local press is all one might hope for."

Mother said, "Pouting is unbecoming, Elizabeth Ann.

You've hardly eaten a bite. You've just sat there brooding and rearranging the peas and carrots."

"She's confronting her muse, dear," Father said, chewing a morsel of steak, medium rare.

Mother rolled her eyes. "She needs to confront her supper right now. Muses can wait."

"On that account I'm afraid I must disagree, Mrs. Barrett," Dr. Blinker's voice intruded. He smiled and doffed his gray derby as they turned toward him, giving mother a pleasant nod. "When the muse knocks, one must of necessity fling wide the door and invite her in, for she is an ephemeral nymph who surely will skip on her way leaving you in the dark clutches of writer's despair."

Father chuckled. Mother forced a faint smile past her scowl. And Libby automatically edited Dr. Blinkers flowery speech to: *Seize the opportunity.*

"I didn't see you come in, Matthew." Father glanced toward the door beyond the lobby desk.

"Err, the alley entrance." His thumb hitched toward the rear of the building. "It's more convenient seeing as I often leave my surgery by way of the back door." Dr. Blinker shifted his view. "I was hoping you'd stop by my office today, Miss Libby."

Caught! Her smile felt stiff. "I didn't forget you asking me to drop by and glance over your latest story, it's just that the day was so very busy. I have an important story to write...and a deadline." It wasn't a lie—not exactly—although she'd conveniently left out the bit about avoiding him on purpose. The statement was factually true. The white buffalo article was not *fait accompli*. She'd written what in her opinion was only a rough draft of the *Curious Incident of the Golden Chip*. She did, after all, have until Thursday evening to expand and polish the piece before the typesetting was finalized for Friday's edition.

Father said, "Have you come to take supper, Matthew? You can join us."

Dr. Blinker glanced toward the lobby and then back, his lips hitching to one side in what Libby thought looked more like apprehension than an easy smile. "So kind of you, Harold. Supper had been my intention, but it just now occurred to me that I'd promised Howard another chance to best me in a round of checkers. Mrs. Wilson sets out a splendid table of crackers and cheese, and canned corned beef that her Dublin sister 'posts'." He returned his attention to Libby. "Yes, my story. Ahem. I'd forgotten about that," he said unconvincingly. "Actually, what I'd hoped for was an opportunity to discuss last night's extraordinary event. I've come up with a few ideas."

Libby's interest perked, but before she could speak, Dr. Blinker said, "A curiosity I discovered among my collection of medical tomes. Something you may very well want to include in the story you are writing, Miss Libby."

"You've piqued my curiosity, Dr. Blinker. Do tell me more."

Dr. Blinker's fingers fidgeted the brim of his derby. "I've come across a small book in my library that may enlighten us on the problem of how such an unusual phenomenon might occur. Rather than try to explain it here, it would be better if we met in my office. Tomorrow morning?"

An educated man like Dr. Blinker giving credence to such a notion? Libby hardly believed her ears. She kept her voice neutral. "I should like to see the book. Might I borrow it?"

"I'd be happy to lend it to you, but you see, it's published in French. You don't perchance read French, do you?" His view flicked toward the lobby, and back.

"A few expressions perhaps. Enough to be annoying." She laughed.

Dr. Blinker smiled. "A pity. So you see, I shall have to translate it for you, but I'm sure you'll immediately grasp the significance of what I've found. It will likely contribute important information to the article you are preparing."

"I'll come around in the morning then," Libby said.

"Splendid. Well, I must run. I'm probably late already." He bade them all good-bye and turned on his heels, settling his hat back onto his head as he strode across the lobby and out the front door.

Father said, "He seems in a hurry. Didn't realize Matthew took his checkers so seriously."

"He did seem distracted," Libby agreed. "I wonder what he's discovered?"

"His eyes were shifty," Mother said, turning back to her plate. "No more dawdling, Elizabeth Ann. Pay attention to your supper."

Father took up his knife and resumed sawing at his steak. "If you're lucky, Dr. Blinker has discovered the *quem ad modum* you've been looking for."

Libby wasn't going to get her hopes up. Dr. Blinker had done it on purpose. He'd been transparently cryptic to excite her interest, and then he conveniently strolled off, leaving her to wonder. That was his way and it carried over into his writing. He was a kind and caring person, and she generally enjoyed his company, but his chicanery sometimes set her teeth on edge. She imagined him being the sort of little boy who'd hide his mother's knitting basket, and then crouch behind the settee giggling as she searched for it.

She picked up her fork, no enthusiasm for eating. The peas were cold, and the mashed potatoes lumpy. The steak tasted good; a little too rare for her liking, but not so red as to bother her very much.

Mother said, "We need to order more lampblack."

Father grunted as he chewed, then swallowed and said, "I'm preparing an order now. I'll include a box of lampblack. Have you read about that new type-setting machine a fellow named Mergenthaler has invented? It's called linotype."

Expertly excising the bone from what was left of her steak, Mother said, "I have. And it's too expensive for a four page weekly like the *Independent*."

Father sighed. "True, true. It would speed up the publication though. We might even fit two editions a week."

"Somerville hardly provides enough news for one edition," Mother noted.

Libby only vaguely heard any of this, her thoughts distracted by Dr. Blinker's cryptic hint that there might be a reasonable explanation for gold bison manure. Movement in the lobby drew her attention. The brash young stranger came down the staircase from the lodging rooms above. Without his heavy coat and hat, he appeared slenderer than before. Dark hair combed straight back, a brown jacket, unbuttoned, over a brown vest crossed by a gold chain. His shoes were polished, and he had left his revolver in his room.

He crossed the small lobby and stopped in the doorway looking around the dining room. Since it was only she and her parents there, his view fell immediately upon her. His mouth quirked in a tight smile.

She averted her eyes and whispered so that only Father could hear. "There he is now."

Father's view slid to one side as he brought a forkful of mashed potatoes to his mouth. Mother was saying something. Libby had blanked it out, but Father had not, and replied without missing a beat, "Yes, dear, I'll include linseed oil with the order." Softer, "He appears to be searching for someone."

Libby glanced up, then back to her plate pretending interest in the food there. "He's checking his watch."

"A meeting?" Father suggested, dissecting another wedge of meat from his steak.

"The first man who stepped off the train?" Libby wondered.

"Possible, but you said you observed him riding out of town."

"Harold, you're not listening to me."

Father raised his voice. "You would like me to purchase gum rubber gloves. Two pair or four?"

"Four."

Libby whispered, "He's starting across the room."

Father looked up as the man passed behind him and took a table against the wall. "Undoubtedly, a certifiable stranger, at least as far as Somerville is concerned." He set down knife and fork and pushed back his chair.

"What are you doing?" Libby shrilled, her voice pitched louder, higher than she'd intended.

Mother glanced up, alerted by Libby's startled tone.

Father grinned. "Certifiable strangers fall under the category of news. I'm a newspaper man and news is my business."

———

Corporal Leland Talbot slouched poutingly in a chair at the back the Billberry Saloon and Billiard Hall sucking a beer and peering bleary-eyed across the table at Jimmy. "Fifteen dollars!" he declared for the fourth or fifth time. "It's a nasty business, Jimmy, I tell you. You sleep cold and wet, you eat cold and wet, the food is wormy and the work is despicable. It's always 'Yes, sir, yes, sir.' Sir says, 'Shoot that Injun," and I says, 'Yes, sir,' and pull the trigger. Sir says, 'Burn that tee-pee,' and I says, 'Yes, sir,' and throw a torch." Leland sucked his beer and slung the foam from his lips. "Fifteen dollars, and for that generous sum of money Uncle Sam expects me to kill folks I don't know who never done me no hurt, burn their homes, kill their stock, scatter their families, take a bullet, lose an eye, addle my brain. All for what?" He slouched deeper into the hard chair as if the weight of his job was pushing him down. "Some silly notion with a fancy name. Manifest Destiny. Fifteen dollars a month. Is it worth it for all the dirt that gets dumped into my soul?"

How to answer that? Jimmy had never been in the army, never harmed another man as he could remember, never much shot a rifle except once in a while at coyotes making their way into Ma's chickens. "The wars are over now. The Indians on reservations."

"They're never over, Jim. Not up here." he tapped his head. "Pine Ridge's a dirty memory what will never wash away."

"You can quit the army, can't you?"

Leland stared into his beer, his thoughts elsewhere. He mumbled something that sounded like, "As if saying the words would make the guilt go away."

"Why don't you quit?" Jimmy said again, louder.

Leland's head came slowly up. "What would I do?"

"Must be all sorts of jobs you could do. You can work for the post office like me. It pays more than fifteen a month." Jimmy thought about the train that came through town this morning. "Shoot, the railroads are booming. Laying track all across this country. You might work for one of them."

Leland grimaced and shook his head. "Don't think I'd be much good at clerking or punching tickets. Don't have size enough to haul track." He tapped his beer mug lightly upon the table top and his continence suddenly brightened. "But you know what I have been considering?"

"What's that?"

He hesitated. "You'll laugh if I tell you."

"I won't."

"Promise?"

"Promise."

Leland thought it over like he was weighing should-he-shouldn't-he, and finally came to a decision. "Well, I heard about that big lump of gold from Lieutenant Danforth. He said it sure looked like the real McCoy."

Jimmy suspected what was coming next.

Leland continued, "I got to thinking if such an animal is out there somewhere, well someone is going to catch him. Why not me?"

Jimmy almost laughed, but he'd promised Leland he'd not to do such a thing. Instead he tried a more roundabout tack to talk sense to the corporal. "How can the lieutenant be certain it's really gold and not, oh, something else?" Jimmy couldn't think of what that something else might be because the buffalo chip really had looked like gold…maybe not exactly like the gold in, say, a double eagle. The gold in coins was refined, poured, and stamped. The gold chip, if genuine, had been somehow *refined* in the gut of a buffalo.

"Lieutenant Danforth said that Dr. Blinker said it was real. Good'nough for me."

Jimmy had to agree. If anyone could identify real gold, Dr. Blinker was most qualified. Somerville didn't have a jeweler who would be an authority in such matters.

In spite of four beer's worth of alcohol in his blood, Leland's countenance turned so intense, Jimmy would have thought him sober as a preacher on Sunday. Leland glanced sideways and lowered his voice. "Borglan and me, we got to talking about it when the lieutenant was away and Timor and Scofield were out back tending the mules. He's in if I decide to bolt, and I think Timor might want in, too."

"In? Bolt? You mean like leaving your post...the depot? Isn't that called desertion or something?"

"What do I owe the government? All I get from them is a tiny paycheck and a wagon load of guilt."

"Even if you do manage to find this white buffalo and catch it, what are you going to do with it? You can just mosey a buffalo along like you can a cow. Put a rope on an animal like that and it'll drag you clear into Colorado."

"We'll build a corral—a strong corral. Keep it penned up."'

"How long do you expect that to last before a landowner or drifter comes along and takes that buffalo away from you, or worse, shoots you and Borglan dead, and then takes it?"

"You're not thinking this through, Jim. All we need to do is keep it corralled up for a couple weeks. I figured it out on a piece of paper. Two or three bales of hay passing through that critter's magical gut will set us both up for life! Me'n Borglan will drift on our way and change our names. Who's gonna know? Army's got no way to run us down, even if they had an inclination to do so. Men up and disappear all the time."

"Where will you go?"

"Can't speak for Borglan, but I thought about heading down to South America. Probably don't have to go that far. The Territories will most likely suit. Albuquerque maybe." Leland became thoughtful, weighing a notion. "You know, Jim, if'n you wanted to join up with us, you'd be welcome." He gave a quiet laugh. "We'll just toss another bale to that buffalo and make you rich, too." His lips hitched to one side in a calculating manner. "Wouldn't hurt to have another pair of eyes, and extra horse and gun."

"I'd not be much help there. I don't own a horse nor a gun." Both were true, and just then he was relieved to be able to admit to his lack of material possessions.

"That's easy 'nough to remedy."

Jimmy grimaced. Gold fever had gone straight to Leland's brain. Well, at least he was able to keep a level head about this white buffalo nonsense...him and Libby and a few others in Somerville. "I'll think about it," he said noncommittally.

And later that evening as he followed the trampled path through the snow back to his house he did think about it, and somewhere along the way his thoughts turned down a trail he did not want to travel. Maybe it was the beer thinking for him, or maybe he was being worn down by all the enthusiasm in town about a mythical bovine out in the flint hills just waiting to make someone richer than King Midas? Whatever the reason, he found himself considering Leland's offer, and in spite of his good common sense, he couldn't help but imagine how life would be different should he come to possess such a wondrous animal—if only for a couple weeks.

When Jimmy arrived home Mr. Suredor and his mother were chatting in the parlor, sipping tea and finishing up the leftover spice cake mom had baked the day before. It was no secret the stableman and his mother —widower and widow—had been seeing each other. Mr. Suredor was well regarded around town, and Jimmy more or less approved of the growing relationship, even if that was none of his business.

His arrival appeared to put a damper on their chatter.

A few minutes later the stableman left for his own home over on Lee Street, and Jimmy put himself to bed while his mom gathered the dishes into the sink. He drifted off to sleep with thoughts of white buffaloes accompanied by his mom humming a Stephen Foster tune as plates and cups clattered from the water to the drying rack.

———

Father set the small snifter of brandy gently upon the table and peered across the chessboard at Libby. "Do you find it so strange?" He wore a slightly puzzled expression. Libby suspected the question was a distraction. Father was pondering a crafty maneuver; arranging the pieces on the chessboard in his head. She moved her pawn with his bishop in her sights, and then the king, three moves out.

"Strange? Not at all. I simply do not believe it."

Scrunched into the corner of the settee, bent toward the light of the best lamp in the parlor, Mother lowered her fancywork and peered over the top of her close-work spectacles. "I thought he was a nice looking young man. He was very polite to your father."

Libby's stomach clenched. "He is a cad, Mother. And in the slight chance that I haven't mentioned this before, I am not pining for a beau, no matter how handsome or polite you may think he is. Anyway, we were discussing his résumé, not his demeanor."

Mother smirked and turned back to her needlework.

"Ahem. Are you finished?"

Libby glanced back at Father, and then at the board, observing she still held a finger upon the pawn. She released the piece and leaned back in her chair. "I mean really. A phrenologist? And he claims to want to establish a practice here in Nowheresville?"

Father ran fingers through his sparse gray hair as he studied the board. "Indeed. Makes one want to scratch his head."

Libby rolled her eyes.

Father sipped of his brandy. "It may come as a surprise to learn that not everyone considers Somerville, Kansas, a back alley at the end of the world, my dear." He moved his castle, effectively blocking her advance on his bishop. No matter, Libby had foreseen the possible parry and was prepared for it.

"But why in heaven's name did you offer up Dr. Blinker as someone he might inquire of? He may oppose the arrival of competition." She slid her bishop in place hoping Father wouldn't perceive her strategy.

Father smiled. "I'm rather certain dentistry and head bumps do not have so much in common as to compete with each other." He moved his queen down one rank.

Libby's thoughts drifted from the game. None of this made sense. Her naturally skeptical brain was scurrying about looking for loopholes in the story. "Let us assume Mr. David Bartlow is the genuine article. What of the other man, his traveling companion?" She positioned her knight.

"He made no mention of him." Father moved his castle one square, opening a path to his king.

She scowled in a manner Miss Penelope would have strongly disapproved. "You might have asked?" she countered. "I would have. Isn't that what reporters do? *Quis, quid, quando, ubi, cur, quem ad modum, quibus adminiculis.*"

Father laughed. "I'm not reporting on a crime, my dear. I was merely welcoming him to town. My only intention was to introduce him to the good people of Somerville through the pages of our newspaper. He seemed agreeable to that. Now, are you going to make your move or pummel me with questions?"

She studied the board, reviewing her strategy while attempting to put the brash stranger out of mind. She slid a pawn into a sacrificial position.

From the settee Mother said, "Mrs. Filbert was by the office this afternoon while you were away, Harold. I meant to tell you earlier. She says there's to be a town meeting in the church tomorrow at half-past-one to discuss what's to be done about that white buffalo."

"What's to be done?" Libby blurted, looking over. "What on earth is there to be done? Arrange for a hunting party? Has the whole town gone daft?"

Father's reply was more reserved. "I hadn't heard that." He glanced at Libby. "It does appear this may be getting a little out of hand. I suppose one of us ought to attend."

"I had planned to rent a gig from the livery, after my meeting with Dr. Blinker, and drive out to Mr. Gannon's place to check in on him and visit with Cochise."

Father's lips tightened ever so slightly. He obviously still didn't think an Arizona Apache would know anything of a Nebraska Sioux's white buffalo legend. "Then I will attend the meeting."

Libby thought a moment. "But I should very much like to be there as well. It may help me put an interesting slant to my article."

Father nodded. "Then we shall both attend, and you can interview Mr. Cochise the day after." He moved his knight. "Check."

Libby startled. She hadn't seen that coming.

Father grinned and tasted his brandy. "You lost concentration."

"Did I?" She sent him a smirk and slid her castle

through the opening her pawn had enabled. "Checkmate."

Father's eyes got big, the muscles of his jaws slackening.

Mother spoke without looking up from her fancy-work, "Did you lose another game, Harold?"

"Indeed he did, Mother." Libby stood. "I'm going to turn in for the night. I have much to do tomorrow. Good night."

Father's view remained on the chessboard, his jaw still unhinged as she went downstairs to the office to stoke the fire in the stove and retrieve a large, smooth rock from atop it. She'd learned long ago that if you didn't have three dogs to curl up at your feet on shivery nights like this, a warm river rock tucked under the blanket by your toes was the next best thing.

DAY THREE
WEDNESDAY

A web of fairy lace had frosted over the window during the night. Libby scraped off a patch of it with the back of a whale bone comb to see a clear, blue sky emerging from the dark shadows of the distant hills. The golden rim of sunlight promised a splendid day ahead. No matter the temperature, with a big sun in the sky and no wind Libby could take on the world.

What to wear? She peered into her wardrobe at the scant selection available to her. She was to going to visit Dr. Blinker this morning and then attend the church meeting in the afternoon. *Business proper but comfortably casual.* Miss Penelope had called it *business casual*, but that was an expression Libby suspected her etiquette pedagogue had just made up. She'd never seen it in print, and as far as Libby was concerned, until an expression had been baptized with ink, it was not official.

Libby eyed the corset with disdain. A fitted chemise offered enough support for her modest figure. She considered and rejected a long shirt. Trains were growing out of fashion and in this weather they were quite impractical. She chose instead a blue, gored skirt with a high hem of gray, buckram cotton; quite modern if not a bit revealing about the ankles, but such was the trend in fashions, at least for women not yet married. She matched it with a simple, mail-order shirtwaist with a bit of ruffle down the yokes and three-quarter length leg-o-mutton sleeves; the day looked to be warmer than any in the past week. A frill of blue and yellow ribbons beneath the tall collar added a splash of color. Beige, doeskin boots that matched her gloves completed the attire.

Pinning her lapel watch in place, her gaze fell upon the youthful tintype of Father wearing a circus master's frock. Behind him an elephant posed upon a round platform, and in the distance the words *Hankly & Witherspoon Circus* emblazoned a banner across a large tent. Libby hardly recognized the wise, newspaper editor of today in that young man of yesteryear.

A final examination in the tall mirror—an extravagance which was really too large for her tight room—produced a satisfactory nod, and Libby left her bedroom to face the day ahead.

Sitting at the kitchen table reading his *Harper's*, Father glanced up and cast a disapproving glance.

"What?"

"If not for those boots, you'd be almost indiscreet."

She lifted her skirt to the top of the boots, examined one of the clunky heels, and then her father. "It is nearly the twentieth century. This is what woman are wearing in New York City."

"Need I remind you, you do not reside in New York City."

From the stove Mother said, "Don't pay any attention to your father. He still thinks this is 1865. You look quite fashionable, Elizabeth Ann. I've been thinking myself if it isn't time to raise the hem on a few of my dress."

"I think you should," Libby said.

"I think you should not," Father countered.

"Fuddy-duddy." Mother turned back to the bacon sizzling in the skillet. It filled the air with a wonderful aroma, and the stove filled their quarters above the newspaper office with enough heat to battle the cold attacking the window panes.

"What are your plans for the day?" Mother inquired.

"First I intend to visit Dr. Blinker's surgery to learn what astounding discovery he's made that would explain how a buffalo could produce such marvelous manure."

"Is that skepticism I'm hearing in your voice," Father inquired from behind his magazine.

"I didn't know Dr. Blinker could speak French," Mother said, bringing breakfast plates to the table.

"Who would not be skeptical?" Libby replied. "You'd think every soul in town would be skeptical. They're not. They believe it's genuine. They've become obsessed with the notion of becoming rich."

"That's how the expression *gold fever* came about," Father noted, retrieving the coffee pot from the stove and filling their cups.

"At the end of it, I'm sure you will find a reasonable explanation, Elizabeth Ann."

"I intend to. And after my visit with Dr. Blinker, I will attend the town meeting with Father. In-between I'll do a bit of investigating. I want to speak to Mr. Wilson and Sheriff Bainbridge, then stop by Pealgramm's to see if Jimmy has heard anything."

"Jimmy is such a nice boy," Mother said, nibbling a crispy strip of bacon.

———

It was not a place she enjoyed visiting...much like Mr. Tappermounty's macabre temple of death, only different.

Different in that here no dark rituals took place; no bloody alters of steel and porcelain, no pallid cadavers awaiting chemical infusions and whatever else Mr. Tappermounty employed in his grim business. The specter of this place was not death, but pain. Pain was the business of the day, or at least a part of Dr. Blinker's business. The croquet stake that stood beyond the wickets of pain was a hoped for cessation of torment and a "right proper set of choppers" as Bo Huffman the blacksmith once declared.

Dr. Blinker sat at his desk at the back of the small surgery, beyond the ominous chair of black leather and nickel plated levers. It's padded armrests had suffered the death-squeeze of many a man and woman—herself included—offering up their teeth to the slow grind of Dr. Blinker's dental engine humming beneath the furiously pumping treadle. Libby fancied it the Dentist's Dance; a one step jig accompanied by the music of clanking metal and braided cord whirring though nickel plated pulley wheels of varying sizes.

A glass-fronted cabinet held brown bottles, glass vials, and rubber-stoppered tubes. Another shelf showed paper bags from various suppliers of dental medicinals, a pair of mortars and pestles—one large, one small—and a balance scale with two shiny dishes suspended on either end of a brass beam. The things of dental alchemy, Libby mused. The lowest shelf displayed an armory of unpleasant weapons: things with points and barbs, cutting things and yanking things. Her shoulders tensed and she looked away thinking of Mr. Gannon. At least these pulling things weren't all rusty.

Alongside the cabinet was the door to the back room that housed a small furnace and a workbench where Dr. Blinker blended his amalgams and fashioned replacement teeth. Next to the door resided Dr. Blinker's large desk with a myriad of cubbyholes, ledger slots, and tiny drawers. He turned from the desk now as she entered and smiled, rising to his feet.

"Miss Libby! I'm so pleased you are here." He hurried across the room and took her elbow, escorting her past the odious black perch. "Here, let me fetch a chair for you." Dashing back to the front, he took up one of the chairs from what might be called a waiting room, only it wasn't a room proper, simply a small corner with a bright carpet and two nicely upholstered chairs.

The room was toasty and she loosened her scarf and her coat and removed her gloves. "I'm interested to hear what you've found, Dr. Blinker. You were quite cryptic last evening."

"I still wasn't certain about what I'd discovered and did not want to give you a false hope. Since then, I've taken time to more carefully translate the text. I think I've found something startling." He paused for her reaction. She was careful to appear professional, and not show skepticism.

"Yes? What is it?" She asked, alert to any trickery the good doctor was about to spring on her.

He picked a slim volume that lay open upon the desk.

"I didn't know you spoke French."

"Speak it, no, no. I'm afraid I could never get my tongue to cooperate." He smiled. "Reading it, however, is quite a different matter. You see, some of the most modern developments in the field of dentistry are coming out of Europe; France in particular. In dental school," he pointed to the certificate of graduation from the *Philadelphia Dental College* framed in polished walnut on the wall above the desk, "I was required to study the latest scientific papers, and many of those had been published in French. So you see, my hand was forced." He smiled again.

That made sense and eased some of her skepticism. "It is in a book about dentistry that you made your discovery?"

"No. Not dental but bacterial. Somehow this book found its way into my possession and followed me from Philadelphia to Kansas at the bottom of a steamer trunk. It bears the stamp from the college library. I must have borrowed it at some point and then forgot I had it and failed to return it."

"Bacterial? As in Van Leeuwenhoek's animalcules?"

"Not, exactly. More like Louis Pasteur's investigations into infectious properties of certain bacterium. This small volume contains the results of the investigation into the bacterial world by another Frenchman by the name of, ah, err, Monsieur Jules."

Libby was intrigued, her skepticism melting like snow on a warm rooftop. "Go on."

He glanced to a paper on his desk upon which he'd written several lines with his Waterman Ideal Fountain Pen that lay beside the paper. "According to Monsieur Jules's scientific inquiries, there appears to be a certain bacteria that thrives in certain soils rich in certain minerals. It is able to ingest these minerals, which would be deadly to another species of bacteria, but is changed within this bacteria's protoplasm into inert molecules of gold. Monsieur Jules discovered the specie in a vein of gold, leading him to postulate that the veins had been deposited over thousands of years by many millions of generations of the bacteria."

Libby's jaw slackened. "Amazing." She was uncomfortably confused. What Dr. Blinker said actually made sense—sort of. Yet none of it made any sense at all! Her brain rebelled at the notion that any animal could poop gold nuggets! "If true, how do you explain the buffalo's excretion? A bison is not a bacteria."

"Ah, now here's where a bit of speculation comes in, Miss Libby. Suppose there is a bacteria living in these hills that is able to glean molecules of gold from the soil and form them into golden nodules within its protoplasm the same as Jules's marvelous wee beasties do, and let us suppose further that these bacteria can be taken up by the roots of the indigenous grasses. And then—"

"The white buffalo eats the grass," she said, following his logic. She frowned. "That still doesn't explain anything."

Dr. Blinker nodded. "True, true. The process would require certain morphological changes within the buffalo's alimentary canal to allow it to assimilate those tiny bits of gold into a single lump." He shrugged. "What we have here is an arrow that may point us in a direction. Unfortunately, I do not have the answer you seek, but being the competent newspaper reporter that you are, I'm sure you will run the trail down to its end." He thought a moment, his eyes brightening with an idea. "You might include the hypothesis in your article with an appeal to your readers for suggestions as to how the buffalo might accomplish such an amazing feat."

Libby had expected a sly ruse, and instead had gotten a scientific suggestion that actually made sense of something nonsensical! More perplexed now than when she'd arrived, Libby said, "I will consider doing just that." She rose and fastened the buttons of her coat. "Thank you for giving me yet another puzzle, as if I hadn't enough to deal with already." She looked at the book resting there on his desk, the title indecipherable except the word *Terre*, which was so similar to the word terra that she suspected it meant land or earth. She attempted to put the rest of the title to memory but at that moment Dr. Blinker discarded the paper containing his notes and it fell upon the cover.

"Sorry if I've burdened your day unnecessarily," he said, hiding a small grin. She suspected he had rather enjoyed it. "Will you be attending the meeting this afternoon?"

"Indeed, I will. And you?"

"But of course. I wouldn't miss it for a pot of," he smirked, "buffalo manure."

Libby rolled her eyes. He chuckled and took her elbow starting her toward the door. Suddenly remembering something, he halted and said, "Oh by the way, might I ask a favor of you?"

She knew instantly what was coming. "Your latest story?"

"If you could be so kind?" He stepped back to the desk, opened a drawer and withdrew and sheaf of paper half an inch thick, punched and bound with brass staples. "I've titled it, *The Adventures of John Steele and the Crater Monsters of the Moon.*"

"Crater monsters of the moon?" She took it from his hand trying not to show reluctance.

"Intriguing title, don't you think?"

"Intriguing. How does Mr. Steele acquire the moon?"

"Balloon, of course." He seemed surprised she would have to ask.

"Of course," she said doubtfully.

"It's a scientific romance. The genre is becoming fashionable in Europe. Shelley, Doyle, Verne. And in this country, too, among the more cosmopolitan cities back east. Even our own Mr. Twain with his clever *Connecticut Yankee!*" He smiled at the manuscript in her hands. "I did enjoy writing it. Perhaps with some professional editing," he hinted, "it may find its way into print."

She glanced at the sheaf of paper noting that it was of quality bond, and that Dr. Blinker had acquired a typewriting machine. The text was crisp and easy to read;

much more legible than his last story, which had been written on inexpensive foolscap with a common dip pen, not his new Waterman. "I'll look it over when I have some time. Perhaps next week."

"Wonderful. I'm anxious for your learned review of the yarn. Oh, you've forgotten your gloves." Dr. Blinker retraced his steps and plucked them from the small table, handing then to her.

"Thank you."

————

"Stop squirming Dick or I'm liable to nick off your neck wart again."

"Sorry, Howard. It's just sometimes that woman can be so down right infuriating I can hardly stand it. Winnie and Hazel Overmier are both cut from the same bolt."

Howard Wilson chuckled as he expertly glided the razor under Dick Balin's chin and down his throat, skimming off shaving cream and whiskers. "I don't see as Winnie is anything at all like Hazel."

Dick didn't dispute that except to observe that, "Both those women busy-bee-buzzing about town putting their noses into other folk's business just about gives me the hives."

They laughed and Howard admonished Dick again about the perils of squirming while his razor was employed about his neck.

"Did I tell you she telegraphed Brad—that's her brother—about the buffalo and his inestimable dropping?"

"Hadn't heard."

"First thing after Hazel popped into the shop to announce what happened here with that Injun and all.

Brad sent a telegram back to her today. It was a long one. Must have cost him all of a dollar and a half to send."

"Did it put to rest the silly notion?" Howard inquired.

"I dare say not! More like it dumped a bucket of kerosene onto Winnie's fire. Brad said he heard of some similar stories from some of the miners he works with there in Cripple Creek."

"No. That can't be," Howard said, carefully scraping around the large brown wart on Dick's neck.

"Yes indeed! Brad wrote back as if he believed it all. He said that one of the miners he knows claims there's something called a Ra Beetle that lives in the Sahara Desert in Egypt. He said that once a long time ago all those Egyptian pyramids were covered over with pure gold and that these Ra Beetles went and ate it all off, and to this very day the A-rabs who live over there find little gold beads of Ra Beetle poop in the desert sands."

"He put all that in a telegram?"

"And more."

"Hmm. Wonder what Holmberg thought of it taking it down?"

"Likely cost a dollar and a half to send!" Dick repeated.

"Tell you what, Dick, don't let on about that Ra Beetle. Keavy might get wind of it. She's already pressing for me to go buffalo hunting."

"Haha—Ouch!"

"Warned you."

"Too late to shut that gate. Winnie's already told Hazel Overmier."

"Oh my. The bull's out of the pen." Howard sighed, "Leastwise I'll be prepared for it when I get home tonight. Here, put a finger on this cotton ball while I fetch the styptic powder."

———

Having run out of milk for his coffee, and not wanting to trudge all the way home for a pint from this morning's milking, Bob Heelcroft hung the "Be Back Soon" sign in the window and went down the street to Saunder's Grocery Store for a can of condensed.

Kip Saunder was arranging canned peaches on the shelf when the bell announced Bob's arrival. "Morning, Bob," Kip called as Bob rounded the other side of the shelf where canned milk was kept.

"Howdy, Kip."

"Run out again?"

"One of these days I'll just have to learn to drink it black."

Kip slid the last can of peaches in place and then strolled around the corner where Bob held two cans in one hand debating over a third in his other hand. Ought he cache one in reserve for the next time he ran out? In the end Bob decided against it. The next time he needed a can of condensed milk, he could always dash down the street for it. These days he was never so busy that he couldn't afford to leave the shop unattended for fifteen minutes. He grimaced. Fact was, he hadn't seen a paying customer in two days.

Kip said, "Going to the meeting today?"

Bob frowned. "I expect Betty will drag me along to it."

"Might be interesting to hear what folks are planning to do."

"Planning? What's there to plan?" Bob asked.

"Whal, you know, like what're we going to do about that white buffalo."

"We?"

"Whal, you know, the folks of Somerville."

"Don't tell be you've bought into that story, too, Kip?"

"Naw, not me, but Hazel Overmier says that Tapper-mounty believes it, and so does Dr. Blinker."

"Hazel's a gossip tornado. And when it all blows over in a day or two, poor Reverend Overmier is left cleaning up the wreckage left in her wake."

Kip laughed. "Ain't that the truth. Sheila was in this morning and said Woodrow took off to poke around the hills for a day or two."

"Hard to believe Woodrow Tappermounty would take such a tale seriously." Bob drew in a breath and made a display of expelling it loudly. "I think I'll take these," he said, starting for the cash register. He paid for the condensed milk, tucked the cans in the pocket of his coat and turned to the door then paused and looked back at Kip Saunder. "Guess you and me are the only two men left in town keeping a level head about this nonsense."

"Reckon so. Just the same I'll probably wander on over to the meeting for a listen."

"Suppose I'll see you there, then," Bob replied unenthusiastically.

He strode up the sidewalk to his watch repair shop, glad for the clear sky and a warm sun. The boardwalk had been swept and the snow was melting quickly as it usually does in this part of Kansas. The road was muddy. Another day and the strong Kansas sun would take care of that, too.

In spite of the pleasant manner in which the day was shaping up to be, his mood was gloomy. He didn't want to attend the meeting but Betty would insist on it. Judging by the murmuring he'd heard so far, most of the town would be there. That meant the prospects for conducting any business today was vanishingly small. That meant another afternoon without a coin going into the till. That also meant he'd have no solid excuse to give Betty why he ought not to attend. He sighed, and not for the first time wondered if the time hadn't come to move on down the line? A man had to earn a living. Towns like Salina and Hays were growing, unlike Somerville.

Pondering all this, Bob Heelcroft stepped down off the boardwalk to cross Lyman Road. A glance to his right showed him the new schoolhouse at its end. That had been a hopeful dream for the folks of Somerville. Instead it had blasted a huge hole into the town's budget; one it might never climb out of if the bonds failed. He frowned. Salina was looking better and better.

Beyond the schoolhouse he spied a small cloud of smoke far out over the flint hills. Who would be out there this time of the year, he wondered briefly? Then he reached the front door of his shop and the sobering reality of business—or the lack thereof—took over his thoughts as he went into the back room to fetch a can opener.

———

The boardwalk along Bridges Road was a sporadic affair with wide gaps where vacant lots awaited new business to put down roots. Bridges road itself was quickly dissolving into a long, muddy stretch as the snow sacrificed itself to a bright sky, its vapors rising to the heavens like those long-ago spirits of the three hundred defeated Spartans to their Elysium Fields. *Molon Labe!* Libby smiled, tucking the metaphor away in her brain to be used in a future article. The mud was not so much a deterrent as it was a challenge. By holding to the south side of the road, which lay in the shade of the few buildings there, she skip-jumped patches of snow managing to keep her shoes unscathed from the mud.

Suredor's Livery, Feed, and Sales loomed large at the edge of town. Within its dark, chill interior dust motes glinted in the light through high, dingy windows. Normally the large door brightened the building. Presently it was shut against the cold. The stove in the corner near Mr. Suredor's desk threw off barely enough heat to keep his work corner warm. She looked about for the proprietor. "Mr. Suredor?" she called.

A rustling-scratching noise down at the end of one of the aisles ceased and Tommy Cassidy's face peeked out from a stall. "Hello, Miss Barrett," he called, slinging the long handled rake over his shoulder and coming over.

"Hi Tommy. What are you doing here at-" Libby looked at her watch "-at ten forty-five? Why aren't you in school?"

His face brightened in the dusty light. "Miss Pickering said we could all go home early on account of the meeting across the street, at the church."

"Did she?" This was shaping up to be a larger affair than Libby had first imagined.

"Yes, ma'am. Mama said on account of I'm not in school I could come here and do some chores for Mr. Suredor. She and pa will be at the meeting."

"I must say, your industriousness is to be commended, Tommy."

"Yes, ma'am. That's what pa says, too."

"Is Mr. Suredor here?"

Tommy pointed down a connecting aisle. "Yes, ma'am, but he's real busy doing his books. He said I should muck out the stalls and try not to disturb him too much."

Libby glanced to the desk near the stove and wondered why Mr. Suredor wasn't doing is bookwork where there was a bit of warmth? "Do you think he'd mind if I disturbed him?"

Tommy shrugged then grinned. "Probably bite your head off." He laughed.

Libby smiled. "I'll have to risk it."

Tommy went back to his chores and she went in search of the stableman. As she approached the back of the aisle the sound of quiet murmuring drew her on. A few steps further and the murmur took on the shape of words and a familiar melody.

"...my money on de bobtail nag, somebody bet on the bay."

Libby stopped at the last stall. Frank Suredor was perched upon his racing sulky, his feet tucked into the stirrups and a copy of *Horse & Harness Racing News* open before him in the spill of warm sunlight through a dingy south window.

Real busy doing his books indeed!

His face hidden behind the newspaper, Mr. Suredor didn't see her. With barely a pause, he began singing the verse again.

"De Camptown ladies sing dis song..."

Libby rejoined with, "Doo-dah! Doo-dah!"

Mr. Suredor's bespectacled face peeked over the top of the paper and grinned. His voice got louder and together they ran through the song. At the end they had a good laugh.

"We make a half decent duet, Miss Libby."

"I'll bet my money on that," she retorted. "Tommy told me you were very busy doing your book work."

"He did?" Hmm. Reckon he must have misunderstood."

"I reckon he must have. *Horse & Harness?* My guess is you're doing your *bookie* work."

"Never too early to start at it. Spring is right around the corner."

"You going to race at the Franklin County Fair again this year?"

"Most likely that one, and a few others. I've been

working with that young pacer I bought last spring. He's a good one. I'm thinking I might have another Joe Patchen in the making."

Libby looked impressed. "That would put Somerville's pin on the map."

"Indeed it would." Mr. Suredor patted his ample belly. "If Lightening Strike works out like I suspect he might I'll have to find a young, lightweight feller to run him for me."

"Or you might consider a young, lightweight woman?"

"A female driver? Hmm, there's a thought. Never heard of such a thing, but don't know of any rules again' it." His forehead furrowed and he pondered the idea a moment. "What is it I can do for you, Miss Libby?"

"I would like to hire a buggy for tomorrow morning."

"You'll have to get in line then. Business been brisk this morning. Unusual for this time of the year."

"So it's begun already," she said.

He nodded. "Yesterday Mr. Tremont took out the buckboard and today Mr. Allison rented the gig. Later today Zach Canton will be using the spring wagon. That's all I have on hand. Both saddle horses are spoken for, too, and the rest of these animals are privately owned. Folks getting awful itchy of a sudden to track down a mythical white buffalo."

"You don't believe the story?"

"Tell you what, Miss Libby. Been around livestock my whole life. Seen and smelled and shoveled enough manure to bury a little place like Somerville up to its eaves, and not one bit of it ever looked like gold except on the rare occasion I'd sell a wagonload of it to someone wanting to dig into his vegetable garden."

"The story hasn't even been published yet."

"News of that kind don't need a newspaper to spread.

Word of it has likely already escaped our little burg and is burning its way across Kansas to every town within fifty miles of Somerville."

Fifty miles was an understatement. Winifred Balin's telegram went all the way to Cripple Creek, Colorado!

Mr. Suredor said, "You aren't thinking about hunting down the critter yourself?"

"Of course not," she said, appalled at the very idea she'd fall prey to such silliness. "I only wanted to check on Mr. Gannon. He had come into town that same night with an awful toothache and Dr. Blinker pulled the tooth with a pair of rusty pliers."

"Blinker mentioned something along that line."

"Dr. Blinker has been here?" she asked suspiciously.

"He was by this morning to say he wanted to collect his trap later today, after the meeting."

"I'm not all that surprised he believes the story."

"Blinker claims the gold chip is genuine and he's discovered scientific proof how it might have come about."

"Yes, he told me about it. His theory will be explained in this Friday's edition. You are on the subscription list. You can read all about it."

"You gonna write it, Miss Libby?"

"I am."

"Then it will be a dandy story. Your words managed to pry open the town council's tight fist and float that bond to build us a new schoolhouse."

She winced. "And they'll not stop reminding me that I broke the bank."

He smiled. "It'll all wash in the end."

Libby was anxious to change subjects. "How shall I make it to Mr. Gannon's place tomorrow? I suppose if I start early I could walk, although that will take most day there and back. I shall be needed at the newspaper to help with the printing." It was looking as if her interview with Cochise would have to wait.

Mr. Suredor thought a moment. "Got an old folding top Studebaker out back under a tarp. I set it aside last fall to grease the hubs and never got to the job. Tell you what, Miss Libby. Right after the meeting I'll dig it out of the drift and get her ready for you."

Libby's hopes rose.

His expression pinched. "Except I don't have a horse to pull it…hmm?"

And her hopes fell, but then Mr. Suredor's dilemma countenance brightened. "I do have Lightening Strike."

"Your young pacer? Oh, but I wouldn't want to take the next Joe Patchen."

"I wouldn't let him out to just any Tom, Dick, and Harry, but to you, Miss Libby, you'll be sensible with him. Keep him under a firm rein. He'll want to step out some, and that'll suit fine enough. Just let him know who's in control."

"I don't know what to say except thank you."

He waved that off. "You'll be helping me out. Lightening Strike's been closed in his stall for some weeks now. A bit of exercise will do him a pleasure."

Libby left Frank Suredor with a little over an hour remaining before the town meeting was to begin. She wanted to use the time judiciously. Father and mother, and maybe even Sarah—now that school had been canceled—would be busy setting type for the print run. She could use the hour visiting Sheriff Bainbridge to discover what news he might have learned about the gold chip and the deceased Indian, or she could return to the office and help with picking letters out of a bin and arranging backward sentences…. The frown she felt upon her face would have appalled Miss Penelope; her course of action becoming crystal clear.

Sheriff Bainbridge it would be!

———

Snow on the distant hill had lost its fresh-fallen sparkle. Patches of brittle prairie grass poked through in scattered clumps and the path between house and barn was quickly becoming a muddy track.

Tom Gannon noted this only peripherally from the window, watching Cochise ride away from the house. The Apache gave the mulberry tree a wide berth and averted his gaze from the graves beneath it. That was Cochise's way. The dead and ghosts were a real part of his world.

With a cut-down, two-barrel shotgun resting across his thighs, the old Indian reined turned onto the snow-buried trail that led from the ranch into the flint hills. Tom's view shifted toward the distant smudge of smoke rising into the sky. Two days it had been there. Most peculiar for this time of year. His view touched upon the tree again and the headstones beneath it. His lips cut a grim line that sent a twinge through the raw, empty socket in his jaw.

A large slice of his life lay beneath the snow under that big, bare-branched tree. Another sliver of it now rode away into the hills seeking a campfire in the middle of winter where one ought not to be.

The two—the gravestones and Cochise—were the flint and iron that sparked the memory…

Cassie was twenty-three with Jonathan, their first born, still on the breast the morning Captain Tom Gannon led a small contingent away from the fort to aid Burns in rounding up the Apaches who had managed to escape the day before and flee the canyon into the bleak desert east of Phoenix. It was to be a mopping up detail.

Arriving at the killing grounds, the sight of so many dead, both white and red, was enough to shrivel the heart of even the most hardened of men. Women and children had been among them. Whole families died together. Bullets fired in battle do not discriminate.

Tom divided his men into threes and fours while he scouted along an escarpment of shining cliffs. A young corporal holding a bawling infant in his arms rode dazed across the killing ground. He glanced at Tom as their horses passed, his eyes glazed by the carnage. There were no words to speak in the midst of so much death. A thought went through Tom's mind; they would have to find a wet nurse for the infant... He thought of Cassie and Jonathan again.

This Arizona Territory was a wide, burning land that for centuries had belonged to Mexican herders and the free roaming Apache. It seemed a rule of nature that nothing might remain unchanged. More and more white settlers had begun moving in, and with them came the military to protect against Indian raiders such as these souls, twisted in death, stiff beneath the shriveling sun. Tom grimaced. One would have thought there'd be rattlesnakes, scorpions, and great lizards enough for both whites and reds.

A muted sound pulled his view to a mesquite hummock against the rock ledge he'd been following. It might have been nothing; some animal maybe? He listened unrewarded a moment longer and was about to ride on, but something held him there. Senses sharpened, his boot quietly touched the ground. Revolver in hand, Tom stalked toward the mesquite. The shadow of a shallow cave behind the mesquite halted him. Signs on the ground told of recent activity. Splotches of dried blood drew the picture in Tom Gannon's brain.

A muffled whimper emerging from the shadows

confirmed his suspicions. He halted at the sight of wide, terrified eyes of a woman huddled as far back as the declivity would permit. She hugged a baby to her chest, a hand over the infant's mouth. The woman looked to be younger than Cassie but the baby might have been the same age as Jonathan.

At her side lay a man no older than the stricken corporal Tom had passed earlier. The Apache's dark eyes showed not fear but challenge. He was unarmed except for a skinning knife clutched fiercely in his fist. The taut grimace of pain pulled at his face. He'd been leg-shot, the bullet having broken the long bone and then passing through, which was fortunate for him. The woman had attempted to set and splint it. She'd done a good job doctoring him. Tom didn't think he could have done any better under the circumstances. Even so, the man would never again stalk the high trails hunting rangy mule deer as he had before the battle. His war-making days were over, and that was a good thing.

It had been the woman and baby, Tom decided years later, that compelled his next decision. He holstered the revolver, which immediately eased some of the tension upon the woman's face. The man remained determined to defend his wife and child with the small knife.

"You have gotten yourselves in a tight fix here, Cochise."

The man didn't understand English. Equipped with only a few words in Apache, Tom tried Spanish instead, a tongue he grasped only slightly better.

"I can take you into camp and have the surgeon fix that leg or I can leave you here. If I take you in you will be made a prisoner."

The young warrior grasped the meaning of that and vehemently shook his head.

"I didn't think so." Tom went to his horse and came

back with a canteen and an army issued blanket. Their wary eyes tracked him as he extended the gifts. "I don't need to tell you that the desert gets cold when the sun moves off," he said, seeing his Cassie and Jonathan instead of the smudged-face woman.

She received the gifts without a word, but Tom knew they were grateful to have them. It was going to be a tough go of it for these two, and there'd already been enough killing and hurt on both sides.

Tom Gannon spun about at the sound of approaching hooves. Fear returned to the Apaches' faces. Tom dropped a suspender strap off one shoulder, slung his holster belt over the other, and strode out around the mesquite.

"Captain Gannon, sir. I thought that was your mount. Everything all right here?" Corporal Meyers inquired. One of Burns's men accompanied him. Tom didn't know his name.

"Just stopped to water the lilies, corporal." Tom grinned lifting the suspender back over his shoulder. The men laughed. Tom said, "I suspect we've gone far enough this direction. Any Apaches making it this far will have scattered to the hills by now. Locate Sergeant Becker and tell him to send a dozen troops down to the river and reconnoiter eastward to those buttes over yonder, and then return by way of the opposite bank."

"Yes sir."

"I'll be along directly."

The troopers rode off. Tom turned to his saddlebags and returned to the cave with a plug of tobacco and a wrapper of hardtack.

"You'll be safe enough here tonight. I suggest you move out soon as you're able to. There will likely be troops through this place later." There wasn't anything left to say. They'd either make it or they wouldn't. Tom had done what he could. He turned to leave.

"*¿Cómo se llama usted, señor?*" The man asked.

"*Me llamo* Gannon. Tom Gannon."

He nodded. "*Gracias* Tom Gannon."

The memory faded like the swiftly melting snow upon the rolling hills. Tom remained watching from the window of the house he and Cassie had built together until the hills closed behind Cochise.

———

"It's not like he was carrying a bank check with his name written on it, Miss Barrett."

"You have made no effort to identify him, then?"

Sheriff Bainbridge gave an impatient grunt. "He was an Indian. How in the devil do you propose I go about identifying an Indian who wanders into town outta nowhere and then dies?"

Libby was frustrated and confused by the sheriff's lack of interest in the poor man who had stirred such a whirl of excitement in town. "If indeed he is Sioux as Lieutenant Danforth has suggested, perhaps a letter to the Indian Agent at Pine Ridge might provide information? Surely he had family who would desire to learn of his fate. Would they not be entitled to his possessions?"

"I got more important business to attend to than trying to identify a dead Indian."

Libby glanced about his office. The three jail cells were unoccupied, their doors open. Toby Snyder, his part-time deputy, was sweeping dried mud from the floor, feigning no interest in their conversation. Sheriff Bainbridge himself sat tilted back in his chair, boots upon his desk near a humidor, a scowl on his face and a smoldering cigar between his fingers. Plainly her arrival had been a major upset to his *important business*.

"Yes, I see that you are quite busy. Since you have no new information for the readers of the *Somerville Independent* on the matter, I won't take up anymore of your time, Sheriff," she said, inserting just the slightest undertone of sarcasm, which the sheriff either missed or ignored. Libby inclined her head at the safe in the corner of his office. "Is it in there?"

"It is, Miss Barrett."

"May I inquire as to why you believe the gold buffalo chip is safer here than down the street in the bank's vault?"

"For the simple reason that here I," his finger touched his chest, "can keep an eye," the finger moved appropriately, "on that." He pointed at the safe bolted to the floor. "Any more questions?"

"No, Sheriff. I believe you have answered them all."

———

Libby emerged onto the boardwalk in front of Sheriff Bainbridge's office and glared back through the window at the officer at his desk displaying the motivation of a contented pig in his wallow. He'd been tight-lipped and antagonistic, but then, when had she ever known him to be anything but cantankerous?

Across the street the Plains Hotel's wide porch and brilliant, white-railed balconies gleamed in the morning light; a bright jewel among Somerville's gray clapboards. The hotel occupied most of Paramount Avenue and a good portion of Lyman Road. Indignation pinched Libby's face at the idea the town council might even consider sacrificing such a grand establishment—grand by Nowheresville, Kansas standards, that is—for a stark, brick bank building. Certainly Mr. Demoy would have a word to say about the conspiracy should an army of axes and crowbars arrive to raze his property.

She sighed aloud to herself, "You are such a lovely sight."

"The view from back here is kind of nice, too," a man's voice declared.

Startled, Libby whirled to find herself face to face with the man from the train. She recovered her poise with her next breath and said, "I was referring to the hotel."

He glanced at the hotel and then back, his bold eyes slowly assessing her form. "I wasn't."

Libby was certain there was not much to appraise beneath her heavy coat, fastened to the top button. "That is quite obvious, Mr. Bartlow, is it not?"

He gave a slight bow and said, "I see that that old newspaper coot is passing about word of my business here."

"That old coot is my father," she informed sternly.

"In that case, I apologize for the derogatory comment."

"Accepted. Now, please step aside."

He remained steadfast, grinning. "I have a better idea. Why don't you and me go off somewhere and get better acquainted?"

"I think not. Good day, Mr. Bartlow."

He moved ever so slightly to impede her passing. "You are going to that meeting?"

"You've heard?"

His smiling eyes caught the sunlight. It was a hand-some face, she thought briefly and at once chided herself for allowing such a notion to even crack open a door in her mind. "Word gets around. Something about a wondrous buffalo, a dead Indian, and gold."

"Correct. Now, please step aside. My business requires that I attend the meeting also."

He thrust his arm to the porch column halting her yet again. "A meeting like that will be of no consequence, and you and me are just starting to get to know each other."

It was the second time he had stopped her, sparking Libby's ire. Two was twice too many. "Mr. Bartlow, you will allow me to pass or I shall call for the sheriff."

His smile tightened and his eyes hardened ever so slightly. "I would not like that."

So far it had been an encounter of words, and with such weapons Libby was more than able to engage the battle, but now something had changed. Bartlow had cast banter aside and was escalating the contest. Her breath shortened as a twinge of worry replaced what at first had been mere annoyance.

"Oh, there you are, Miss Libby," Lieutenant Danforth's voice rang out. The tall officer was striding down the boardwalk from the direction of the army depot. He halted at her side, cast an innocent smile at Mr. Bartlow and then turned his attention to her. "If Ah recall, we were going to attend the meeting together?"

A bright blue wink told her had assessed her situation and was offering an avenue of escape. "I was awaiting your arrival, Lieutenant Danforth," She replied. "*Dr.* Bartlow and I were just now discussing the meeting." She cast a smirk of victory but there lingered a remnant of worry. She had avoided this skirmish, however, she was certain others lay ahead.

"You are new to town, are you not, Dr. Bartlow?" Lieutenant Danforth inquired.

"I am," Bartlow allowed briefly, his roguish smiled fixed on her in a way that confirmed Libby's prognostication.

Libby said, "Dr. Bartlow examines bumps. On the head."

"Bumps? How unusual," Lieutenant Danforth drawled easily.

"Sometimes I even make them, sir," Bartlow added lightly, the undercurrent of a challenge plain to Libby's ear.

"Ah would enjoy discussing bumps with you later, Dr. Bartlow, but Miss Libby and Ah must be on our way. Will you be attending the meeting?"

"Maybe."

"Then *maybe* we will see you later. Good day." Lieutenant Danforth crooked an arm, which Libby accepted. As they strolled off she stole a glance over her shoulder. Bartlow leaned against the post, watching them. Libby quickly averted her face and said, "Thank you. Is this what is meant by the cavalry to the rescue?"

"Ah spied your situation, and how the Indians were circling. Ah considered it my duty as an officer and a gentleman to offer aid."

"He arrived on yesterday's train. There was another man traveling with him but they pretended not to know each other. The second man has remained low and I have not seen him since."

"Quite a feat in a town the size of Somerville,"

"My thoughts exactly."

They crossed Paramount Avenue at Bridges Road. Once past Dr. Blinker's surgery and out of sight of Bartlow, Libby released Lieutenant Danforth's arm not wishing to add yet another snippet of gossip for Hazel Overmier and Winnie Balin to spread about town.

Ahead, past General Henry Somerville Park, folks streamed into the Somerville Methodist Church. Hazel and Reverend Overmier bounded about the steps greeting them as if this were a regular Sunday morning meeting.

"Who has mustered this meeting?" Lieutenant Danforth asked as they joined the press of people ascending the steps to the wide porch. Hazel Overmier spied them. A smile burst upon her face and she abandoned Mr. Carson Clark with whom she'd been conversing and rushed over.

"I don't know," Libby said as Hazel arrived flashing a mischievous grin that forewarned of another thread of gossip about to be spun about Somerville.

"Lieutenant Danforth and Libby," she declared, her bright, conspiring eyes taking them in as if appraising a pair of crystal lamps and trying to decide how the two would look together upon her fireplace mantle. "I am pleased you two could come."

You two. That was not a good sign. Libby deflected the insinuation with, "We were both going the same way. My, you have a crowd. How will you ever fit them all?"

"We're bursting at the seams," she said happily. "The exciting thing is, there are many heathens here who have never set foot inside a church before."

Lieutenant Danforth chuckled. "Perhaps your husband ought to change his strategy and preach sermons about buffalo chips of gold rather than heavenly streets of gold?"

Hazel favored him with an unenthusiastic smile and suddenly spied someone else whom absolutely required her attention. The crystal lamps didn't quite meet with Hazel's approval after all, Libby thought happily. "That went over like a wing-shot turkey."

Still smiling, Lieutenant Danforth said, "Routed the savages, did Ah?"

Had he read her thoughts? "Are you always this intuitive?"

"It's called military strategy, Miss Libby."

Whatever did he mean by that?

Inside, Libby spied Father saving a chair for her in the center of a packed row. Lieutenant Danforth veered off toward a couple of his troops standing against a wall chatting with Jimmy. The little church was indeed *bursting at the seams*, the overflow stacking against the walls, two and three deep in the corners.

She worked her way past averted knees. Father said, "I was beginning to think you wouldn't make it."

"I was delayed. *Your* Dr. Bartlow derailed me."

"My Dr. Bartlow?" Father eyebrows raised. "I see you managed to get back onto the track."

"The cavalry arrived just in time." Libby inclined her head toward the small collection of soldiers.

"Do tell. I suppose I ought to have a word with the sheriff." Father glanced about. "I don't see Walt."

"I spoke with him a few minutes ago. He did not seem inclined to attend."

"I suppose someone has to mind the town. It appears everyone else is here."

Libby knew most of the faces by name. Ava Pickering sat with Dick and Winnie Balin. Bo Hoffman and Warner Pealgramm had their heads together, talking. Malcolm Demoy and Ben Alexander, the land agent, were earnestly conversing. Libby wondered briefly if Mr. Alexander, a registered land attorney, had been consulted with by the town council about the razing Mr. Demoy's fine hotel? She stopped herself. Razing the Plains Hotel had not been established…yet. It was still only her speculation. Keep to the facts, she chided herself.

Across the sanctuary was Alice O'Meara and two of her girls happily chatting with several men gathered about them. The Wilsons sat near the front, the Heelcrofts and Cassidies two rows behind them. Libby was surprised to spy Sheila Tappermounty among the crowd. Sheila was a tall, thin, gray woman who like her husband, rarely smiled.

Libby's view traveled around the church. Its door stood open as did every window. Heat was in no short supply, but oxygen might very well have been. The tail end of the throng pressed inside seeking places to stand. The last two were Dr. Blinker and, to Libby's surprise, Dr. Bartlow! They seemed to be getting on amiably. Dr. Blinker to point out a few square inches of floor space, which Dr. Bartlow immediately appropriated.

Libby whispered, "Dr. Blinker produced a slim volume written in French, by a French scientist who claimed that a certain kind of bacteria might be the cause of the gold chip." She inclined her head toward the narthex. "Look, there he is now, and Dr. Bartlow is with him."

Father glanced over and then whispered, "I shall like to know more about this Frenchman and his theory."

Just then Dr. Blinker abandoned Dr. Bartlow and ascended the aisle to the lectern at the front of the church. The murmuring got quiet.

Was Dr. Blinker conducting the meeting? Had he been the one to call the town together? Libby leaned near Father's ear and whispered, "Scooped again."

Father responded with a cryptic smile. "Let's not be hasty in our prejudging. It's all in how he works the crowd."

Libby said, "Am I hearing the voice of an old circus barker?"

His smile widened. "I was quite the hand with a crowd back in the day."

Dr. Blinker open the meeting with a quip about Somerville suddenly getting religion, which generated halfhearted sniggers. Libby readied her notepad and pencil. As the crowd quieted, he got right to the point, expounding on what had occurred Monday evening, skipping only the episode with Mr. Gannon's tooth.

A Miss Penelope disapproved frown creased Libby's forehead. *Scooped*! Dr. Blinker's drone became background noise as Libby began rewriting in her head, grasping for ideas to bring something fresh to her piece for Friday's edition. She despaired. Her last hope was that Mr. Cochise could add an enlightening snippet of insight that she could insert before the story was set to type and printed.

"I have in my library documented evidence that such an amazing phenomenon might occur," Dr. Blinker's proclamation generated a bit of excitement.

Father appeared to be more interested in critiquing Dr. Blinker's style than content. "The insertion of a pause would have heightened the response," was his only comment.

"He has devastated my story."

Father merely smiled.

"No one will buy a single copy!"

"Think not?"

Dr. Blinker continued, "And I have learned that our own Mrs. Winifred Balin has received a telegram from the Colorado gold fields reporting a similar knowledge amongst the gold miners with who her brother is acquainted."

"Whom," Libby corrected. "With *whom*."

Father chuckled

Jasper Hennigan shot to his feet and said, "If all this can be true, what are we to do about it?"

"Yeah," Another broke in. "Rightfully that buffalo ought to belong to us, to Somerville."

The grocer, Mr. Saunder, said reasonably, "There are people like Dave McClaine here who have lived here from before the war. Why hasn't he or anyone else ever found a golden buffalo chip before? I think this is becoming wild talk that needs to be tempered with some common sense."

A few agreed with that.

Keavy Wilson stood and cast her view about the crowded church. "I'll tell what I've been t'inkin'. T'is is the very sort of mischievous a leprechaun might be a'playin' on all of us. Now ye might laugh at the very notion but it is true how the little folk play such pranks. T'ey'll pay ye a gold sovereign and ye'll tuck it away in ye'r pouch and come mornin' all you have is ashes or dried leaves. I've seen it with me very eyes as a lass. If it is all true and we capture the white buffalo we'd all be livin' on a pig's back in two ticks, but before we t'row it all up, I say we peek in on t'at gold chip to be certain it ain't turned to a pile of ashes."

As silly as it sounded, Libby thought leprechauns a more reasonable explanation for the gold chip than the digestive workings in an albino bison's alimentary canal.

Keavy sat, having spoken her mind. Some scoffed and some applauded. Dr. Blinker patted down the commotion. "Words of wisdom, Mrs. Wilson. And to Kip's question, I cannot answer scientifically as to why no one has yet to discover a gold chip, but I am certain most of you here are aware of Mr. Darwin. Perhaps we have witnessed a genuine demonstration of his hypothesis? Need I recall to you Mrs. Balin's telegram from the gold fields?"

"He's pushing the people like snake oil salesman," Libby said.

"True, true," father replied, "however, I have stood in the presence of more talented hawkers. He has missed several opportunities to capture the hearts of his audience."

"Who would be the owner of such a beast should we capture it?" Bob Heelcroft asked in response to Betty's elbowing.

"The critter ought to belong to the town," someone interjected. "To We The People!"

A few mumbled in agreement.

And yet another countered, "The buffalo will belong to the man who corrals it!"

An eruption of hurrahs drowned out the mumblers. Immediately disputations arose and Libby scribbled furiously to capture the arguments flying back and forth.

Mr. Suredor took to his feet and declared, "This bickering will be a moot point in a few hours. I've hired out all my horses and conveyances to men you might very well call claim jumpers. Mr. Tappermounty headed out yesterday. Theodore Beasley, Lemle Carter, Wallace Krowe, and Hex Bradshaw all left town this morning. Amongst them, they had enough food and water to last a month."

Anger rattled the windows, especially from those men who didn't own a horse or carriage. Libby suspected that included most everyone in Somerville. The crowd appeared on the verge of stringing up the stableman on account of his poor planning, as if Mr. Suredor had been remiss to have not prophesied a stampede on his stock and trade.

"Sorry, folks, but I'm clean out of livestock," Mr. Suredor said, casting warily about for the nearest window.

With shouts and gesticulations, Dr. Blinker brought the meeting back to order.

The owner of the DK Ranch stood, wide hat in hand, sun darkened face looking like old leather. David and Kimberly McClaine were one of the first settlers in this part of the Flint Hills and their ranch covered half the county. The town of Somerville had been established on a small corner of that ranch, which Mr. McClaine had deeded over to General Henry Somerville after the War.

"Sounds like you folks have stoked up a head of steam to go on a hunt for this white buffalo. I'm not one to discourage adventure nor preach the virtues of common sense. That's Reverend Overmier's trade, and seeing as we're in his church I'll pass it on. Fact is, if I had followed that advice I'd still be in Ohio turning dirt behind a plow and mule. What I will say is that Me and Kim have been over fifty years in these Flint Hills, and in all that time never once have come across a buffalo of any but one color. Not saying it can't happen. I believe God has a sense of humor and if He wanted to make 'em green or purple, well I would not dispute the matter with Him.

"In like manner, I've never found a buffalo chip worth the effort it took to gather it up except to toss to a chip fire. All that being said, I'm not going to pass judgment one way or the other except to say this has the feel of someone at the table with a card up his sleeve, but I can't make any sense of the why of it. I hear from some of you it was an Indian what found the thing. We haven't had much to do with Indians in almost a decade now, and if he was Sioux he probably drifted on down from Pine Ridge after that unpleasantness a year or so back. Can't say as I'd blame him wanting off the government feed trough."

Libby wore the point of her pencil to a nubbin attempting to record all of what Mr. McClaine was saying. If she parceled it out in small bites, she could stretch it out for at least three more editions!

"I'm standing here being long-winded when I ought to get down to the point. I've got most of a thousand head bedded down on winter pasture and half my wranglers off the ranch 'till spring. That has left me with something like forty head of horses I can let out to you folks who want 'em. I think five dollars a week is a fair price."

Twenty or more hands shot toward the ceiling to claim a spot on Dave McClaine's offer.

Father whispered, "That's going to turn up the heat under the pot."

"And when half the town flees to the hills, who will be left to buy our newspaper and read my story?" Libby asked.

A mischievous gleam lit Father's eyes, a cunning grin lifting his lips. "I'm thinking we shall have to increase our print run by at least twenty-five percent."

Libby rolled her eyes. What was Father thinking?

Mr. McClaine wasn't quite finished. "Very well. I'll have a couple wrangles pull together a remuda and drive 'em into town tomorrow afternoon. Any man who wants one will have to provide his own tack."

Mr. Owen Wright, owner of Wright General Store and cousin to Bob Wright, had springs attached to the bottom of his shoes. He sprang to his feet in a flash announcing that he'd recently received a shipment of saddles and bits from Dodge City and would sell the tack to any buffalo hunter in need at ten percent off!

The sudden earthquake inside the church was a mass rush for the door, but the aftershock that came next was even more startling! Father bolted from his chair and proclaimed in an unfamiliar voice of authority. "Listen, listen, listen!"

The rolling cadence coming from the normally soft-spoken newspaper editor stilled the seismic tremor. Father scooted sideways past averted knees to the main aisle and strode to the lectern giving Dr. Blinker a nod and a gentle shouldering aside.

"Before all you fine folks dash off in a haphazard

pursuit of this amazing bison, this wondrous gift from the blizzard of '93, harken to what I have to say. Would you leap to build a store without a plan? Would you lay a rail line without a survey? Nae, you certainly would not. So why would you embark on this momentous enterprise without the proper information in hand?"

Father stepped out in front of the lectern and slowly scanned the crowd. "My dear friends and neighbors, I stand on a precipice, on the verge of violating a solemn promise made to myself many years ago when I entered upon this most sacred of professions." Father's dramatic pause gripped the crowd. Even Libby sat half mesmerized. "Do you know what that hallowed promise was?

Silence.

"I shall tell you," Father continued after an insufferably long moment. "The promise I made those many years ago when I embarked upon the consecrated duty to bring the news of the world to the hamlet of Somerville was simply this: I promised that I would never disclose ahead of publication the contents of any story I intended to print in an upcoming edition of the *Somerville Independent*.

"Why, you might ask, would I make such a pledge?" Father began to pace. He paused suddenly and thrust a finger toward Mr. Tebor sitting in the front row. "Because of you!" His pacing resumed, halting again, "And you!" he said, visibly disquieting shy, Miss Janice Ream. Father peered across the sea of faces, riveted eyes, breath captured within stilled lungs. "Because of all of you," he intoned with a dramatic sweep of his arm. "My conviction was, is, and has always been, the news shall be cast out to everyone at the same time, not divvied up privately to the advantage to a select few."

Father scanned the packed church like an Indian Scout casting his dark view across some distant horizon.

He continued in a low, even tone. "I dare allow that we have assembled here half the town, perhaps more, so in fact I do not feel I am shattering my promise utterly. I would hardly call this a *select few*, but instead a gathering of the finest and best; people who have as their intent only to bless the town of Somerville with hope and prosperity as we forge ahead into the new century a mere seven years from now."

Libby cringed. This wasn't 1868 nor was it the *Hankly and Winespoon Circus* come to town. Father's emoting skirted precariously near that of a Kickapoo Indian Medicine Company barker peddling magic elixirs; his locution and dramatizing absurdly dramatic...and he was enjoying it! Curiously, the crowd was delighting in it, too, responding like puppets, dancing on cue to whatever emotional string Father's fingers pulled.

By chance there was a piece of paper on the lectern. Father seized it and rattled it aloft. "*Information*. I said it before and I'll say it again, when you hold Friday's edition of the *Somerville Independent* in your hands you will be holding the accumulated scientific discovery that we have got together over the—err—um, last two days. A metaphorical treasure map containing the dying words of a Sioux warrior fleeing the final moments of the battle of Pine Ridge, wandering alone across the desolate prairie, his soul tormented by the horrors of remembrance. You will read about how he discovers the wondrous white buffalo that at once lifted his spirit from the depths of despair to the heights of hope!"

Libby shrank into her chair wanting to disappear.

"We shall lay before you scientific proof how such digestive alchemy might occur, discovered by a brilliant French doctor laboring in the laboratory of a famous French school of—err—scientific proving.

"We reveal exclusive interviews with the now-tamed

savages of this land who tell of hidden Indian legends of the dark past.

"Indeed, unarmed with the startling facts discovered and transcribed by my daughter, L. A. Barrett." Father swept an arm toward Libby putting her at the center of attention. She struggled to smile and dare not meet their gazes. What was Father thinking? "Unarmed," his voice boomed, "with this information will put you at a great disadvantage."

Father came to a dramatic halt. The silence that followed sucked the breath out of the church, every face a magnetic needle pulled toward Father's great magnetic attractor of the north.

Now his voice droned low with conviction, as a few of Libby's instructors at Winfield College had employed when making a salient point. "A successful hunt for our amazing white buffalo requires—nae, demands—that each one of you…" at this juncture he pointed and identified a few of the people by name. "Each one of you be armed with all the facts, and facts are what this Friday's *Independent* with provide."

Silence ensued. Father cleared his throat and straightened his spine. "To that end, I have come to a decision. To do my part in this pursuit, I will not be selling this edition at its regular price of one nickel, although the pearls of knowledge it contains is easily valued at thrice that small amount. No, not one nickel. Not four cents. Nor even three cents!" He scanned the crown with a fervor Reverend Overmier could only hope to achieve, during one of his hottest sermons. "This week I intend to provide each one of you with all the facts we have uncovered for a mere two cents."

Father arrived at the conclusion of his pitch. The silence immediately broke and excitement rattled the windows. Folks came to him and shook his hand and slapped his back. Some told Libby that she was a blessing to Somerville and how they looked with anticipation to reading all her articles. Libby's cheeks burned; she wanted to escape to her room and lock the door. But she endured, and as she and Father left the church she noted that Bartlow was no longer in the building. Instead, Sheriff Bainbridge shadowed the narthex, as if waiting for them.

"That was a convincing spiel, Harold," Sheriff Bainbridge said as they emerged into the cold, a pale winter sun lower in the sky now, an edge of it eclipsed by the livery stable's roof. "You could sell fleas to a dog."

"I feel it my civic duty to help the fine folks of Somerville achieve their goal, one they have plainly set themselves to pursue regardless of what you or I advise. The secret to one's success, Walt, is to help others achieve success of their own."

"Hmm." Sheriff Bainbridge scowled. "Or maybe set 'em up for a swindle? Makes me wonder if you didn't arrange the buffalo show to drum up sales of your newspaper?" The sheriff tried for a light, even jocular tone, but Libby sensed that was only a cover for something unspoken. "What exactly is it you have discovered?"

Libby said, "You suggest a clever crime, Sheriff. One more apt to flow from the inventive pen of a writer like Doyle than from the editor of a four page weekly."

"Who?"

Father said, "Should I come across evidence of a mendacity, Walter, you shall be the first person I will inform. Was there some business you wished to discuss with us?"

"No, no business, just curious to see what kind of turnout Blinker's meeting got."

"Speaking of swindles, Sheriff, what does Dr. Blinker have cooking?" Libby asked. "It was he who admonished hushing the event, and in his next breath it is he who publicizes it?"

"Blinker's a queer duck, Miss Libby. He's got one foot on the ground and the other chasing moonbeams." He shook his head. "He's an agreeable fellow; he just needs to decide on a course and keep to it. I was of two minds like him when I was younger. Moved cattle, hunted meat for the army, panned a little gold, bull-whacked from Marysville to Laramie before the railroad come through. Never married, never made much of myself, drifting from one career to another, and here I am long past sixty years old with an empty poke and a bad back."

"Sheriff," Keavy Wilson hailed from the narthex, "might we have a word wit' ye?" She strode over leading a pack of women six or seven strong, ignoring or perhaps not caring that she was intruding. "We wish to be havin' a look at t'at gold item in y're safe, if ye please."

"Why on earth do you fine women want to look at it?"

"Somerville is rushin' like a Kansas cyclone to find t'at beast. Before we send our men out on t'is adventure we want to see for certain it ain't just a leprechaun prank."

Libby was prepared for a harsh reply. Instead, Sheriff Bainbridge sighed and said "Appears I'm outnumbered. All right ladies, come along and have a look." He said good-bye and led the flock away.

Father called, "Should you discover dried leaves, Walt, let us know. Leprechauns inhabiting the Kansas Flint Hills will be an even grander story than a buffalo excreting gold."

The sheriff raised an acknowledging arm. Libby said, "He was unusually compliant."

"I sense a bout of nostalgia has laid Walt low. Remi-niscing often has that affect. Rarely does life follow the plan we set for it when we're young and the future lies distant."

"Or he's hiding something." Libby watched the ladies hauling Sheriff Bainbridge off to jail, mystified at the change that had overshadowed Somerville in only a short three days. "Gold chips and Leprechaun tricks."

"The title of your article?"

"Hum? No. Just thinking. And speaking of articles, *Father*, what on earth were *you* thinking promising scientific evidence and exclusive interviews? I have none of that."

He chuckled and they began to walk. "Do you not intend to interview Mr. Cochise in the morning?"

"To paraphrase the words of a former circus barker, 'Cochise is Apache, not Sioux'."

Father said innocently, "If I recall, it was you who proclaimed that a minor detail? I will reserve a quarter column for your expanded revision. We'll set the type soon as you have written it tonight."

"Tonight? You want me to make it all up before the interview?"

"We'll frame the story as speculation based on an overwhelming weight of facts."

"In other words, you want me to lie?" Libby stared at him certain she was seeing a stranger.

"Think of it as a work of fiction," Father countered. "You're quite capable."

"Miss Libby and Mr. Barrett." Lieutenant Danforth hailed coming alongside them, promptly ending their discussion.

"Good afternoon, Lieutenant," Father said brightly. "I heard how you gallantly rescued my daughter from the attentions of our recent arrival."

A smile lighted Lieutenant Danforth's handsome face, his blue eyes giving a twinkle—definitely a twinkle—Libby thought. "You can hardly fault Dr. Bartlow's attentions." The lieutenant beamed his smile at Libby.

"No, no. Of course not," Father agreed.

"Typical male bantering," Libby scolded, but in fact she enjoyed it; something she'd never admit to out loud. To divert the topic onto a less personal track, Libby asked Lieutenant Danforth what he thought about the gold chip affair?

"Ah had not taken a stand either to the left or to the right of the matter when Ah arrived here, but after listening to Mr. Barrett's excellent presentation Ah'm now leaning a mite in the direction the wind seems to be blowing."

"Not you, too?"

Lieutenant Danforth smiled. "Only leaning, Miss Libby. Ah'm not prepared to abandon my post and join Somerville's posse to capture the bountiful bovine."

"I should hope not, Lieutenant. I rather think Gibraltar might fall than you succumbing to this *gold* fever."

He laughed. "Why thank you, Miss Libby. Ah take that as a compliment."

Libby winced. Had she said too much? Lieutenant Danforth did not need any encouragement from her to stir his obvious romantic interests.

He turned to father. "You have a gift for capturing an audience, Mr. Barrett. Have you ever considered seeking an office?"

"Office?"

"Ah'm speaking of politics, sir—Governor Harold Barrett. And Miss Libby can act as the State's Official Hostess. Our country is falling into what some are calling the Great Depression. We need men who can lead us out of it, a man who can capture the imaginations of the people. Ah do have certain influential connections who can come alongside you."

Father stopped and gave the lieutenant, a startled look, his mouth agape. "Politics! You ought to be tarred and feathered for using my name and that word in the same sentence," and then he laughed and the subject of Father becoming governor of Kansas fell by the wayside. At the corner Lieutenant Danforth said good-bye, bowed curtly to Libby, said he hoped to see her again soon, then turned and strode up Paramount Avenue while Libby and Father headed south.

"He has his sights trained on you, my dear," Father commented.

"He does not," Libby retorted without conviction. "Don't start down that road with me, not now when I have to clear my mind of the day-to-day and turn it to the low estate of writing fiction."

———

And a very low estate it was indeed.

Libby pondered. She struggled. She paced, and at intervals stared long out the window seeking inspiration from the vacant lot across the street. An hour passed without even an opening sentence appearing upon the paper. It irked that Father had imposed this task on her. She stalked the floor for another half hour. How did one fabricate such a fable and pass it off as fact?

Libby collapsed onto her chair despairing. Hunched over her desk her view fell upon the neatly type-written manuscript that Dr. Blinker had thrust on her.

The Adventures of John Steele and the Crater Monsters of the Moon.

Desperate for inspiration, Libby snatched up the thin sheath of papers and began to read.

———

The painful ordeal ended...finally. Every word Libby penned was truthful, yet on the whole, the article contained not a grain of new information, only mountains of speculation, supposition...and obfuscation in abundance. Out and out lies...none. For that Libby was quite proud of how she'd wrangled the piece into shape; it flowed well, even logically. Considering the scant shards of evidence she had to work with, she had built a convincing edifice...

Rising from the chair, Libby sighed.

Whose foundation rested upon nothing more than shifting sand.

Her eyes, strained from the hours working in the weak light of the desk lamp. "Fiction," she scoffed under her breath and carried the neatly penned gibberish to the composing table where Mother and Father were still hunched, plucking letters from the bins. Sarah Saunder had gone home hours ago, before night had pulled its dark curtain over the town. That had been—Libby glanced at the wall clock—five hours ago. She dropped the pages onto the platen in front of Father.

He glanced up from his tasked, blinking to get his eyes to focus on her. "Finished?"

"In more ways than one," She said tiredly. Any vitality she may have possessed had fled hours earlier.

He took the pages and adjusted his spectacles while she leaned against the heavy Washington Press massaging her eyes. She could use fresh air. Even more, sleep.

"Not bad."

"It's horrible."

"Shall we let the reader decide?" he suggested.

"I had to fight my way past moon monsters and fainting Martian princesses searching for inspiration."

Father smiled. "And was Dr. Blinker's yarn—what is it he calls it? Scientific Romance?—of any help?"

"It's horrible; littered with adverbs, redundancies, and inconsistencies. The premise is utterly ridiculous. Three fellows acquire a balloon and launch themselves to the moon. Upon opening the gas valve, they bring the basket to earth—err, moon—within a crater where they're immediately set upon by green machine-men made of clockwork and tin.

Father chuckled and mother said that Dr. Blinker has a vivid imagination.

"It gets even more fanciful. The machine-men have taken prisoner a beautiful princess who, by chance also arrived in a balloon from the planet Mars, accompanied by her faithful eunuch, Kagor. Kagor is killed, of course."

"Naturally," Father agreed.

"Princess Duavare, and a chest of gold, which she'd recovered from the royal treasury of a Marsian enemy king, have been seized by the mechanical moon men. John Steele, protagonist and leader of the expedition, and coincidentally a Kansas dentist when not romping about the moon, orchestrates a clever diversion that sends the machine-men chasing a red herring, whereupon Dr. Steele rescues Duavare, retrieves her treasure, and flees back to the balloon and escapes the moon."

"Isn't the basket quite a bit heavier by now?" Father wondered.

"I suspect it might be," Libby allowed.

"And had not Mr. Steele expelled a sufficient amount of gas to bring the basket to the moon's surface?"

Libby sighed. "The plot has more holes than a colander."

"How does he return to Kansas?" Mother asked.

"Apparently the moon's aether towed them until they found themselves suspended over Topeka at which moment Dr. Steele releases more gas and settles the balloon in a cornfield, only a few miles from where they had ascended."

"Ah-hah," Father chuckled, "Thus validating Rowbotham's hypothesis!"

Libby said, "So it would appear."

Father rose and carried her pages to his desk, "I will just take a pencil to this and it will be ready to set."

Mother said, "You're all done in, Elizabeth Ann, and you have a full day tomorrow. Your father and I can finish up here."

"You sure it's okay?" She didn't like leaving them to complete the task she always helped doing, but in her weary state, she would certainly mix her Ps and Qs, as Father often admonished not to do.

"You go on to bed," Father said. "I'll leave two inches for whatever you manage to glean from Mr. Cochise."

"And if I glean nothing?"

"We'll fill the space with an advertisement. Or perhaps that block we use to announce the annual Fourth of July concert in General Somerville Park."

"That's five months from now."

"Never too early to remind folks of the Fourth!"

DAY FOUR

THURSDAY

G roats, a side of fried ham, a cup of coffee. Somerville may not be anything more than a small dot on the sprawling Kansas map, but since his arrival here Davy Bartlow had eaten hearty, and at half the price as he would have paid for breakfast at Manny's Restaurant back in Hoboken.

He'd taken a table by the window of the Broken Arrow Cafe and ate unhurried as he skimmed a three-week old copy of the *Somerville Independent*. There had been several back issues to choose from out of the wrinkled stack on the food counter. It wasn't much of a newspaper by any measure Bartlow was used to; four pages of small-town chatter and lots of advertisements from local businesses and mail order houses back east.

Most of the articles had been written by L.A. Barrett, that cute piece of calico he fully intended to get to know better—much better. He grinned allowing his imagination to construct a tantalizing plan along that line.

The newspaper contained an editorial on page three and a short couple of paragraphs on page four titled *Wisdom of the Ages*, both of them written by Harold

Barrett—the skirt's father. The remainder of the rag was laden with town gossip, recipes, and reprinted stories from larger newspapers back east, all properly credited, and all old news to Davy Bartlow.

Finished with breakfast, Bartlow lingered over his third cup of coffee watching the street past the window. Paramount Avenue was unusually congested for such a small burg as Somerville. Since his arrival, the south end of Paramount Avenue had been the quiet side of town. Today, the plebes of Somerville were stoked to catch themselves a white buffalo and get suddenly rich. Davy Bartlow grinned. Sheep everywhere loved to be shorn.

He'd spent most of yesterday wandering to get the lay of the land—to locate a likely spot to set up practice, he explained when asked. Most of the town activity lay to the north, near the railroad tracks...and the army depot

Tucked between Bo Huffman's blacksmith works and Alice O'Meara's Gentlemen's Club and Social Garden, the army depot was a trivial post; four buildings, a corral, eight mounts, five troops, and one officer named Danforth. Danforth had been the one who'd intruded upon Davy's advances toward the intriguing newspaper reporter and Bartlow had put the lieutenant's name on a mental list of unfinished items to tend to before leaving Somerville.

Lifting the coffee cup, he caught sight of a buggy turning onto Paramount, heading south. Libby Barrett sat upon the seat sawing the reins to a fast-stepping stallion, the horse plainly wanting to exercise its legs. Its gait was odd in a graceful manner. Bartlow was unfamiliar with such movement, but then horses were not his preferred mode of travel. He favored trains or trolleys, or even walking if the distance was manageable and the weather agreeable. He'd ride a horse only if no better means were available to him. Unfortunately, Somerville, Kansas offered few alternatives.

"L.A. Barrett." He said to himself, grinning as she rolled out of town.

Putting a quarter on the table, Davy Bartlow left without waiting for change.

———

The stableman, Suredor, was bent over his desk searching through papers and making notations in a ledger book when Davy entered the nippy stable and stood by the stove warming his hands.

"Gray skies," Bartlow said.

Suredor glanced out the dusty window. "If the sun don't push through by noon, you can figure on snow tonight."

"Heard you had a howling nor'easter come through last week's end."

"Well, we don't call 'em by that name, but the results are the same. That's just Kansas for you, Mr. Bartlow. If you've a notion to establish your trade here in Somerville, you can figure on burning in the summer, freezing in the winter, and dodging tornadoes in between."

Bartlow laughed and asked about the horse. "He's not mine, you know. Borrowed it from a friend who said I'd likely need one to get around these parts."

"He's enjoying his oats. Don't think he liked the train ride much, but he's settled in."

"Might take him out to look the area over. Somerville appears to be expanding to the north. I might poke about up there, but I'm thinking the south would be more agreeable."

"Lyman Road or Bridges is where I'd look to set up a

practice," Suredor advised. "I don't see much growth north or south any day soon, at least not before the century turns."

"What lies south of here?" Bartlow asked casually as if not having any particular interest other than moving the conversation along.

"Not much. Just a long, empty road and a few farms. Some cattle and sheep ranches. Winfield is down that way, near the state line. Indian Territory once you cross over. Mr. Gannon has a little ranch about five-six miles that way."

Just a long empty road. Bartlow held back a smile. "Think I will take a ride to look about before that weather moves in."

"I'll fetch your horse for you, Mr. Bartlow."

———

Wolves had been by to visit during the night. They'd come out of the hills from the east, circled the barn, the house, and then scouted out the chicken coop. Tom Gannon studied the signs in the snow from the window, sipping his coffee. He hadn't heard any ruckus and figured they'd not found anything worth stealing, and like a band of Comanches had drifted off for easier pickings.

Tom lifted his view to the hills beyond the corrals, gray beneath the low skies. It wasn't uncommon for Cochise to be gone days on end, but generally not in the winter. He grimaced at his reflection in the window. Like himself, Cochise wasn't a young man. Come cold weather he preferred to stay under roof and near the stove. Tom finished his coffee, drew on his coat, and took along a rifle in the event any of those four-footed *Comanches* had lingered.

The two horses stood hipshot in their stalls casting only a fleeting glance as he entered the barn before turning back to pick at the last of the hay at the bottom of their feed boxes. He pitched in some more hay and broke the thin sheet of ice that skinned the trough.

Finding nothing amiss here, Tom took the frozen path through the snow to the chicken coop. By the tracks, it was plain the Comanches had stalked his hens but the wire remained intact. Most of the gals were inside the hutch. A couple hens had emerged to scratch at the frozen ground. Tom tossed them a coffee can of grain and then took the trampled path back to the house, poured a second cup of coffee and sipped it peering out the window.

The hill had brightened some. Here and there splotches of sunlight broke through the clouds. Warmer weather might hold for another day or two. Enough time to check on his small herd wintering in the boxed pasture. Tom didn't think the wolves would try for the thirty head there. The cows were healthy, well fed, and Kinsey, the big Texas bull, was protective of his harem. Kinsey would allow no mischief from a pack of marauding four-footed *Comanches*.

Comanches...Apaches...that was the past; another world he'd lived through and come out on the other side. A twinge of concern pulled at his lips. He'd be lying if he didn't admit he was growing worried over Cochise's absence. Ought he go look for the old Indian or give him another day?

The jingle of chains and crunch of wheels on the crusted snow out front turned his attention from the kitchen window.

Tom set his coffee cup on the table and went through the parlor to the front door. "Good morning, Miss Libby," he declared coming out onto the porch. "This is a surprise." His smile narrowed with concern. "Everything okay with your mother and father?" He stepped down and took the reins from her as she returned the buggy whip to its holder.

"Everyone is healthy and well, thank you, and you're looking chipper. Much better, I must say, than your deplorable condition Monday evening."

Tom grinned. "I was in a pretty poor shape…in more ways than one. My jaw started feeling better almost at once but my head…well, that's another story. Don't think I'm likely to look upon a bottle of John Barleycorn for a good long while." He took her hand and helped her down. "Come on inside out of the cold."

Libby paused inside the parlor looking around. "It hasn't changed since—" she hesitated. "Since the last time I was here."

"Since the funeral," Tom said finishing what he knew she'd had been about to say. "I wanted to leave it like Cassie had it arranged. Cochise and I, well we mostly keep to the kitchen these days. Can I get you a cup of tea to warm you? Got coffee in the pot if you'd rather."

"A cup of coffee sounds good," Libby said. "The ride out was under gloomy skies but it appears old Mr. Sol intends to show his face today."

"He's welcome in my book."

"Oh, here. I brought this for you. It's last week's edition." They went to the kitchen and Tom poured coffee while Libby shed her coat and gloves.

"To what do I owe the pleasure, Miss Libby?"

Libby took the cup in both hands, clearly relishing the heat of it. "Two reasons, Mr. Gannon. Firstly, I wanted see that you were recovering from your bout with Dr. Blinker."

He laughed. "Hadn't thought of it like that."

"And secondly," she looked about, "I wanted to ask Mr. Cochise a few questions but I see he isn't here?"

Tom motioned to the table clearing places for her and himself. "Cochise is off somewhere right at the moment. He's been gone since yesterday." Tom saw the tilt of disappointment on Libby's lips and added, "I'm expecting him back soon."

"Does he do that often?"

"Often enough. It's his way, but generally not when there's a foot of snow on the ground. What is it you wanted to talk to Cochise about?"

"I suspect you have not heard what happened in town?"

"Haven't had a word. Not many folks come out to visit. Fact is, you're the first in over a month. What's happening in Somerville that would bring you all the way out here to talk to Cochise?"

"It all began right after you left town Monday evening…"

Libby told him everything, not leaving out a single detail, referring once or twice to the notebook she brought with her. She finished by reiterating, "The buffalo chip was solid gold," and then waited for his reaction.

Tom had not interrupted the telling, struggling to hold back skeptical grins or even outright laughter. He hunted for a clue to turn the yarn back onto her so he wouldn't appear naive, but if it was a prank, her deadpan face wasn't giving anything away.

She said, "I don't blame you for looking at me like I belong in an asylum. Every word of it is true."

In all the years Tom had known Libby Barrett he'd never known her to spin fanciful tales. Her newspaper writing had always been honest and nailed to the wall with facts. "You've confirmed for yourself that this buffalo chip is true gold," he asked.

"As much as I could confirm such a thing. As I said, the town council was there, and so were Jimmy Winchell and Lieutenant Danforth. We all saw and touched it."

"Hmm." Tom considered. "The Indian who had it, he died there in Wilson's Barbershop." It wasn't a question, but a restatement of what she'd told him.

"Almost at once, after mumbling about the white buffalo still loose out in the Flint Hills somewhere."

"This is what you wanted to talk to Cochise about?"

"I'd hoped Cochise might have some knowledge of legends among the Indians of such a thing ever happening before. If so, it might somehow verify this most unusual occurrence."

"No telling what he might know. If there are tales of such things as your white buffalo, I've not heard them." Tom thought it over. "Who was it that claimed the thing was gold?"

"That was Dr. Blinker."

"Where is the chip now?"

"Sheriff Bainbridge has it in the safe at his office."

"And what became of the Indian?"

"Mr. Tappermounty took him straight away to the mortuary and put him in a coffin because of the deadly illness. The coffin is behind the mortuary in that shed where he keeps the hearse."

"Dr. Blinker diagnosed the illness right there in the barbershop?"

"He thinks the Indian died of…" Libby flipped back a page in her notebook, "Aboriginal Hemorrhagic Fever."

"Hmm. It seems fortunate Dr. Blinker was at hand."

Libby rolled her eyes. "Yes and no. The next morning he announced the event far and wide, even though he had admonished we say nothing about it. He's managed to turn Somerville into a 49er's camp with everyone eyeing everyone else as if they were claim jumpers. Right-minded men have lost all sense, scrambling for a grubstake to rush off and capture this buffalo! I've never seen such a commotion."

"I'm certain a few level heads will prevail," Tom said.

"A few, perhaps." She thought a moment. "Sheriff Bainbridge has not bought into the gold rush and neither has Jimmy Winchell. Father thinks it a dodge and he intends to capitalize on the moment."

Tom went to the stove for the coffee pot, thinking over what Libby had said. Everything she'd told him sounded off except for the sudden case of gold fever that infected the town. He'd seen sane men lose all control over the smell of gold. If there was game being played on the town, he could not see a reason for it. Nor could he see it happening without some townspeople in on the prank. He refilled their cups and asked if any strangers had appeared in town.

His question startled Libby. "It's odd you'd ask that. Two men arrived. On Tuesday's 11:10. They were traveling together but made a point as to not appear so. They both were traveling with horses. One of them remained in town. The other left on the road toward Topeka."

"East." Tom turned to the window, scanning the hills.

"Does that mean anything to you?"

"Cochise went to scout smoke east of here. Maybe when he gets back we'll have a better notion of what's going on. I'll ask him about any Indian stories he may have heard about white buffaloes and golden chips."

"Father doubts an Apache would know about Sioux legends."

"I suspect your pa is right about that."

Libby came to the window. "You're worried, I can tell."

She was perceptive. "A little, maybe. It's not unusual for Cochise to go off for a few days. It's his way. He likes being alone, yet he likes knowing there is a place he can come home to. But not so much in the winter. When the cold moves over these hills Cochise stays close to bed and stove." Tom inclined his head at the cot in the corner of the kitchen, then looked at her and smiled. "It's only been a day. I expect he'll come riding in this afternoon."

"I find Indians to be confounding. They keep themselves all bottled-up inside. I don't think I could manage that if it had been my home and my land that had been taken away and I'd been gathered onto a government reservation. I can understand how something like that Medicine Dance movement came about. Maybe the reason Cochise goes off alone is so nobody sees him crying?"

That had never occurred to Tom. He did not believe lamenting over the past was the reason Cochise liked to be alone. Men who thought deeply about things, who pondered dreams and ideas, tended to find their own company more agreeable than that of crowds.

"Cochise isn't feeling sorry for himself, Miss Libby. He's not out in those hills crying over what was. He's out there hunting." Tom's real reason for concern was that sometimes the hunter becomes the hunted.

"Well, I need to be on my way, Mr. Gannon. Father will just have to use that Fourth of July announcement to cover the two-inch hole we'd hoped Cochise would help fill. Father's planning on a large print run for tomorrow's edition." She gave a small smile and a large sigh. "We shall be busy late into the night running sheets of paper through old Mr. Washington."

Tom walked Libby to the buggy, gave her a hand up, and passed the reins to her. "This is Suredor's new trotter, is it not?" he asked eyeing the sleek lines of the young stallion.

"It is indeed. Meet Lightening Strike. He's feisty and a bit of a handful, but there is something exhilarating feeling the wind in your hair."

"Indeed there is Miss Libby. Enjoy it." He smiled and for an instant saw Cassie at that young age. "By the way, did you see the Sioux after Mr. Tappermounty put him in the coffin?"

Libby looked appalled at the very idea. "I did not. The man was contagious." She cocked her head and gave him a wondering look. "Should I have? Is it important?"

"Oh, probably not. Just curious. Have a safe ride back to town. Tell Harold and Dorothy hello."

"I shall." Libby turned Lightening Strike from the rail onto the lane that led back to the main road back to Somerville.

———

At long last the prodigal sun had returned home to shine warm upon her shoulders, dissolving the morning's grayness to bright blues. The road ahead lay steamy and drying.

Enjoying Lightening Strike's brisk pace and smooth gait, Libby played with words and images, mentally constructing and rearranging sentences.

Wind, traffic, and three days of temperate weather had defeated winter's Leviathan whose lingering bits of hide lay scattered across the hills in a patchwork of white and brown.

Her thoughts drifted and she tucked the literary exercises away in that special compartment of her "writer's" brain where creative snippets were kept for future use. It was while rummaging through that attic of metaphors and similes, observations and rehearsed repartees, that she came upon a recently labeled box: *smoke in the hills.*

Immediately the memory from two days previous flashed a magic lantern show upon the screen of her brain. Cochise had observed that same gray smoke she'd spied from the boardwalk! Suddenly the event took on an importance she had overlooked.

Ought she return to Mr. Gannon's place and tell him about this new puzzle piece?

Just then movement drew her eye. A rider descending the hillside came onto the road and halted a few hundred feet ahead of her. Dr. Bartlow! Warning tingled up the back of her neck as she brought Lightening Strike to a reluctant stop, for the young stallion had been enjoying his afternoon trot.

Bartlow nudged his horse alongside the buggy and gave a charmingly disarming smile. "Why, if it isn't Miss Libby Barrett, the Rose of Somerville. Or do you prefer L.A. Barrett?"

She ought to have felt flattered at his obvious interest. Instead, a sense of alarm tightened her grip upon the reins. "You have been investigating me, Dr. Bartlow."

"A question dropped here and there," he allowed. "Your byline is in every issue of the newspaper."

"What brings you out of town? Was it to enjoy this lovely weather and the inspiring Kansas scenery?"

"That's it exactly." His face widened; the smile somehow taking on a devilish leer in Libby's mind. He said, "I must admit the scenery has made a sudden improvement."

"Only if you like snow and cold."

"Are you cold? Shall I climb up on that seat beside you and we can both warm ourselves?"

His boldness was shocking, yet somehow flattering. Libby chided herself for allowing such a notion to creep into her imagination. She wasn't a lonely spinster who craved affection, even if only from a rapscallion.

"We can get to know each other without that pesky army officer coming between us," he continued.

"Oh, is that all you want? To get to know me?" Libby played innocent. "In that case there will be a winter Masquerade at the music hall on the 18th *instante menses*. I will see to it that your name appears on my dance card. Now, if you will please move aside, I have a busy day ahead of me."

"Whatever it is you have planned for today cannot be as entertaining as what I have planned for us."

Sudden tightness gripped Libby's chest. She forced a faux smile and said, "I think you have changed my mind, Dr. Bartlow."

His eyebrows rose with interest. "That, girl, is the smartest thing you've said so far."

"Your name will *not* appear on my dance card! Please move aside."

"Don't get sassy with me." He reached for Lightning Strike's bridle.

Libby snatched the buggy whip from its holder and snapped Bartlow's fingers, near Lightning Strike's ear.

Bartlow yelped.

Lightning Strike startled at the *crack* of the whip and took off at a gallop. Libby barely had time to gain control of the reins.

Thrown back by a buggy wheel, Bartlow's horse reared and spun. "Damn you, woman!" he yelled sawing the reins. Bartlow dug in his heels and came on at a pounding pace, looking ungainly in the saddle until he'd regained his composure. Libby turned her attention to the long, empty road ahead and leaning into the wind, urged Mr. Suredor's trotter on to greater speed.

The smart, little Studebaker hummed like a well-oiled Singer, stitching a jolting seam as it skittered dangerously upon the rutted roadway. Libby knew she ought to slow to a safe speed. She was driving a buggy, not Mr. Sure-dor's lightweight racing sulky. But the pounding of hooves gaining behind her spurred her on to reckless-ness. Lightening Strike's muscles rippled beneath his sleek coat, his gait a beautifully choreographed dance between clockwork precision and the power of locomo-tive pistons.

The buggy bumped and swerved. Libby leaned hard to counter a tilt, setting it with a bounce back onto all four buzzing wheels. As fleet as Lightening Strike was, the weight of the buggy was too great for the racing stal-lion. Bartlow was upon her tailgate!

And then the frightening hammering of hoofbeats diminished. Libby cast a glance over her shoulder. Bartlow had veered off the road, heading into the hills. Libby eased back on the reins slowing the reluctant stal-lion to a safer pace. Puzzled by Bartlow's retreat, she spied the reason on the road up ahead. Approaching was, at first appearance, a caravan of wagons and outriders. The caravan turned out to be three wagons.

She pulled the buggy to a halt at the side of the road and adjusted her scarf, and the bonnet, which had whipped off her head, saved by the purple ribbon tied about her neck. Another rearward glance confirmed that Bartlow had made his escape into the hills.

The lead wagon stopped. Bo Huffman took up most of the seat with his eldest son, Castor, nearly as large as Bo, sitting beside him. Two more wagons and a company of four riders accompanied them—most of Bo's family, and a couple men Libby did not recognize. Bo identified them as cousins from McPherson, and then proclaimed that he and his kin were going to find that white buffalo, sell the shop, and move to Colorado Springs, right next door to General Palmer.

Libby wished them luck and the caravan moved on.

Bo was anxious to be on his way for now other *prospectors* were coming up behind them. She got Lightening Strike moving again, holding a tight rein. He'd had a taste of racing and wanted more. Libby had taken a bite out of that same fare and had no desire for more…at least not soon. One morsel was all she wanted. She kept an eye out for Bartlow but he'd gotten skittish by the sudden traffic. The hills had become a busy place, the number of riders swarming them increasing as Libby neared Somerville.

Coming into town, Libby gazed upon a tumult of horses and wagons, people rushing and calling, the clatter and bang of activity as she'd never seen on the usually humdrum Somerville streets. General Henry Somerville Park had turned into a market where David McClaine's wranglers hawked horses to a surging tide of men wanting them.

Libby returned Lightening Strike to Mr. Suredor and answered without elaborating, "Yes, he did seem to enjoy the exercise."

She wove her way through the crowd—many more folks she suspected than actually lived in town—to the newspaper office where she found Father in shirt-sleeve, on the boardwalk staring in shock, much as Pharaoh must have appeared watching his Hebrew slaves marching away toward the Promise Land.

"Are you all right?"

His hypnotic gazed turned slowly toward her. "We will be lucky to sell two copies."

"Come inside." Libby took his arm. He followed with the dejected languor of a child who'd just watched a circus train whistle past without even leaving a colored flyer fluttering in its wake.

Father sunk into his chair, pushed his spectacles up the bridge of his nose and peered at Libby. "Not seen anything like this since word came that Sherman was on the march. No one's got the time to read a newspaper. We won't sell two copies."

"It's the fever. The whole town's come down with it."

"You can blame Dr. Blinker for that," Mother said, working the lever on the Washington Press. *Clunk...growl.* The platen slid out and Sarah Saunder carefully peeled off an inked sheet of newsprint and lifted it to dry upon the clothesline strung back and forth across the ceiling. Mother positioned a fresh sheet upon the platen. "Your gibber-jabber at the meeting yesterday didn't help either, Harold," she added pointedly.

Father winced and sunk deeper into his chair.

Libby said, "I think there is more to it than that. I'm sure those two strangers are somehow involved."

Clunk...growl.

"I don't see how," Father said.

"I saw smoke in the hills the other day. Somebody is camping up there. Cochise saw it, too. He went to investigate. That was two days ago, and he hasn't returned. Mr. Gannon is worried, although he didn't admit it."

"That can mean anything...or nothing at all." Father thought it over a moment. "I suppose it is worth bringing to the Sheriff's attention."

"You might also mention that that Dr. Bartlow accosted me on the road back from Mr. Gannon's place."

"Oh, my!" Mother declared. "Are you all right?"

"I am unharmed thanks to Mr. Suredor's beautiful stallion and the sudden road traffic."

Father straightened in his chair, suddenly energized. "That I will tell Sheriff Bainbridge, and at once! Campfires are one thing, but my daughter's safety is something else entirely."

Libby said, "Dr. Bartlow does not act or speak like an educated gentleman," but to herself, Libby admitted the experience held a certain excitement that was generally lacking in Nowheresville, Kansas. His attention might be considered flattering, even. Immediately, and not for the first time, Libby chided herself for allowing such thoughts room inside her head. "I suspect Dr. Bartlow is a fraud,"

"You are allowing your emotions to speak," Father observed.

"I'm still upset."

"I take it then that you were not able to interview Cochise?"

Clunk…growl.

"You take it correctly." Libby removed her coat and hat and rolled up her sleeves, donning a work apron. "You shall have to run that Fourth of July announcement after all."

Father rose from his chair and took his coat and hat off the hook. "First I will have a quick word with Sheriff Bainbridge." He glanced about the busy office and shook his head. "If you're correct about some nefarious happenings, perhaps we can rescue ourselves from this two-copy day."

———

Tom Gannon let the horses into the corral as he mucked out the stalls and hauled water. A couple barn cats appeared at Tom Gannon's feet, mewing and rubbing against his leg.

The dog wandered in. He was a loner and never lingered longer than it took for Tom give the mutt a brisk scratching behind the ears. Today the dog sniffed around the empty stall where Cochise's horse usually resided, and then sat thumping his tail on the dirt floor as if overseeing Tom's chores. Cochise had named him Turkey Killer. Tom just called him Turk.

After a while Turk went back to sniffing the stall.

"I'm getting some concerned myself," Tom told the dog. "Reckon if that old Indian don't drift in by tonight I'll just have to go hunt him down and fetch him out of whatever trouble he's gotten into."

Turk wandered outside and the cats drifted off, too.

Later, Tom fixed dinner and ate in the quiet, hearing the soft, familiar creaks of the house settling down for the night. Far out in the hills the Comanches howled. Tom glanced at the empty cot across the room.

He gathered the dishes into the sink, washed them, then carried two lamps to the table and spread open the newspaper Miss Libby had brought. Afterwards, he stood outside the back door peering at the stars, thinking over what Miss Libby had told him about the dead Indian and golden buffalo chip.

He scanned the moon-bright hills hoping to spy a rider coming in from the shadows. None appeared and he went back inside, filled the stove's firebox with wood-enough to last the night, and extinguished the lamps.

The stars have all fallen to earth, Libby mused, peering from her bedroom window at the far-off hills twinkling with the stardust of a hundred campfires…men, boys, and not a few women in search of a magical animal guaranteed to bring untold riches to whomever could toss a lasso around its mythical neck. She exhaled a wistful breath, giving the vision a pragmatic edit—and then managed to fend off the claim jumpers wanting to steal the magical beast away from them.

The street lay cold and empty beneath the bright moon, its silver light painting shuttered storefronts in ghost-gray tones. The darkened windows along Lyman

Road that she could see past Wilson's Barbershop roof were the closed eyes of a gasping town whose life essence had been drained out across the hills in a hundred flickering lights.

Libby gave a small shiver. The temperature had fallen. She envisioned cold people huddled around campfires, wrapped in blankets, hands turned to flickering heat; all because of an animal that promised a treasure. *Treasure?* Libby smirked up at the big moon. "John Steele had to travel all the way to you to find his treasure...and the love of a Martian Princess. The folks of Somerville only have to venture a few miles."

There was a proverb hidden somewhere in that, but Libby was too weary to tease it out. She crawled under her heavy quilt, snuggled her feet against the warm river rock, and with thoughts of white buffaloes, Martian princesses, and golden chips, fell asleep.

DAY FIVE
FRIDAY

W arley Blinker dreamed he was in Philly, back in his cozy rooms at the Hampton, snuggled in his feather bed beneath a mound of blankets, the steam radiator cracking with warmth, driving the night chill through the plaster wall and brick veneer, back outside where it belonged.

His half-dreaming state didn't last long. The rope bed sagging in its crude, wooden frame prodded him fully awake to face another grimy day in this frigid Kansas wilderness. He hated his clothes smelling of smoke and the constant fare of tin can beans and stew eaten off of tin plates, washed down with weak coffee from tin cups, devastating his digestion. The rough food and squalid living condition he could almost manage without complaint but squatting bare-ass in the cold to relieve himself...well, only keeping the promised reward at the fore of his brain prevented him from calling quits to this affair and fleeing to the closest railroad depot that would rush him and his rented horse back to civilization.

Giving a groan, Warley Blinker marshaled reluctant muscles to *march*. With a wince he sat up, steadied himself with a hand upon the edge of the rude bed frame, and lifted one at a time to set stockinged feet on the floor…that is if hard-packed dirt could properly be called a "floor".

He eyed the pile of blankets on the "floor" against the stone wall of this tiny eight-by-eight enclosure called a line shack. From Warley's experience shacks were flimsy things made out of old wood, pasteboard, and a few sheets of tin to keep rain from washing out the place. This shack was made from something called post stone, and about as solid as a bank vault. The thought of bank vaults stirred up unpleasant memories, which Warley put quickly out of mind. "You awake, Matthew?"

"No," the pile of blankets replied, stirring a mite.

Warley smiled. "There's daylight in the window, the smell of coffee in the air…and I have got to take a piss, so, awake it is for me."

"While you're about business, take a piss for me, too," his cousin mumbled from somewhere beneath the blanket mound.

Warley laughed, shoved his feet into frosty shoes and reached for the coat hanging from a peg. It held the night's cold and made him shiver when he drew it on and buttoned it up. "I wish you would have had the good common sense to have arranged this venture for some-time in June or July."

The blankets stirred again and Dr. Blinker's face appeared amongst the folds. "You never did care for camp outs, War. Aunt Suzy always used to say you were a 'feather bed and silver spoon child…"

"'Born to a canvas a pewter family.'" Warley stared a moment into the past, aware of a distant sadness approaching. He steered his thoughts away. "I am hoping this gambit takes care of the canvas and pewter part. Three years in the Pennsylvania State Penitentiary surely did not help my financial situation. Even so, June would have been more favorable month."

Dr. Blinker exhaled a breath that hung in the air like frozen steam. "June would have been too late."

"Yes, I know. Just saying." Warley tied his shoe laces and picked his bowler hat off the crude table, brushing at a speck. He reluctantly set the cold hat upon his balding head. "Geese it's cold. June or July," he muttered unlatching the door—if such a fixture with gaping slits between the boards sprung on leather hinges might truly be considered a proper door anymore than hard dirt might be considered a floor.

The Donatalli twins sat near the fire energetically feeding the flames as if attempting to keep all of Kansas warm. They glanced up when Warley emerged from the stone cabin. Antonio said, "Sal and me were just discussing which one of us was going to drag you an' your cousin outta there."

"You'd have had your hands full if you'd tried. I smell coffee."

Salvador Donatalli reached for a cup and filled it for Warley.

"Thank you, sir."

The twins were a handsome pair with black hair, dark eyes, and youthful olive skin. They were somewhere in their late twenties, Warley reckoned. He'd never asked as it was none of his business. What was his business is knowing they were both competent with a knife or a gun and ruthless when provoked; a line over which Warley was careful not to cross. Generally speaking, Tony and Sal were an amiable pair so long as you didn't get cross-wise with them…and they came to him cheap. Angel had owed him one and the Donatalli twins were his payback.

"Where's the doc?" Sal asked.

"He ought to be along directly." The twins ran with

the Faggini gang out of West Jersey. They'd earned a reputation making life miserable for the Gallo boys who controlled east Philadelphia. Angelo Faggini had been making moves into Philly and Sal and Tony were part of the muscle the *Angel of Death* employed. Warley surveyed their camp. He didn't see Askook. Woodrow was over by his buckboard, rolling blankets and arranging them in the wagon's bed.

A few hundred yards across a snowy swale sunlight had set the tumble of stones there aglow. The place looked warm and inviting compared to here where shadows lingered long into the morning. Warley had half a mind to hike to those stones and perch like a lizard absorbing their heat. But walking any distance didn't appeal to him, and there was still deep snow along a shadowed ridge he'd have to cross over. He took a sip of coffee. "Where's Snake?"

Sal shrugged. Tony said, "Heard him moving about some before I crawled outta my blankets. That was around dawn. Maybe he's taking a leak?" Tony laughed.

Warley drew his watch from a vest pocket and wound the stem. "Dawn was about an hour ago. A leak that long would surly make a mighty flood." Tony's remark reminded Warley of his own extended bladder.

Sal poked at the fire with a stick. "Snake probably found himself an audience…three squirrels and a couple rabbits…and is giving them a performance…act two, scene three of *Margo the Magnificence on the Thames*…or whatever the hell it is he calls it."

Tony chuckled and elbowed his brother who was grinning at his own cleverness.

Woodrow Tappermounty tottered over pressing a hand to his back, moving like he'd slept on a stone or two under his bedroll.

"Hard night?" Warley asked.

Tappermounty turned his palms to the flames. "Too old for this nonsense. Should have stayed home and only pretended to have gone off looking for our albino bovine."

Sal filled another cup and handed it up to the frowning mortician. "You'd have had to hide out with Snake, if you had worked it that way, Woodrow."

Tappermounty accepted the cup and glanced around. "Speaking of Askook, where is the Indian?"

Sal shrugged. Tony offered his hands to the sky.

Warley shook his head. "No idea, but I do know that if I don't see to business, my bladder id going to bust." He set his cup on a flat stone and strode off for the nearest bush. When he returned from answering nature's summon, Askook stood with the others in the narrow circle of heat. Sal kept the fire roaring at the hurt to several nearby bushes whose limbs had been severely shorn.

Warley said, "Decided to rub elbows with us plebes, Snake?"

Askook Connor struck a pose and fixed a patrician smile upon his face. "I endeavor to circulate amongst the crowd, to shake the hands that so enthusiastically applaud." He took a bow and sloshed coffee on his fingers. "Ouch!"

Everyone but Tappermounty laughed.

Askook noted his scowl. "Ye doth disapprove, Sir Keeper of the Bodies? Still upset with my performance of Monday night?"

Tappermounty's frown deepened. "Shed ragged tent? Across yon Jordan? Whatever were you thinking, Snake? You overplayed your part and nearly ruined the show."

"The lines popped into my head as I lay there dying. I must have memorized them once, but I don't remember where. Perhaps one of The Bard's excellent plays?"

Askook shrugged. "Or perhaps not." His smile accentu-ated his high cheeks and deep-set, dark eyes. At first glance one might suspect Askook's lineage to include Asian blood somewhere down the line. Warley knew differently. It wasn't an oriental infusion, but a blending of Algonquin Indian with feisty Irish that had shaped Askook Connor into the animated actor whom Warley had by chance met one evening in a cold alley warming himself before a small fire behind the Chestnut Street Theatre.

"It is unimportant from which of my many perfor-mances I learned the line. What is important is how it added a dramatic touch to my dying." A grin cut his sly face. "I relish dying on stage. One can do so much with death to steal a scene."

"Snake, you're so full of horse shit I'm gonna have to put on galoshes," Tony declared. "If you're such a wonderful actor, what are you doing out here playing to a one-horse town like Somerville?"

"Signor Antonio, many a times and oft in the Rialto you have rated me…"

"Cut the crap, Snake."

Askook deflated and concluded softly, "Shylock, *Merchant of Venice*, Act 1, Scene 3," He sighed. "Your perception cuts to the quick, Antonio. Truth be known, I was a wee bit down on my heels when the fortuitous encounter with Warley occurred. My financial situation at the moment being, ahem, in rather poor repair, I accepted the role he offered. The pay was, or shall I say *will be,* good and the character an easy one for me to perform. I've played Indians in the past. Several times, in fact. And Jews as well. It's the nose, you see." He turned his head in profile. "A gift from my mother's branch of the family tree."

Tappermounty grunted and carried his coffee back to

the solace of his buckboard, alone with only himself, his obvious preferred company. Warley had a thought, and it brought a grin to his face. Mr. Tappermounty's usual dealings were with quiet folk, not lively ones as engaging as the Donatalli twins or Snake.

Cousin Matthew's rotund form filled the narrow doorway of the "shack" just then. He'd donned his long, gray wool coat and wrapped a scarf about his neck in such a manner as to covered his ears as well. A gray, narrow-brimmed hat topped his head. He moved stiffly to the fire and stood in its heat frowning and shivering and burring and hugging himself, and generally letting it be known how thoroughly woeful was his condition.

"June or July," Warley reminded him by way of a gentle jab.

Dr. Blinker ignored him. Salvador Donatalli dug through the canvas sack, retrieved a tin cup and banged it a couple times on a stone to dislodge the debris that had accumulated at its bottom. "Coffee, doc?"

"Coffee is quite necessary," Dr. Blinker replied burnishing his arms in an obvious display of attempting to warm them that made Askook laugh.

"Me thinks the good doctor doth protest too much," he intoned as though casting his voice to a crowded auditorium.

"Think whatever you wish, Snake!" Dr. Blinker's harsh reply mellowed and his view narrowed questioningly. "Why is it people call you Snake? Does it not annoy you?"

Askook rolled his narrow shoulders. "It's my name… my Algonquin name, that is to say. I was never told why my mother had insisted upon it. She did not like Sean, my father's choice. Something about the sound of Sean Connor did not appeal to her indigenous ears."

"But Snake did appeal to her?" Tony Donatalli

sounded both incredulous and combative. Warley wondered what had irritated Tony this morning? He frowned recalling Angel's warning.

"Go figure that one out," Askook replied giving another shrug.

Dr. Blinker pulled a gray lump of hair from his coat pocket and tossed it to Snake. "You left this in the shack. It startled me. Thought I had lain my head down on a dead rat."

Snake laughed, put the stage wig on his head and did a quick and shoddy Indian dance around the fire, the wig's braids whipping about like gray snakes. He settled back in place and cast the wig away. "I won't need that old prop again, thank god." He looked up at Dr. Blinker. "Complain about the cold all you want to, but until you swoon into two feet of snow in the middle of a frozen road, you don't have any room to gripe."

Sal handed the coffee cup up to Dr. Blinker. "How much longer are we gonna have to hang around here, Doc?"

"It shan't be long now. When I left Somerville yesterday, most half the town was already out searching. I expect word from David most any time now."

Tony refilled his cup. "I don't reckon Davy's in any hurry, him sleeping in a warm bed, eating hotel food," he paused and then added, "and dallying with the ladies." The growl Tony gave that last part was a clue to Warley as to what had gotten stuck in Tony Donatalli's craw. Tony fished through the pasteboard box and drew out a can of beans pretending to read the label. "So what do we have here for breakfast? Hmm. We can have beans or…" he drew out a second can. "…beans."

"I believe I will have beans this morning," Sal replied and tossed another branch into the fire.

Warley was hearing discontent coming from both of

the Donatalli twins and was beginning to see what Angel had meant when he'd given his warning the afternoon they'd struck their agreement.

Dr. Blinker rolled his eyes, glanced at the shack with its shabby door askew, and fanned the air in front of his nose, "Should any of you gentlemen need to strike a match, please do not do it inside that building. You're liable to ignite an explosion." He grinned at Cousin Warley.

Sal laughed and Snake grinned. Tony was not in a humorous mood this morning.

"I do believe I heard a few barking mice coming from your side of the shack, too," Warley retorted.

Dr. Blinker sighed. "Looks like I will have to pass on the steak and eggs this morning and have the beans as well. Self defense, you understand." His view shifted. "And you, Snake?"

"Decisions, decisions. Put me down for the beans and remind me when this performance is over to have a talk with my agent about my dining requirements the next time I am on the road."

Tony tossed the cans back into the box. "I don't want to eat any of 'em this morning. I'm tired of beans."

Dr. Blinker said, "I've brought along canned milk, canned asparagus, canned peaches, and canned stew." It was clear that the provisions weren't impressing either of the twins. "There is a sack of flour," he added hopefully. "We can make biscuits or a cobbler. I think I have a can of blueberries somewhere around here."

"I don't want anything that comes out of a can, and I don't want to cook. That's women's work."

Sal said, "Speaking of women, you might have brought a couple of 'em along with you."

"Sorry, but I'm fresh out of women these days."

Warley said, "Explaining what we were doing out here might have proven inconvenient."

"I can surely enjoy the tender company of a woman about now," Tony allowed. He took a moment to count back. "It's been over two weeks."

"You'll live," Warley said kindly enough, although sympathy was not what he felt toward Tony's plight. "I went over three years while at ESP."

"Maybe so for you, but I'm not locked up in no penitentiary."

"Yet," Askook noted stoically.

Tony ignored him. "I don't see any reason I shouldn't ride to Somerville and pick me up a woman right now." He went broodingly quiet.

Warley grimaced. Angel had warned about the twin's changeable nature. *It's like they each have this track switch inside them that when thrown put them on a siding called mayhem.*

Dr. Blinker said, "The cure you're seeking can be found at Alice O'Meara's Gentlemen Club."

Askook said, "There was that fetching reporter lady." He kissed a finger and pressed it against an imaginary air skillet, making a sizzling hiss. "Hey Doc, what's her name?"

"Her name is Libby Barrett, and she is off limits to you gents."

"You got a claim on her, Blinker?" Tony challenged.

"My only claim is her friendship. She's not to be molested. Besides, you haven't time for any of this rutting nonsense. I suspect David will be bringing word soon enough."

Warley was impressed by the firmness in his cousin's voice. The Matthew he'd grown up with back in Pennsylvania had been a soft-spoken fellow hesitant to confront anyone head-on. The west had toughened his cousin.

Tony glared at Matthew; a glaze hardened the younger man's eyes and his fingers started twitching as if seeking a trigger or knife. Fortunately, there weren't any firearms within reach. Tony's Smith & Wesson in its fancy armpit holster was over by the Donatallis' bedrolls, and the little slide action .22 leaned against the shack's stone wall.

Warley said soothingly, "This will be over soon enough, Tony. When we're done here we'll all go back home and have us a grand time."

Tony impelled Warley with an evil stare. He shot to his feet and strode toward the shack."

"What are you doing?" Warley asked worriedly.

Tony grabbed the Winchester and wheeled around, racking the slide. "I'm gonna hunt something other than beans for breakfast," he snarled and stomped off toward the valley.

Sal said, "There goes your audience, Snake."

"Huh?"

"Never mind." Sal poked at the fire and a long breath escaped his lips "Lucky for you Doc, he's only going to shoot rabbits."

Cousin Matthew looked confused and a good bit relieved.

Tappermounty came up behind Warley. "What was that all about?" He peeled off the wrapper and stuck a square of spruce gum in his mouth watching Tony striding out into the valley, the little gallery rifle swinging at his side.

Askook said, "Signor Antonio seeks a young damsel to void his rheum upon...or something like that. I'm pretty sure The Bard had something else in mind."

Dr. Blinker said, "That young man is quite unpredictable."

Warley heard the slight tremble in his cousin's voice

and nodded slowly with a new respect for Angelo Faggini's warning.

Sal said, "Best not to get crosswise with Tony. You challenged him and he held back. You were lucky. A word of advice, Doc. Stand clear of him from here on out. Tony don't forgive, and he don't forget."

———

Cochise did not return during the night. Grimly, Tom Gannon hurried through the morning chores. Afterwards, he saddled Colby and led the horse to the house, tying him to the rail.

Inside, Tom gathered biscuits, jerked venison, and a canteen. He shed his canvas work coat for the heavier buffalo one and took the carbine down from its pronghorn rack above the door. The holster belt on the wall peg held his eye a moment. He rarely carried the revolver these days. Not much need for one now with the land mostly tamed and the Indian problem settled, not like it was twenty years ago. Tom considered, then plucked the handgun from its peg.

He filled his saddlebags with the supplies, added a half-full box of .38 cartridges and slid the Winchester into its saddle holster. Eyes fixed upon the gap in the hills where he'd last seen Cochise heading, Tom stepped into the saddle and moved out, past the bare mulberry tree overshadowing the gravestones. He did not look at them.

Tracking the Indian would not be easy now with the snow melting and what there was left of it trampled by coyotes, wolves, skunks, foxes, turkeys and...he grimaced. He had almost added white buffaloes to the list. Definitely not. The smoke Cochise had gone to investigate had been to the northeast. For an old Indian fighter like Tom Gannon that was a good enough to start him on his way.

————

Libby awoke with the rosy blush of dawn in the sky. The quiet street beneath her frosted window lay silently somber, as if awaiting the lonely appearance of Mr. Tappermounty's hearse emerging from the darkness. Libby shook the thought from her head. Being morose was not in her nature. Something was afoot in Somerville and she intended to discover what it might be.

Despite her best of intentions, the morning languished beneath an oppressive cloud so unusual for Somerville. Even Nowheresville, Kansas was a busy place on a Friday morning. Not today.

Father stood at the window for long intervals staring at the empty street, shuffling back to his desk from time to time. "We are going to go bust," he'd mumble to no one but the ghosts of the newspaper world. Libby struggled to focus as she sat at her desk attempting to compose a follow-up article to the awful piece of fiction she'd cobbled for today's edition.

The task eluded her. Even the ticking of the clock distracted. The heavy iron printing press stood silently laughing at their hubris. No need to print the extra copies that Father had hoped to sell. Too few folks remained in town to buy the copies already printed, and in a day or two, when winter's chill dragged everyone back to their warm homes and glowing stoves, no one would want to read about Somerville's Folly anyway. Some might even consider hanging Dr. Blinker...and Father...for having encouraged the misadventure.

"We're going to go bust."

"You had no way of knowing, Harold." Mother called

from the back room where she was washing rollers and bottling ink.

"I had wagered on the simple-minded nature of man and his predilection for greed. I had not considered the whole town, thus infected, would act like a herd of buffalo," he winced, "and propel themselves over a cliff of cupidity.

"Of what?" Mother shrilled.

"Covetousness, dear."

Libby said, "It's only some ink and paper. This is surely not going to be the cause the *Independent's* demise. Consider it a lesson on 'counting chickens'."

The distant whistle of the 11:10 floated through empty streets. Father glanced at the clock and then rose from his desk chair and went out front to the newspaper stand by the door. The cash box made a familiar clatter as he worked the latched. He returned counting the small pile of coins in his hand.

"Eight cents," he declared. "four newspapers sold all morning." Father sighed and murmured once more how they were going to go bust.

Libby turned back to her desk feeling an otherworldly unease she couldn't describe or put a finger on. The quiet of the empty town crashed like brass cymbals inside her head. Productive concentration was useless. She shot abruptly to her feet and went for her coat and scarf. "Perhaps brisk air will clear the cobwebs," she said, pulling on her gloves.

"Collect the mail while you're out, will you Elizabeth Ann?" Mother said.

"If Mr. Winchell is even in town to collect it from the train," Father added glumly.

That Jimmy might have succumbed to the fever never occurred to Libby. The possibility was one more demon to trouble her spirit.

Paramount Avenue lay desolate before her; a long empty track leading to the AT&SF depot whose lonely platform was a perfect metaphor for what insanity looked like. Libby might have followed that thought into a briar patch of similes. Today her heart just wasn't in it. Her view wandered up one side of Paramount and back down the other side spying here and there a solitary figure. In Libby's imagination everyone looked as lost as she felt.

She crossed Bridges Road feeling she was intruding where only ghosts dare tread; a stage setting with all the actors vanished. In door windows hung "closed" signs: Dr. Blinker's Surgery, Hibbner's Department Store, the Music Hall, the Mortuary—Mr. Tappermounty had been one of the first to flee town in search of scatological riches —but the bank was still open for business. Libby peered through the glass at lonely Mr. Havendish inside the teller's cage, staring from beneath his green eye shade and not a depositor in sight. Clark's Saloon was open for business, and like the bank, no one was spending money there.

She crossed Paramount at the corner and peeked into the window of the watch repair shop. Bob Heelcroft had succumbed to the fever. Libby was pretty sure it was Betty's prodding that had compelled him to join the hunt.

Pealgramm's General Store was open for business. Somehow, Libby knew it would be. Faith renewed, she stepped inside and stood alone amongst all the merchandise. Jimmy's mail window looked forlorn. Mr. Pealgramm, who always appeared promptly at the sound of the door bell, did not appear.

"Hello?"

Only quietness…and then the heavy thump of footsteps and Helma Pealgramm came through the back door, her full cheeks aglow, her blue eyes smiling. "*Fraulein* Barrett, *gut morgen.*"

"Good morning, Mrs. Pealgramm." Libby looked about the desolate store. "Is Mr. Pealgramm not here? Is he unwell?"

Helma's eyes pinched and she explained that her husband had gone off on his foolishness.

The news startled Libby. Not him, too! A stalwart pillar of Somerville had developed a wide crack. So much for having good common sense. Libby felt disappointment but couldn't tell if what Helma was feeling was annoyance or mere humor from it all. Father's prognostication came back to her with a twinge to her stomach.

"Jimmy?" she asked, her throat tight. It couldn't be! Not Jimmy, too!

Mrs. Pealgramm's never-failing smile deepened the dimples on her cheeks. "*Herr* Winchell outside, back on dock."

Relief crashed over her and her foundering ship of faith righted itself. "May I speak with him?"

"*Ja.*" Mrs. Pealgramm's plump hand beckoned at the back door.

Through a cluttered office and out another door, Libby found Jimmy shuffling boxes to a covered area against the building, away from the edge of the loading dock where a recent delivery had deposited them.

"For a moment I feared you had become one of them," she said.

"You mean out there?" He glanced at the hills past Somerville's last residence at the end of Lyman Road. "Got this close." His thumb and finger came together almost touching. He grimaced, looking embarrassed. "Leland almost talked me into going along with him and Vinny Borglan. Said that Josh Timor was in on it, too."

"Leland Talbot from the army depot?" Had the fever

had affected the army as well. "Did Lieutenant Danforth give them leave?"

"I'm not sure. Leland looked kind of sheepish when I asked him about that."

This was more serious than Libby had suspected. If soldiers were abandoning their posts to scour the hills for this beast, then no one was immune to the madness. "What stopped you?" she asked.

Jimmy's cheeks reddened even though already flushed from the cold. "I don't know. Maybe I was afraid to go along? I didn't believe Leland and the others got permission to leave. I think they saw this as a good way to get free of the army with money in their pockets. I didn't want to be a part of that."

"Sensible of you. Lieutenant Danforth will be madder than a wet cat when he finds out."

"And I didn't want to go off leaving the store for Mrs. Pealgramm to handle by herself. Mr. Pealgramm sort of put the place in my hands before he left. Anyway, I have got to collect the mail whether or not anyone is here to receive it. Who would do that if I went off for a week to hunt an animal that probably doesn't exist anyway. If it does, that poor critter has probably already been scared into the next county."

"I can't believe he fell for it," Libby said sharply.

"Don't be to harsh. Mr. Pealgramm has a sister and mother in the old country he wants to bring over. He can't afford the passage."

Across the street in the corral behind the sheriff's office where Sheriff Bainbridge kept his horse, movement caught Libby's eye. The sheriff had emerged from his back door, Dr. Bartlow with him! Libby backed against the wall behind some barrels, tugging Jimmy by the sleeve with her.

"What?" Jimmy startled.

"That's David Bartlow with the sheriff. The stranger from the train?"

"So what if it is?"

Libby gave him an abbreviated account of what had occurred on her way back from Mr. Gannon's place. "Father reported his behavior to the sheriff," she told him.

Jimmy peeked through a gap between the barrels. "Why isn't the man in jail?"

"That's what I want to know."

There were two horses in the corral where normally only Sheriff Bainbridge's animal was kept ready at hand in the event he needed it quickly.

Bartlow led his horse from the lean-to and adjusted the girth strap. The two men talked a while and then with a nod of agreement, Bartlow swung up onto his saddle. The sheriff opened the gate to the alley.

Libby and Jimmy remained hidden as the sheriff returned to his office. Soon as he'd gone Libby hurried down the loading ramp and out onto Lyman Road in time to see Bartlow turn onto Schoolhouse Road toward Capital Highway.

Jimmy said, "Walt had no intention of arresting the cad."

"Aiding and abetting." Libby stared down the empty road.

"Why would Walt do that?"

"I don't know, but I intend to find out. Something more is afoot here than a dead Indian with a lump of gold and a silly story about a white buffalo."

"But what could that have to do with Walt and the stranger?"

"There were two strangers, remember. One left town and Bartlow remained."

"You still think they were traveling together?"

"I'm sure of it, Jimmy."

"But the sheriff?"

Libby scowled in spite of Miss Penelope's dire warnings. The puzzle was missing too many pieces. They returned to the loading dock. "Jimmy, can you think of any way I can get another look at that gold chip? If I could see it in daylight instead of lamplight it might help me to determine if it's genuine. We have only Dr. Blinker's word on it."

"Sure. That's easy," Jimmy said. "Walt has it in the safe."

"Easy?" she asked, her skepticism showing.

"Well, sure."

"It's locked in a safe. How is that *easy*?"

"Well, the safe belongs to the town of Somerville, and so does the building. Walt, he's only an employee. The Town Council has access to both the building and the safe, and since I keep the books and write up the minutes to the meetings, I do, too."

"Now that is convenient." Libby's voice lowered, her tone suddenly conspiratorial. "Would you open the safe for me?"

Jimmy hesitated. "I suppose," he equivocated. "I don't see where I'd be breaking any law so long as we don't actually take the gold chip." He thought a moment. "We'd have to do it when Walt is away from the office."

"A distraction?" she suggested.

"Already got one." He grinned. "What time is it?"

Libby tipped up her lapel watch. "Almost Twelve."

"Walt takes lunch at Harbournes' around noon every day."

"Jimmy, you're wonderful."

"Gosh, no I'm not. Just helping a friend. Like you said, there's something not right going on and I want to know what it is, too."

Libby recalled something that had lingered at the back of her brain and now she brought it forward to examine it a little closer. "When I visited Mr. Gannon yesterday he asked if I'd seen the Indian's body after Mr. Tappermounty and put it in the coffin."

"That is a strange thing to ask. Why do you suppose he wanted to know?"

"I have no idea. Do you think it's important?"

"Hmm. The Tom Gannon I know is not a man to ask frivolous questions."

"No, he isn't. I think maybe it's time for me to find the answer to it."

"Libby, you're not thinking…"

"Oh, yes I am. If it was important enough for Mr. Gannon to ask, then it must be important to find the answer."

"For us," Jimmy said.

"Us?"

"Sure. I guess if I'm going to open the safe for you, well then I'm going to help you open that coffin, too."

———

Tracking Cochise would not have been easy even in the best of conditions. An unshod horse leaves a lighter trail than one wearing iron shoes. Now the task was double hard. The ground had been snow covered two days earlier when Cochise left the ranch. The snow had swallowed the tracks and then melted them away. Riding a looping pattern, Tom spied a single track on a patch stiff grass where wind had swept it clear early on. He found another hoof print in a shaded drift. The signs were scant; a hoof print here, a snapped twig there. It was enough to point Tom in the right direction.

It had been years since Tom had tracked an Indian

and his skills had grown a cover of rust that he had to polish off now as he worked the trace east and north. The day warmed. He shed his coat, the sun comfortable upon his shoulders as he bent his view to the ground. Twenty-five years ago on a day like today, it had been Crazy Horse and his warriors he'd tracked. The racing years... the swift decades...where had they gone?

Movement in the brush snapped him out of his memories. The marauders were out there and were alert to his passage. Colby sensed them, too, and sidestepped nervously.

"Easy boy." Tom laid a hand upon the horse's withers. "I see them." Glimpses of the gray stalkers moved amongst the scrub. "The Comanches are trying to surround us," he said, drawing his carbine from its saddle scabbard and moving the lever just enough to catch a flash of brass in the chamber.

The wolves came stealthy at first and then all at once. Six or seven of them burst into view, circling, fangs bared, dark eyes focused. The hunters were hungry.

Tom flung the carbine to his shoulder and fired and fired again, the finger lever ratcheting fresh shells into the chamber as fast as the Comanches came at him.

————

Where shelving rock had collapsed, sunlight pushed deep into a cranny warming the stones of a natural shelter...and Cochise, who lounged upon his blanket tending a small fire beneath the rabbit he'd snared earlier. From this concealed place he kept watch on the men across the intervening swale. They moved aimlessly about their tents and the old line shack, sometimes hovering near the fire, which was kept burning hot for the little warmth it offered. Their numbers had grown over the last couple days. There'd been three when Cochise had found them. Two more arrived a day later, and another the next day. Now six men wandered about, turning hands to the heat, smoking, drinking...waiting.

Cochise took care not to reveal his presence; building his fire on the backside of the leaning rock during the day, allowing it to die back to a bed of hot coals when darkness came upon the land.

Their being here was strange. At first Cochise put it off to a hunting camp, but the men had shown no interest in that activity. The only shooting they accomplished was at tin cans and bottles, and the occasional fleeing rabbit, which they most often missed. Cochise would have abandoned the affair had not the Death Shaman, the one called Tappermounty, arrived together with another man. The few times he'd met the him, he had not struck Cochise as one who would suffer the inconvenience of sleeping in the cold without a good reason.

And then there was the strange, little man who had arrived with the Death Shaman. He looked Indian, but...?

One night Cochise stalked around the head of the valley and moved in close enough to hear their words. The little man who looked Indian spoke as a white man. Cochise hunkered in the shadows to watch him prancing about the fire casting long shadows as his arms gestured and his face made shapes of anger and then surprise, his words both furious and then joyful. Cochise suspected the man was loco. When the crazy Indian finished his prancing and beckoning, and his speech came to an end, the other men laughed and clapped their hands. The Indian smiled and bowed many times and waved his hands above his head. Were all these men loco, too?

Determined to learn the meaning of all this, Cochise had returned to his secret place across the valley to ponder what he had seen.

Now taking in the sun's warmth and tending his roasting rabbit, the distant sound of rifle shots brought his head about. One...two...he counted eight shots followed by the sharper report of a revolver. Afterwards no more shooting. A quick glance assured him that the men across the valley had not heard. Cochise knew the voice of that rifle.

Tom Gannon was coming.

———

Armed with broom, determination, and spying eyes on the sheriff's office up the street, Jimmy attacked the stubborn mud clots that had dried hard as sugar candy on the boardwalk out front of Pealgramm's store. He swept and scraped and pounded, his efforts ineffective...and that was the plan. His purpose was not victory but reconnaissance. The sidewalk skirmish merely a diversionary tactic. Waiting near the window for Jimmy's signal, Libby played with the metaphor of a military battle, nipping it here, tucking it there.

At 12:12, Jimmy ceased his attack. Setting the broom aside, he gave a nod. Libby set her mental editing aside, too, joining him out front in time to see Sheriff Bainbridge turn into Harbournes' Restaurant, three buildings up from his office. Using his official Town Council key, Jimmy let them into the sheriff's office through the back door. Their footsteps sounding alarmingly loud in Libby's ears, nearly as loud as her pounding heart. She'd never in her lifetime done anything as daring as breaking and entering. Jimmy appeared calm, but Libby was sure his heart was rebounding off his ribs as well. He went straight to the safe and she, according to their plan, went to the window to keep watch. Jimmy had said that lunch usually consumed half and hour to forty-five minutes, but there was always the chance some necessity might summon Sheriff Bainbridge back to his office sooner.

Jimmy called for her a few minutes later. She came back and knelt at his side as he lifted the heavy, hide-covered lump from the safe to the floor and peeled back the wrapping. It looked exactly as it had the first time she'd seen it. The shape was definitely that of a buffalo chip—the same as a thousand others like it that had once strewn the Flint Hills before the buffalo had disappeared. Undigested bits of grass pricked it here and there, and the color was undeniably gold. Libby set her bag aside and removed her gloves placing them atop the safe so that she might better feel the texture of the gold chip.

Jimmy said, "Well, what do you think? Does seeing it again answer any of your doubts?"

"No." Libby said, disappointed. "It looks like gold buffalo poop…but it can't be, can it?"

"Dr. Blinker thinks it is."

"And he has that book that backs up his belief," she agreed.

"Then that settles it. Let's put it back and get out of here before someone see us." Jimmy began wrapping the chip.

"Wait a minute." Libby glanced at her watch. They had time yet. "I want to try something." She hefted the heavy lump and carried it out behind the office where a cord of firewood was stacked. Setting the chip on the splitting stump, Libby retrieved the ax leaning against the pile and took aim."

"What are you thinking!"

"I want to know for sure it's really gold." She swung the ax down. The buffalo chip rebounded off the stump. Jimmy recovered it and their heads came together over the lump. The gouge left by the ax showed the gleam of metal, bright and true! It was the silvery glint of *lead!*

"It's a fake," Jimmy declared.

"Somebody went through a lot of trouble for a prank," Libby said, a mix of wonderment and vindication in her voice.

They returned it to the safe and Jimmy spun the tumbler. The sound of footsteps on the boardwalk, and the metallic rattle of a key startled them. Grabbing up her bag, she and Jimmy rushed down the hall and out the back door. Jimmy turned the locked even as the front door was opening. They fled across the corral, bent through the rails, and sprinted across the street and up the loading ramp behind Pealgramm's store, falling against the wall of the store breathlessly.

"That was close." Libby looked at her watch. "It's one o'clock already!"

"Time flies, they say" Jimmy replied sounding as shaken as she felt.

"I knew it couldn't be real!"

"But why? What's the point?"

"I have a bad feeling about all this. If the chip is fake, then the whole drama with the dead Indian has to be fake, too."

Jimmy's eyes enlarged. "Are you saying the Indian didn't die?"

"That is exactly what I'm saying."

"But Dr. Blinker verified that he was dead. And Mr. Tappermounty did, too, by the fact that he put the body into a coffin and out in that cold shed behind the mortuary to keep."

"Did he?" Libby wondered.

"You think that's a ruse, too?"

"I don't know. I still need to fit the pieces together, but…"

"Dr. Blinker said the Indian died of a deadly disease,"

Jimmy countered, "and that he needed to be put away quickly, before anyone caught the illness."

"Dr. Blinker also said the buffalo chip was real gold," Libby reminded him. "But neither you nor I have seen the body."

"Tom Gannon's question," Jimmy said.

"He suspected something right off."

Back inside, Mrs. Pealgramm "tsked-tsked" at Jimmy and pointed out the office door at Mrs. Tinsley and Mrs. Lorange hovering near the mail window. Jimmy hurried apologetically out front, donning his official postal cap as he appeared behind the window and ruffled through the mail sack of letters and packages.

Libby said to Mrs. Pealgramm, "I am surprised that Mr. Pealgramm has gone out to hunt for the white buffalo. I'd heard him say it was all foolishness."

Mrs. Pealgramm's ever present smile never faltered as she explained how Warner wished to deliver his sister and mother from Berlin to Kansas, but that steamer passage to New York, and then by rail to Kansas cost too much *märks*. She shrugged. "Warner wishes to find money to make the passage."

Libby regretted that his adventure was destined to fail, but didn't mention the sham to Mrs. Pealgramm.

Official postal duties fulfilled, Jimmy emerged from his mail cubical looking chagrin. "Going to have to stay here until my window closes at five-thirty."

Libby took his arm and moved out of earshot of Mrs. Pealgramm. "It's better we wait until dark before risking a second break-in," she said quietly, still shaken from their narrow escape from their first one even though, she rationalized, it wasn't really a *break-in* if Jimmy possessed the key and the authority...more or less...to enter the building and open the safe, was it?

Jimmy agreed to meet at 5:45 for the next phase of

their investigation and Libby returned to the *Independent's* office. Mother and Father looked sullen, playing tick-tack-toe on the back of a half-printed sheet of newspaper.

"This is a gloomy place." Libby shed her coat and scarf. "It's only one edition? You're both acting like you lost the business to the tax collector."

Father looked up as Mother drew a circle and struck a bold slash. "Eight copies," he replied. "We sold more during last week's blizzard. It's not the money," he sighed, "it's how poorly I read the mood and mind of the crowd. I am falling down on my game, I fear."

"Want to hear some good news?"

"What news, Elizabeth Ann?" Mother asked hatching out a new grid.

"The gold chip that put all this into motion is not Au. It's Pb."

"Huh?" Mother said.

"Pb?" Father paged through his mental encyclopedia and suddenly perked up. "Lead?"

"Jimmy and I verified it just now."

"How?"

"With the strike of an ax."

"No. I mean, how did you get your hands on it?"

Libby grinned and burnished her fingernails upon her shoulder. "I merely broke into Sheriff's Bainbridge's office while he was away and cracked the safe."

"You burgled his safe?" Mother sounded shocked.

Libby's grin faltered ever so slightly. "I wish it was so *audace*." She sighed. "The truth of the matter is, Jimmy had a key to the back door and he knew the combination."

Father sprang to his desk and snatching up a pencil. "We shall expose this charade to the nation—err, at least to the county. It will be an *Independent* exclusive. The shocking story might even find it's way into one of the large eastern newspapers!"

———

From his higher vantage, Cochise spied the rider long before the men across the valley became aware of him. Judging from his brisk pace, the rider appeared to be a man on a mission. His arrival instantly excited the sleepy campers who for days had lain about like lazy dogs. They gathered around to hear his words. Afterwards, tents came down, chairs folded, blankets were rolled, bound, and heaved into the wagon. A horse was led to harness and within an hour the campsite had broken apart. The Death Shaman and the loco Indian climbed into the wagon. Blinker stepped up into a buggy. The rest of the men mounted their horses, and the party rode away.

Cochise watched the riders bend their trail toward the north, toward Somerville. He eased from his den, stretched, grabbed up his shotgun and limped down a well-trampled path into the secluded swale where his hobbled horse grazed dry grass.

Soon the horse was saddled and ready to travel. Before Cochise rode away, he removed the strand of red beads he wore about his neck, hung them conspicuously upon a scrubby branch, and snapped a stem to point toward the valley.

———

Tom Gannon traced the scant trail over shelving flint stone and across ground moist from snowmelt. The afternoon's quiet was broken only by the creak of saddle leather and the sound of his horse's hooves. Cochise had taken no effort to hide his tracks, few as they were; a hoof print here, a twisted twig there, the rare gray blaze of hoof upon a slope of stone.

The sun's warmth crept off his shoulders and shadows moved like the slow hands on a clock. Noon was long past when Tom came across the first clear signs on the sunny side of a hill where a trickle of water issued from a cut of naked rock. An unshod horse had entered the gap into a small swale set down between two hills. The ground was trampled. The horse had been hobbled and had grazed here, and then freed of its fetters had been ridden away...maybe two hours earlier, Tom reasoned by how the brown, brittle grass had lifted. What had kept Cochise here? Other than it being a natural shelter from the wind, with proper grazing and water for the animal, Tom saw nothing compelling about the place...

A glint of red caught his eye. He nudged his horse forward and untangled a strand of beads from some scrubby brown branches. Near the beads a snapped branch pointed Tom's eyes toward a trampled path up a slope. Dismounting, he followed it a short distance to a wide slab of rock leaning over a bed of dead coals and some scraps of bone and fur. The shelter had been well chosen, open to the south and protected from the north and west. From here Cochise had a wide view across a shallow valley and the hillside beyond where the old, stone line shack stood.

A few minutes later he rode into the abandoned campsite. Six or seven men had recently bivouacked here. The coals of their fire were still warm. There'd been a heavy wagon and a lighter buggy judging by the width of the wheel. A small corral made of rope still in place had held their animals. Strewn about were bottles and cans, scraps of paper and food wrappers. He picked up a Curtis & Son chewing gum wrapper. Spruce scented. The odor on the paper was familiar but the memory of exactly where he'd encountered it was not at all clear. Tucking the wrapper into a vest pocket, Tom scouted further. A nearby rock, covered with shards of broken bottles and riddled bean cans, told the story of men killing time. He stooped for a small brass shell. Rimfire. .22 short. Hundreds of them scattered about. The place had the feel of a military encampment.

Returning to his horse, he spied something snagged in a naked branch. At first he thought it a dead gray squirrel. Upon examination he discovered a toupee with two long braids. A woman's wig?

Tom remounted and followed their trail north. It was nearly impossible now to separate a single set of tracks from the broken ground, and no longer important to do so now. It was clear where they—and Cochise—were going.

The sky darkened and the temperature dropped. Tom crawled back into his heavy coat. Their trail met up with the Topeka road where the AT&SF railroad tracks ran parallel to it. Tom scanned ahead in the failing light hoping to catch sight Cochise or the men he was following. Darkness moved over the land and a big moon climber higher, casting its slivery a glint along the steel rails and overhead telegraph wire. It felt colder, as if the moonlight was absorbing what little heat remained on the land.

Tom hunkered inside his warm coat recalling a similar night many years ago and far to the north of Kansas. He and a small cavalry contingent had been following a band of Crazy Horse's warriors. Back then Tom knew who they were and why he was pursuing them. Tonight, all he had to go on was the conviction that Cochise would not be out here in the cold following these men if he didn't have a good reason to do so.

Libby donned coat and hat and searched for her gloves. Not finding them in her room, she went downstairs to the newspaper office to retrieve them from her desk where she was certain she'd left them.

Mother stopped her. "You're going out tonight, Elizabeth Ann?"

"I'm meeting Jimmy," Libby said lightly, hoping a casual reply would avert further inquiry.

"It is almost dark," Father said from his desk, stating the obvious.

The graying light past the window announced nightfall in another few minutes. Perfect timing for what Jimmy and she wanted to accomplish.

"What are you two up to?" he asked suspiciously.

Libby grabbed for the first lever that came to mind to sidetrack Mother and Father from derailing her plans. To Father she said, "We are conducting an investigation into the matter of the gold chip, which will give me the facts I need to write a story that will catapult the *Independent* to the front page of The New-York Times!" And to Mother she added, "I shall be well protected under Jimmy's watchful eyes. He's such a nice boy," she added, imitating the inflection Mother always used when attempting to attach Libby to an agreeable suitor.

"Jimmy is a nice boy. He has good sense."

The psychology worked. Libby had hoped; she could almost hear matchmaking clock-work turning in Mother's head. And Father's face brightened at the prospect of far-reaching exposure. "Can you be a little more specific as to how you intend to thrust the *Independent* into the national limelight?"

"Not at this moment, but I will explain everything as soon as I return home. I'm already late." Fleeing further interrogation, Libby dashed out the door flinging the scarf about her neck as she plunged into the early winter's nightfall.

Jimmy was waiting for her on the corner. "What took you so long?" he asked.

"It takes time for a young lady to prepare herself when meeting a gentleman for an evening engagement," she replied lightly, and then seriously, "Mother and Father waylaid me on my way out wanting to know the *Quis, quid, quando*—

"The what?"

The who, what, and when. It took a few strategic moves to extradite myself from their interrogation."

They turned up the alley behind Dr. Blinker's surgery making their way past dark back windows and doors. Libby's trepidation mounted as it had when they broke into Sheriff Bainbridge's office, but this time the tightness in her chest was tempered with a curious thrill of forbidden adventure. The windows in Mr. Tappermounty's mortuary were lit and briefly Mrs. Tappermounty's shadow passed across one of them."

"Sheila's home," Jimmy whispered.

Silvery moonlight glinted along the roofline of the large shed across the alley where Mr. Tappermounty kept the black hearse and a few caskets. The shed's big door was locked, and so was the side door. They pondered the problem.

Libby said, "I don't suppose you have a key to this building, too."

"That would be too easy," Jimmy replied. He stepped back to survey the building. A glint of moonlight drew their eyes to the window. Jimmy attempted to lift it. Stubbornly stuck in place, it finally budged, and then reluctantly creaked and moved up a few inches—probably for the first time in years. Jimmy found a crate in the weeds that fringed the rear of General Somerville Park. It put him at a more favorable elevation from which to muscle the stubborn window wide enough to crawl through.

Libby stepped up and peered into the gloom where the dark hearse loomed ominously. "Can you open the door from the inside?"

"I'll try it." Jimmy moved felt his way along a work-bench encountering things that made dull scrapes or metallic clatter. "A-ha!" Something rattled and a matched flared. A moment later a hurricane lantern's soft, yellow glow showing Jimmy making his way past clutter to the door. He tried the handle, moved the lamp about, and said, "It needs a key from this side, too, Libby."

"Help me through." She gathered her skirt about her and leaned into the window. Jimmy grasped her under her arms and pulled her the rest of the way inside. Over balanced, they crashed against the hearse and landed in a tumble of arms and legs on the floor. The awkward, intimate moment, secure in Jimmy's arms, brought her face dangerously near his. Libby felt a flush of heat come to her cheeks. A part of her wanted to remain in the cozy embrace, but the moment passed and she and Jimmy scrambled to untangle themselves.

"I hope the crash doesn't draw attention," she said, a little flustered as she brushed her coat and straightened her twisted skirt.

"Who's left in town for it to attract?" he said, pointing out the stark reality of this golden chip affair.

"Mrs. Tappermounty," she reminded him.

"Oh, yeah. Guess I forgot about Sheila." He lifted the lantern for a better look. Hand tools hung on the wall and longer ones leaned in the corners in no particular arrangement. Shelves held boxes. A long bench beneath the window had a hammer and saw, and a coffee can full of nails. Three caskets had been stacked against the wall at the back of the hearse…and a fourth one, separate from the others, rested at the end of the workbench.

Jimmy moved the lantern closer to examine the lid. "Nailed shut." He handed the lantern to Libby and attempted to lift a corner. "It's got weight. There's a body inside."

"Whose body?" Libby wondered aloud. "The Indian's?"

"Who else can it be? No one else has died since Mr. Abercrombe passed last September."

She looked at him. "We need to open it." The words struggled out as if resisting her attempt to speak them. "We have to be sure. If it was important enough for Mr. Gannon to ask, then it's important we get the answer."

"Must we really?" He looked as if hoping she'd change her mind. Libby's face remained firm. He grimaced then took the lantern to a corner, rummaged through the long tools there, coming back holding a crowbar.

"This ought to do the trick."

She held the light as Jimmy wedged the bar into the seam. Wiggling it, he got a bite on the wood and pried it up. The wood creaked and the nails gave an awful squall. Libby glanced at the open window, worried Mrs. Tappermounty might hear.

Jimmy worked his way along the rim lifting enough nails for the bar to get a good grip on the lid and with a couple hard yanks it lifted enough to peer inside. Libby and Jimmy came together above the gap, the pale light falling upon the casket's secret. Libby was the first to speak.

"Sandbags!"

"Even this part is fake."

She stared at him. "I should have guessed. Dr. Blinker told me exactly what he was up to."

"He did?"

"This whole affair is nothing but an elaborate red herring, Jimmy. It's Dr. Blinker's story playing out in real life. John Steele has sent the crater monsters of Somerville on a fool's errand in order to vacate the town so that he and his companions might steal the Martian treasure."

"Martian treasure? John Steele?"

"Dr. Blinker's alter ego in his latest story."

"He wrote all this in a story, on purpose?" Jimmy asked.

"Not on purpose, I'm sure. They must have been planning this while he was writing *The Adventures of John Steele and the Crater Monsters of the Moon*. His subconscious simply used the plan for the plot of his story."

"Who are *they?*"

The pieces were coming together and Libby didn't like the picture being painted. "Dr. Blinker, obviously. Mr. Tappermounty has to be in on it, too. And I'm almost positive Sheriff Bainbridge is involved. He made sure to put the chip in his safe so that no one could closely examine it."

"And the strangers from the train?" Jimmy added.

"And the strangers," she agreed.

"Okay, if it is as you say, what is the Martian treasure?"

"It can only be one thing. The gold stored at the army depot. We need to tell Lieutenant Danforth right away!"

Jimmy lightly hammered the coffin lid shut and shinnied out the window.

Libby extinguished the lantern setting it out of the way. Taking care not to repeat the calamitous result of the last time, she made it safely through, with Jimmy's assistance. Jimmy closed the window and cast the crate back into the scrub to hide any evidence of their investigation.

Coming around the corner into the alley, Libby dug in her heels and came to an abrupt stop. A man had moved from the dark shadow of the shed to block their escape. In her haste, Libby almost ran into him.

"You two are out late."

"Sheriff Bainbridge," Libby gulped. She couldn't make out his expression, but if it reflected his tone of voice, it must have been hard and scrutinizing. She stammered. "We're just out for a moonlight stroll." That sounded lame even as said it.

"How romantic. But aren't your hands cold, Miss Barrett?"

"My hands?"

He held out her gloves. "I found these atop my safe. Maybe you can explain how they managed to get there?"

Caught! She stared at the indisputable evidence of her crime. There was no talking her way out of this fix.

Smooth as butter on a hot biscuit Jimmy said, "Oh, that's easy, Walt. I needed to check on some notes that I'd recorded in the minutes of the council's last meeting. Libby came along with me. She must have set her gloves aside and forgot them."

"Hmm. You check your notes with the edge of an ax, James?"

It was Jimmy's turn to stammer.

Sheriff Bainbridge said, "You, Miss Barrett, and me, let's take a little walk." His head hitched toward the steps up the side of the mortuary to Mr. Tappermounty rooms above.

"Oh, but I really need to go home now," Libby said.

The sheriff's hand moved and his revolver appeared, its hammer making three distinct clicks in the cold night air. "Move."

———

At his impatient knock, the door lock made a soft metallic click and a sliver of light fell across the dark landing at the top of the stairs, above the mortuary. Sheila Tappermounty's wary face appeared in the crack, her pinched expression expanding at the sight of Sheriff Bainbridge on the other side of her door. Her eyes narrowed sharply at the sight of Libby and Jimmy there with him.

"What-?" she began.

"Trouble," Bainbridge said, not waiting to be invited inside. He pushed past Mrs. Tappermounty with Libby in hand, roughly swinging her toward the settee and ordering Jimmy to sit as well. "And don't move an inch or I'll hog tie you!"

"You have no right to treat us in such a scurrilous manner!" Libby's trepidation had turned to hot anger as the shock of her sudden encounter with Bainbridge disappeared.

"I'll hog tie you, too, if you don't be quiet."

"What's this all about, Walt?" Sheila asked staring at the two of them upon her settee and then up into his face. "Why did you bring them here?"

"Caught them snooping around inside Woodrow's shed."

Mrs. Tappermounty drew in a sharp breath and shot them another look. Libby winced at its fierce impact. "Did they...?" She had no need to finish her sentence. Bainbridge was already answering the question.

"They opened the coffin. I heard them talking."

"What are we going to do, Walt?"

Bainbridge didn't answer. His silence speaking louder than words could have, his look of slowly hardening resolve turning Libby's blood cold. She could think of only one thing Bainbridge could do! She shivered and forced herself to analyze the problem rationally. If she couldn't overpower a tall, broad-shouldered man like Walter Bainbridge, she would have to out think him.

"For the moment we'll wait for Woodrow and Matthew to get here." Bainbridge glanced at the mantel clock. "It ought not be too long now, if all goes as planned."

"Was that Mr. Bartlow's job?" Libby asked. "To ride out to wherever it is Dr. Blinker and Mr. Tappermounty, and the man in the bowler hat, have gone while your golden chip fraud turned Somerville into a ghost town. And now that it has, your gang can swoop in unopposed and do the crime?"

"You're too clever by half, Miss Barrett."

"Libby's a newspaper reporter," Jimmy said, "and a darn good one. It's her job to uncover the truth."

Jimmy's encouragement emboldened her. "Whatever made you think you could get away with such an outlandish scheme, Sheriff?"

"So far we have," he noted calmly. "You two are only an unexpected problem we'll have to deal with." His unspoken treat was clear.

Libby pulled another arrow from her quiver and aimed it at Sheila Tappermounty. "You and your husband are two of the most respected people in Somerville. How can you countenance such a low deed as this?"

Sheila Tappermounty merely stared, her long, unhappy face giving no hint of what she was thinking. The somber look was similar to that which Mr. Tappermounty always wore. Libby did not know the mortician's wife all that well, and now, desperately seeking to draw the taciturn woman over to her cause, she wondered if Sheila Tappermounty had always worn the mien of a dour scarecrow, or had she once been a bright-eyed, gay young woman who over years of marriage had slowly taken on the dreary reflection of her husband?

With pale hands folded upon the simple blue gray dress, Mrs. Tappermounty's spine stiffened ever so slightly. It was a small movement that managed to square her shoulders beneath the thin brown sweater that she wore. Libby wished she could crawl inside the woman's head and poke around a bit to ascertain if her arrow had nicked a sympathetic nerve. There was no way to know from Sheila Tappermounty's expressionless face.

"Stoke up the fire, will you?" Sheila said finally, burnishing her thin arms beneath the sweater. "It may be a while yet. I'll put on some coffee." Mrs. Tappermounty went to the kitchen.

She's escaping. She doesn't want to face Jimmy and me knowing there could be only one solution to their *unexpected problem.*

———

The quiet thump of hooves came from his right, almost too soft for a man's ears, but Colby had heard it. The horse halted and looked toward the twin moonlit streaks running parallel to the road a hundred or so feet away.

"I hear him," Tom Gannon said softly. He loosened his coat and drifted his hand to the Colt's revolver beneath it. The black land lay heavy with scrub. Scattered patches of snow stood out like leprous sores. It took a long moment for Tom to pick out the rider moving through the shadows coming up the ravine from the culvert beneath the tracks.

Tom let go of a tight breath and worked the buttons of his coat back through their leather loops.

Cochise reined to a stop leaning forward a mite as if to stretch tight back muscles. His long blanket coat hung below his knees. One hand held the reins and the other gripped the short, double barrel gun across his saddle. "I expected you would come by soon, Tom Gannon."

"Now why would you be expecting that?"

"Eight shots. Far off. I know the voice of your rifle."

Tom grinned. "Comanches."

"Hmm. I think maybe so. I see their tracks. I think maybe a hunting pack."

"Well, they won't be stealing chickens anymore." Tom dipped into his pocket and withdrew the strand of red beads. "You lost these." He handed them across to Cochise.

The Apache transferred them to his own pocket. "No lose. I think maybe Tom Gannon need easy sign to read." Now it was Cochise's turn to grin.

"Not hardly."

Cochise inclined his head up the road. "Seven riders. The Death Shaman and Tooth Puller, and five more. One looks Indian but talks white man's words. I think maybe he loco."

Tom's tongue probed the hollow in his jaw. He remembered now where he had encountered that scent of spruce on the gum wrapper in his pocket. It had been on Tappermounty's breath the night Dr. Blinker had pulled his tooth. "What are they up to?" Tom wondered aloud peering at the darkness up the road. His view shifted back. "Ever hear any legends, Apache or otherwise, of a white buffalo that shits paddies made of gold?"

Cochise straightened unexpectedly and peered hard at Tom. "I hear many stories of such legends."

"You have?" Tom's surprise brought another grin to the old Indian's face.

"The stories, they begin not too long after the white man's whisky come to my people's lodges."

Tom laughed. "Now that you mention it, I might have even seen one or two of those white buffaloes myself the other night." His voice hardened. "Let's find out just what those seven are up to."

————

Half a mile east of Somerville the riders turned off the main Topeka highway and halted. The few scattered lights to the east reassured Warley Blinker that Somerville had taken their bait. Now it was only a matter of setting the hook and then skedaddling out of this bleak Kansas wilderness back to civilization. In the hills beyond the dark town, tiny, scattered flickers of campfires gave the impression that the sky had come down and touched the earth. Warley smiled. Human avarice was an amazing thing. Cousin Matthew's scheme had sounded incredible when he'd proposed it, but it had worked...so far. He flexed his fingers inside his double-gloved right hand, almost feeling the tumblers of the simple Victor safe falling in place.

Ahead of them a pair of moonlit streaks crossed Davis Road. Overhead a strand of #8 galvanized wire reflected the bright moonlight. Woodrow Tappermounty moved his wagon beneath the telegraph wire, felt about under the seat, and passed a pair of wire cutters to Snake on the seat beside him.

Snake stepped up onto the tippy seat and stretched his slight form, heels leaving the board. Snip-ZING the wire recoiled into the weeds on both sides of the road.

Snake sat down and returned the cutters. "Me thinks the singing wire no longer carries a tune."

Warley nudged his horse alongside Dr. Blinker's buggy. "We'll take it from here, Matt. You and Woodrow be sure you're not seen coming into town." His view shifted between the two men. "You've got your alibi, be careful not to trip over it. So long as Bainbridge is doing the investigation you'll be in the clear. No doubt the military will get involved. If they should question you, keep it simple, and don't say too much. There should be no reason you two should be suspected."

Dr. Blinker said, "We know what to say if anyone gets nosy. Woodrow and I met out there," his hand indicated a vague direction. "He was afoot on account of having his wagon and gear stolen. We came back to town together sometime after midnight."

"Right. Keep it simple and stick to it."

Tappermounty passed the reins to Askook, stretched out a leg and felt around in the dark for the iron step. He swung to the ground and told Askook to drive to the end of Davis Road and cut the wire to McPherson. To Warley he said, "When you're done with the wagon run it off the road someplace. That'll affirm our alibi. Set the horse loose. It'll find its way back to the stable."

Tony Donatalli said, "We're wasting time. Let's get going before someone comes along."

Davy Bartlow's sardonic laugh came from the dark. "No one is going to come along, Tony. That town snuffs out its candle soon as the sun goes down. All except Alice O'Meara's place on the other side of the tracks." He rotated in his saddle and pointed to the cluster of lights near the army depot. The depot itself looked lonely and dark except for a single lighted window in the barrack.

Tappermounty hefted himself up onto the buggy's seat next to Dr. Blinker. Warley said, "I'll see to it the gold gets split up evenly and that your three shares are buried where we've discussed. The five of us will make our way back to Philly separately, same as we came so as not to draw any attention." He peered at his cousin. "Give it some time for things to cool down before you retrieve it and start buying fancy new type-writing machines and other expensive gewgaws."

"No worry about that, War. Woodrow, Walt, and I are patient men. Besides, I already have one of those new type-writing machines." He smiled. "And I do believe our little adventure these past few days has given me an idea for my next story." His view drifted toward Tony. "And I think I know who I'm going to cast as the villain."

Sal caught his drift and laughed. Tony's scowl only deepened.

The cousins said good-bye and hoped they'd see each other again soon.

————

There had to be something Libby was overlooking! In all the novels she'd read as a young girl, escaping the villain came easily, organically even. The dashing hero bursting onto the scene at the last moment, the clever female working her wiles on the half-witted outlaw. A frown tortured Libby's face, Miss Penelope be damned! There was no simple breakout here, no silly leaping into a carnival basket and being carried away from the evil Crater Monsters. This wasn't fiction. She and Jimmy were trapped in Mrs. Tappermounty's parlor. Sheila Tappermounty sat erect in a straight-back chair, her painfully severe posture—Miss Penelope would have approved— reflected in the scowling creases at the corners of her mouth and unblinking eyes cold as chunks of gray ice. And in-between her and Jimmy, and the doorway to freedom, stalked the strong, scowling, and well armed sheriff.

Sheriff Bainbridge worked out his tension differently from Sheila. Libby had quit counting the number of passages his pacing was adding up to. Back and forth… back and forth…with an occasional pause at the window to move aside the curtain and peer at the dark alley at the foot of the staircase.

She forced herself to concentrate on the problem instead of the creak of floorboards beneath Bainbridge's boots. "My father will be worried. He shall come looking for me," she said. Bainbridge merely turned his silent scowl at her.

Libby elbowed Jimmy. He took the hint and said, "And my mother will come looking, too. Why, this very moment she is likely across the street at Mr. Suredor's house rounding up a search party."

Bainbridge ignored him and peered out the window. He turned abruptly from the window, suddenly animated, and said, "They're here."

Libby's breathing stilled.

"It's about time," Sheila said, sounding as if a heavy weight had suddenly been removed from her.

Footsteps sounded on the outside stairs; the door opened and Dr. Blinker and Mr. Tappermounty entered. The undertaker drew up short seeing Sheriff Bainbridge there.

"What are you doing here, Walt?" and then he understood. "What's wrong?" His view shifted from the sheriff to his wife.

Bainbridge pointed. "Caught them sneaking out of your shed," Bainbridge said.

"Miss Libby," Dr. Blinker croaked, sudden anguish in his voice, startled look upon his face.

"Damn," was Mr. Tappermounty's response.

Bainbridge said, "This changes things."

Dr. Blinker shook his head. "Miss Libby, why couldn't you have left this alone?"

"How could *you* have devised such a preposterous scheme and not expect the truth to be discovered?" Libby struggled to keep a tremble from her voice and her words composed. Tranquility was definitely not the emotion she felt.

Jimmy said, "You set the dominos falling with that moon story you wrote. Libby told me all about it."

"Me?" Dr. Blinker's eyes rounded. He glanced at his two companions and winced beneath their scrutinizing glared. "I did no such thing."

"Certainly not consciously." Libby forced confidence into her words. "Subconsciously, you took what you were planning to do here in Somerville, tossed it into a balloon basket and deposited it in the left eye of the man in the moon."

"Oh, stop this!" Sheila Tappermounty shot from the chair and stalked to the men, cowing them with a glaring scowl that would have made Libby recoil, too, had it been directed at her. "It's too late for blame making. What are we going to do about them?"

What could they do? Libby had known all along there could be only one solution to the dilemma she and Jimmy had forced upon them. They would both have to be silenced. Permanently. Libby shivered. There could be no other solution...except...

An idea that had been stumbling about the shadows inside her head stepped tentatively into the light. Seizing upon it, Libby moved a pawn into its opening position. "You could just simply let us go," she said, knowing the suggestion witless and would soundly be rejected.

Mr. Tappermounty's eyebrows hitched up. "Why might we want to do that?" he inquired.

"Allowing Jimmy and me to go free is the only way all of you will escape the hangman's noose." The boldness in Libby's voice had not been forced, but flowed easily now as that stumbling idea suddenly became clearer.

Dr. Blinker was the first to speak since the others

appeared too stunned by her naively to utter a word. "If we end it here and now, at best all we face are a few years of incarceration." Of the four of them, Dr. Blinker plainly was most distraught over the obvious solution to the *problem*.

Bainbridge said, "I have a different notion, Matthew. We take the two of you out into the hills, shoot you, and let the wolves and buzzards take care of the evidence."

The sheriff's solution cut away some of the supports beneath Libby's poise. She forced a smile and rose to her feet. She had to stand to forestall the trembling that would soon become impossible to hide. Hands clasped behind her back, she crossed her fingers. "The problem there, Sheriff Bainbridge, is that you, Mr. Tappermounty, and dear Dr. Blinker have already been exposed."

Sheila Tappermounty cast a worried glance at her husband. The undertaker's stoic face didn't change except for a slight widening of his eyes.

Libby took that as a hopeful sign and forged ahead, "You see, gentlemen...and lady...I have already written the story of your failed caper." It hadn't failed yet but Libby saw no reason to lighten up on the pressure. If she was going to tell a lie, she might as well make it a big one. "The story lays bare the crime and deception perpetrated upon the good folks of Somerville, and it names the three of you, and the two strangers who arrived by train Tuesday morning. I'm quite certain the exposé will be every bit as compelling as my essay that compelled the town council to build our new schoolhouse." Seeing she had captured their attention, she took a cue from Father's running commentary on Dr. Blinker's church presentation and paused for effect. "The exposé resides safely upon my desk and should anything happen to Jimmy or me, Father will discover it and put it to print, which will put the three—err, four—of you upon the hangman's gallows. Who knows, the piece might even be taken up by the New-York Times." Why had she added that last bit? It was all part of going with the flow.

Dr. Blinker snatched out his handkerchief and patted his brow. Mr. and Mrs. Tappermounty remained unmoved, staring like two scarecrows overseeing the ravens in the cornfield. And Sheriff Bainbridge? His scowl deepened considerably and his hand came to rest upon the grip of his revolver. "You've got it all figured out," he said.

To Libby's chagrin, Bainbridge did not sound at all intimidated by what she'd said.

Nervousness started her pacing; moving seemed to helped control the trembling she desperately wanted to hold back. "Figuring it out, Sheriff, was the easy part." If she couldn't intimidate Bainbridge with exposure, she'd baffle him with rhetoric and sowing doubt among his companions.

"Once I discovered the gold chip was paste, I asked myself who in Somerville had the tools and ability to produce such a fake? Only two men had furnaces and the skill. Bo Huffman and Dr. Blinker. I met Bo on the road on his way out of town to find the white buffalo, so it couldn't have been him. He'd been taken in by the ruse. That left the only other man with the expertise to make realistic items from metal...things like gold teeth?" Her view shot toward the dentist. "In a flash I realized that everything I'd seen of this silly gold chip caper had been described in *The Adventures of John Steele and the Crater Monsters of the Moon.*

"Not true!" Dr. Blinker blurted.

Libby laughed, "Dr. Blinker was the intrepid John Steele. You, sheriff, and Mr. Tappermounty, his brave companions. And as for Somerville? The town was simply removed to the moon and recast as crater monsters. And the treasure? That is clearly the gold kept in the army depot across the tracks. It was obvious, really." She had their attention. "Jimmy and I had only to confirm one final piece of the puzzle, and that we did this evening." She looked to the Tappermountys. "An empty coffin. The ploy has been exposed. Have I gotten it wrong?"

Bainbridge said, "Your cleverness will be your demise. It is true, but I don't intend to spend what years I have left milking cows and picking eggs on the prison farm in Lansing. So you see, Miss Barrett, we still have the problem, don't we?"

"*Au Contraire*, Sheriff. A bargain always has at least two parties. We get something and you get something. Your part of the bargain will be to allow Jimmy and me to go free. If no one is harmed, and that includes Lieutenant Danforth and his men, however few of them remain, then for our part, I promise not to publish the story I have written, nor will I mention a word of what transpired here tonight. In a few weeks and months, the tale of the gold chip will only be a painful memory, and the three of you will have quietly moved on and disappeared into the great western landscape." Libby glanced at Jimmy. "Is that okay by you?"

"Uh, yeah, I'll agree to that," Jimmy answered promptly, hardly in a position not to go along with Libby's gambit.

"Well, Sheriff?" Libby willed her voice to remain even as she clamped hard on her wrist to keep her hands from shaking.

"*Well*, Miss Barrett, I don't much care for the terms you're offering. I kinda like living here in Somerville and at my age have no wish to move on and *quietly disappear*. I'll stick with my plan. I like it better, and so will the wolves and buzzards."

Dr. Blinker stepped forward and declared, "You can't do this, Walt. We all agreed from the beginning that no one was to be harmed. I like Somerville, too, but I'm willing to move on if Miss Libby promises not to publish her story and our names."

Mr. Tappermounty remained silently stone-faced, his wife's expression chiseled from the same block except for a tick at the corner of her mouth. Libby had no clue what they were thinking.

Sheriff Bainbridge continued, ignoring Dr. Blinker's plea. "But now you've complicated things a bit more. No matter. It's a complication easily solved by the unfortunate fire that will burn down the *Somerville Independent* building tonight. Regrettably, no one survives it." His lips compressed ruefully. "I think that will do nicely. Clean and simple with all the loose ends tied up with a ribbon. No one will question a fire and it'll give the fine folks of Somerville another reason to build with brick."

Libby's calm dissolved into panic. "You can't do that! Mother and Father have no part in this. They can't hurt you!"

Bainbridge grinned. "I suspect that is the first truthful thing you've said, Miss Barrett. You have written no story, have you?"

Distant gunshots coming from the direction of the army depot turned Bainbridge's glance to the window and then to Dr. Blinker. "You should have known from the start this wasn't going to come off without someone being harmed."

———

Tom Gannon dismounted at the crossroad and studied the hoof prints; shod, freshly made. He moved a few paces and found the wider imprint of a wagon wheel.

His view lifted to Davis Road, its dark track vanishing in the night. Far off were the few lights of Alice O'Meara place, and beyond that a single dim point that marked the army depot, its buildings and corrals—the legs and arms of the place—lost in the darkness. The signs were plain enough to the old cavalry officer who'd earned his stripes a score and ten years ago tracking renegade Yankees and then hostile Indians. It may be nothing more than men out for a good time at Alice's Gentleman's Club. Tom frowned. He had a bad feeling about all of this. Miss Libby's story about a gold buffalo chip and the strangers off the train seemed too much a coincidence, and he was not a big believer in coincidences.

Cochise emerged from the shadows near the railroad embankment where he'd been searching, dragging a wire out in the weeds. Cochise's limp was more apparent now. Cold weather always made the ache worse.

Tom took the heavy wire and held it to the moonlight. A glint of bright iron showed a sharp edge. "It's been cut with a tool."

"They council here, cut wire, then go two ways." Cochise pointed down Davis Road and then toward Somerville.

"That's how I read it. The wagon and riders are making for O'Meara's place, or the depot, while the buggy, that would be Dr. Blinker, is returning to town."

"You want me follow Tooth Puller?"

Tom shook his head. "Whatever's going on here, Blinker will not want to appear involved. I'm guessing it's the other's who are up to mischief of one kind or another." Tom looked again at the distant lights. "But what sort of mischief might that be?"

Cochise said, "Army keep gold in fort."

"Danforth commands a small contingent. It would be

a bold move to try to take it, but then maybe there's more of 'em than these we've been following."

"Or maybe blue shirts all go away." Cochise pointed toward the distant hills where with a half hundred specks of light from campfires flickered.

"The gold chip might well be the fox, and those people the hound sent out to chase it."

"Not white man's whisky?" Cochise's mouth hitched up with little smile.

"Not whisky. Greed."

Three muted gunshots came quietly from the distant darkness.

"Sounds like they're making their move." Tom swung up onto Colby. Cochise stepped stiffly into the stirrup and lifted his bad leg over his saddle, setting the shotgun across his legs.

———

At the sound of those gunshots, Libby noted a sudden rise in Bainbridge's apprehension. Might they summon succor for her and Jimmy? Would they expose Bainbridge's, Blinker's, and Tappermounty's role in the crime? Her own anxiety ratcheted up when the sheriff's revolver came smoothly from its holster and its hammer clicked back with a sound that would chill the blood of the bravest man...or woman.

"Let's get this over," he said, his voice tight yet strangely calm, any emotion that he might have felt subdued in a manner Libby doubted she could have manage considering the magnitude of the crime he intended to commit. In all the years she'd known Sheriff Bainbridge he'd never come across as an evil man. Distant, yes. Brooding, too. Many times she'd thought him unhappy and regretful of a life misspent on failed adventures, but never had she seen the cold ruthlessness he'd revealed tonight.

"Not in my parlor," Sheila Tappermounty objected, plainly more concerned with saving her carpet than Libby or Jimmy's life.

"No, Walt! I won't permit you to harm these young people." Dr. Blinker sprang between Libby and the sheriff.

Libby secret-signaled Jimmy. Alerted by the small gesture, he stood cautiously and moved to her side.

"Out of my way, Matthew," Bainbridge snarled. "We both know it needs to be done."

"I will not move out of the way. This conspiracy is gotten out of hand. I ought to have known from the start it wasn't going to work."

"It's going to work fine," he shot back. "Just let me handle this."

"I won't permit it." Dr. Blinker thrust out a hand. "Give me that gun."

"I said I'll handle it!" Bainbridge swung the revolver against his Dr. Blinker's head. The doctor staggered and caught himself on the chair Sheila Tappermounty had recently vacated.

The time to make a move was now or never. Whether from sheer fear, or the result of some plan forming in that subconscious part of Libby's brain where such things incubate, what happened next felt so impromptu, she hardly realized what she was about until it was too late to alter the plan set suddenly in motion.

"Dr. Blinker," she said, pointing. "You've dropped your Waterman." As she spoke she bent, pretending to retrieve the prized fountain pen. So unexpected came her declaration and so natural her reaction to it that Bainbridge did not react to the sham until it was too late.

Libby lurched from her crouch, swinging her handbag

into Bainbridge's gun hand. The revolver gave a horrible blast the breadth of a cat's whisker near her ear and Dr. Blinker cried out. Ducking beneath the sheriff's arm, Libby flung open the door. A glance showed Jimmy moving, too, head and shoulders down. Like a Princeton football halfback, Jimmy slammed Bainbridge to the floor and then leaping to her side upon the outside landing they scrambled down the stair steps and out into the alley.

Behind them came a flash-bang that reflected off the rear of the Balin Shoe and Boot repair shop. Libby flinched. Any clear and rational thinking that may have remained with her vanished in a flood of raw, animal panic. Bainbridge fired again. In spite of the deep shadows his aim was spot on, or just damn lucky.

Jimmy grunted and staggered against the building

Libby spun in time to catch him before he slumped, his weight taking them both to the ground.

"Go!" Jimmy said.

"You're hurt!"

"Go, Libby. He's coming."

Bainbridge reached the last step, and then he, too, became one with the darkness. "Don't let him get you. It's up to you now to find help." Jimmy grabbed a support beneath the steps to the repair shop and pulled himself deeper into the cold gloom beneath them.

As desperately as Libby wanted to remain with him, to help him in whatever way she might be able, to stay meant certain death for both of them. She squeezed his hand and then moved out. The alley was too dangerous now with Bainbridge stalking the shadows there. Libby went the opposite direction, feeling her way through the narrow passage between Balin's establishment and the ice house next door. At the corner, Libby scanned the dark length of Lyman Road. Not spying Bainbridge, or anyone else upon the empty road, Libby dashed across it to the alley behind the Plains Hotel and hurried through the quiet dark. She had a plan now. First, inform the night clerk at the train station who could telegraph for the Doctor Brownlee at McPherson, and then advance to the army depot to aid Lieutenant Danforth as best she could.

Obscuring the more salient details these in plans was her desperate need to find help for Jimmy, and Dr. Blinker. The gunshot that had been meant for her still rang her ears. Dr. Blinker had been an accomplice in the whole nefarious gold chip business, but in the end he'd defended her and Jimmy. That brave act allowed for their escape, and might very well have resulted in his own demise.

When she reached the end of the alley where it spilled out onto Capital Road, clearer thinking had overcome the primitive part of her brain that had impelled her from the moment that first shot had exploded near her ear. She lingered in the shadows where she felt safe. The sensible thing to do was to return home by way of stealth and shadows. Libby vetoed that idea. Sheriff Bainbridge might be waiting there for her to appear, to carry out his threat to burn the building to its foundation with her and her family inside it. Disturbingly, Libby had no clue where the sheriff might be. He'd been as quiet in his pursuit as she'd been in her flight. So long as she stayed away from the newspaper office her parents would remain unmolested. Of that Libby was certain.

She studied the street from the corner of Murry's Meat Market. Was Bainbridge likewise observing from some dark nook waiting for her to make the first move…a hidden bishop positioning himself to take a knight? Is this how a deer felt sensing a predator on the stalk? Libby drew in a long breath and dashed across Capital Road, up the steps of the train station platform, and through the side door. Falling against the door, she slammed the locking bolt in place...and exhaled.

"Mr. Beltorie...Mr. Beltorie."

No reply from the night clerk who tended the key when Mr. Holmberg was off duty. Libby moved cautiously down the dim hallway to the quiet waiting room with its empty benches looking forlorn in the muted light of a single lamp. "Mr. Beltorie?"

Light showed under the door to the AT&SF station master's office. Libby slipped behind the counter, past the desk where the silent telegraph key resided next to a pad of paper and a stack of blank telegram forms bearing the Western Union's letterhead.

The door was unlocked, but no one inside. Libby was about to back out when she heard a thump. She whirled, giving a gasp at the sight of a bundled form trussed up with rope in the corner of the room, peering at her with bulging eyes, a cloth stuffed into his mouth.

"Mr. Beltorie!" Libby rushed to his side. "You poor fellow, what have they done to you?"

"Mumph flup glub mum."

"Oh, right, let me remove that." Libby worked the wadded handkerchief from his mouth. Mr. Beltorie drew a huge breath as if starved for oxygen.

"There were two of them with handguns," he blurted. "Thank goodness the waiting room was empty. I'd been receiving a wire from Topeka when the key went silent. Investigating the connection, I didn't hear them until a revolver appeared in my face. They forced me into the office and bound me hand and foot!" He sounded more miffed than frightened.

"It's the gold chip. Somerville has been played for a dupe. The white buffalo is nothing more than the carrot to draw the people out of town leaving the army depot, and the government gold, wide open for an attack."

Libby worked at the knots as she spoke. They were unyielding and tougher than walnuts.

"Something didn't smell right about that story," Mr. Beltorie said.

"You're more perceptive than most of Somerville's residents. It was a ruse to steal the army gold, orchestrated by Sheriff Bainbridge, Dr. Blinker, and Mr. Tappermounty. Blinded by the shine of gold the town fell for it in spite of impossibility of it." Libby had no success with the knots. Rummaging through the necessities in her hand bag, she chose the penknife over the nail file—she always kept the little blade sharpened—and began sawing at the ropes turning Mr. Beltorie's hands blue.

"You must send a wire to McPherson at once. Jimmy Winchell and Dr. Blinker are badly injured and need a-" She stopped. Had a door open? Were those footsteps? Was her imagination playing tricks.

A chill wind snaked along the floor and brushed against her hand.

———

His leg afire, a warm dampness was running into Jimmy Winchell's shoe. With one hand twisting the belt wrapped around his thigh to keep the makeshift tourniquet tight, he forced himself not to think about the blood he was losing as he made his way down the alley, grasping for support wherever his free hand could find it. He had lain in the shadows only long enough for Sheriff Bainbridge to stalk past the porch's supports. When Jimmy had thought it safe, he'd removed his belt and attempted to staunch the bleeding. His efforts weren't very successful. He needed help, and there was only one place he was sure he'd find it.

A darkening fog obscured Jimmy's thoughts and

blurred his eyes. He stumbled out onto Bridges Road and somehow managed to make it across to the boardwalk. The distance had not been great, but it felt a monstrous journey just then. He tumbled up the first step and almost fainted. Impelled by the memory of Libby fleeing from the murderous sheriff, Jimmy clawed his way up the steps. The buildings on either side of Paramount were dark except for one. Focusing on that single point of light in the black, enveloping fog, he willed himself to regain his footing.

Consciousness was swiftly slipping away by time his hand fell upon the doorknob, the door unlatched and he fell into the *Somerville Independent's* building.

Out of the swirling gloom came cries of surprise and the incoherent clamor of startled voices, among them he thought he heard his mother's cry? Jimmy wondered if he'd died, and decided he had not. His leg still hurt too bad. He was moving—being carried to be exact. Someone was turning the tourniquet tighter also.

"Oh Jimmy, Jimmy," It was definitely his mother's wailing.

"Let me take a look at this," another voice intruded. Male. Mr. Suredor?

"Jimmy, where is Libby?" That was Mr. Barrett.

His head cleared a mite when water touched his lips. "Sip it slowly," Mrs. Barrett advised. "You're going to be all right," she assured. Jimmy wasn't as convinced as Mrs. Barrett tried to sound.

"Oh Jimmy, Jimmy." A soft hand clutched his hand.

"Looks like the bullet went clear through. Missed the bone. I've seen worse," Mr. Suredor said. "Damn Blinker for running off on his damn fool adventure right when we need him."

Jimmy forced words to his throat. "Blinker shot. Tapper's rooms over mortuary," he managed to say.

"What about Libby?" Mr. Barrett demanded again.

"Sheriff after her. He wants to murder us."

"Bainbridge? He did this to you?"

Jimmy found it easier to simply nod. The fog was lifting a little, enough to make out the faces bent over him.

"We must find her, Harold!" Panic had swept aside the assuring tone in Mrs. Barrett's voice.

Mr. Barrett snatched his coat and hat off the tree and dashed for the door.

"Here, take this with you," Mrs. Barrett said.

He paused and looked at her. "That relic has seen neither ball nor cap since Appomattox. It'll take half an hour to clean and load even if I had the fixings, which I do not." He cast about and then dove into a corner flinging aside odds and ends. An old Stars and Bars on a flagpole crashed to the floor. A moment later Mr. Barrett reappeared brandishing a long sword sheathed in shiny steel.

"Be careful, Harold. Find our daughter!"

Mr. Barrett plunged out into the cold.

Mr. Suredor said, "I'll go fetch the Doc Brownlee from McPherson. One of you ladies keep this tourniquet tight. Wrap that wound and keep pressure on it."

Positions shuffled, but who stood where now, Jimmy didn't follow. The fog rolled back smothering him in a soft, black, comfortable nothingness.

———

Warley Blinker cursed, and for the third or forth time cupped his hands to his mouth warming his fingers.

The small depot storeroom offered a view of the rail yard and the dim windows of the train station across the tracks. Davy Bartlow gave an impatient growl and turned from the window. "'Victor safes' are a walk in the park.' You said so yourself. What's the problem?" Davy's nerves were growing rawer by the minute. There'd been gunshots from town. Others surely heard them, too. There wasn't supposed to be any need for guns if the break in had played out as they'd planned it. Davy glanced at the two soldiers on the floor; one bleeding and the other working desperately to staunch the flow. So far nothing had gone as planned.

Warley cut Davy a sharp look. "In this cold I can't feel the tumblers." His voice leveled and took an accusatory tone. "I had not planned on the cold." He glanced to the man on the floor. "If you hadn't been so quick-tempered with that gun, we could've forced him to open it."

Davy shifted his view from to Warley to the soldier. "He went for his gun. What did you expect me to do? Sing him a lullaby? Anyway, I owed him."

"Shut up and keep watch." Warley put an ear and his fingers back to the lock.

"Maybe that one's lying? Maybe he knows the combination, too."

The corporal tending the officer's wound cast Davy a panicky look. "I don't know it and that's the truth. Only Lieutenant Danforth knows the combination, and the commandant at Fort Leavenworth."

Sal, who had taken a position outside the door to watch the dark road in front of the storeroom, poked his head in and said, "Snake is back."

"Where's Tony?" Davy returned his attention to the window and the dimly lit train station across the way in the shadows of the empty rail yard.

Sal said, "He's still down by the corral. I seen him move a moment ago when the wagon come in through the gate."

"Damn," Warley cussed softly, brushing his fingers upon his coat.

Davy had a snide remark ready but held back. Railing the cracksman would only delay things longer. In spite of his own growing impatience, Davy knew that Warley Blinker was as anxious as they all were to finish the job and get down the road. Davy's thoughts halted. A shadow had passed by one of the station's windows. Someone had entered the station master's office where he and Tony had bound and gagged the night clerk.

"Looks like trouble on the way."

Warley glanced up from where his ear pressed close to the dial. He didn't speak, didn't break his concentration.

Davy said, "I'll take care of this." He hitched up his collar and moved out into the cold night.

———

Behind the door and pressed hard against the wall, Libby stopped breathing. The quiet footsteps from the waiting room halted just outside the office door. Mr. Beltorie, still hopelessly bound, stared at her. She caught his eye and shook her head. He understood her signal and averted his eyes...just in time. Someone cautiously pushed the half-opened door wider and the narrow gap between it and the jamb darkened. Sheriff Bainbridge came a step into the room, stood silently there for a long moment. Libby dare not breathe even though the stale air in her lungs had begun to burn.

"Sheriff," Mr. Beltorie blurted sounding relieved.

Bainbridge gave a soft growl. If he did nothing to free him, it would be plain to everyone that he was in on the crime. If he still hoped to cover his tracks and remain sheriff of Somerville and live out a peaceful and comfortable life with his ill-gotten wealth, then Mr. Beltorie would have to be shut up...permanently...as he had intended for Jimmy and for her.

Mr. Beltorie's mouth gaped and his eyes went suddenly huge. The blast from Sheriff Bainbridge's revolver answered her question. Mr. Beltorie jerked once and slumped. Libby stifled a cry, almost revealing herself. In spite of her pounding heart she willed herself to remain frozen there, behind the door, her thoughts terrifyingly clear. The ruthless demon that had possessed Sheriff Bainbridge would stop at nothing now until she had been silenced—and Jimmy, too, if he had not already succumbed to his wound.

She'd witnessed murder cold and calculated. Her head began to spin, every nerve in her body sparking at once. She felt faint. She needed to breathe! So desperate had her situation become that she was hardly aware of the door closing until the latch clicked. Libby exhaled and the tears came in trembling release. No. Not now! She swiped her eyes. It was too late to help poor Mr. Beltorie, and clearly she could be of no practical help to Lieutenant Danforth. She had no weapon to oppose them. Her only hope was to flee; to survive this nightmare and return to the fight with the only weapon she could expertly wield...the pen. Pen and ink would mete out justice against Sheriff Bainbridge!

Libby listened. All was quiet. Bainbridge had left the building, or was he laying in wait? Had he set a trap for her or was he indeed gone, resuming his search through Somerville's dark alleyways?

She spied a key on the station master's desk, tip-toed to it, and silently slipped it into the door lock, ever so softly turning the bolt. She heaved a deep breath and exhaled again. At least she felt a little bit safer. It would take time and a strong shoulder to burst through the stout door.

Moving quietly, she extinguished the desk lamp. Trying not to look at Mr. Beltorie's body, she crossed to the window and standing aside, peeked out at the dark rail yard. Empty as church on Monday morning. Libby slipped the window latch and raised the sash. Careful to avoid another window disaster as she had with Jimmy, she gathered her skirt, carefully hefted a leg and perched briefly upon the sill. Only then could she summon the will to gaze upon the body in the corner. "Poor Mr. Beltorie," she said softly...or had the words been only a thought?

She found footing on the platform outside the window and in an ungainly Miss Penelope *never-approved* manner, extracted herself from the window into the night.

There was no sign of Sheriff Bainbridge on this side of the station. So far so good. Moving swiftly along the station wall that shadowed the bright moonlight, Libby arrived at the corner and stopped to listen. She peeked around toward the front of the station and Capital Road, which lay dark and quiet a dozen or so yards farther on; a mere sprint across the platform and down the steps. She calculated her chances. Once across the road she could reach the Plains Hotel where she knew she could find help. Or, was Sheriff Bainbridge waiting for her just beyond the station's far corner?

There were just too many unknowns, but one thing Libby was certain of, she couldn't remain here shivering and undecided. She made up her mind to attempt the dash, and crept along the east side of the station. Poised for the final, desperate sprint, a distant pounding arrested her. It grew louder and vaguely familiar. Hoofbeats, yes, but more than that—the rapid, familiar cadence of a race-horse! Lightening Strike! A shape emerged from the cold gloom far down Paramount Avenue; a swift, sleek phantom pulling a tall-wheeled skeleton of a vehicle carrying a man bent to the wind. Mr. Suredor! The racing sulky came clearly into view. Libby was about to dash out and flag Mr. Suredor, but at that instant the nimble sulky swept around the corner, one wheel lifting off the road and then dropping firmly back as Lightening Strike propelled Mr. Suredor out of sight in the direction of McPherson.

Her sudden rise of hope crashed and faded as the ghostly sulky melted into the gloom and winter's chill seeped back deep into Libby's bones. Mr. Suredor's urgency appeared to border on panic. What could have driven him to such recklessness? Had bodies been discovered? Jimmy? Dr. Blinker? Were the few folks left in town alert to the crime in progress? A spark of renewed hope reversed Libby's decision to flee. News was in the making here. L. A. Barrett did not let danger get in the way when an important story was breaking right under her nose! Her reporter instinct began to take over and sharpen her thinking and subdue the primitive —yet wise—urge to flee.

A steel rod of determination stiffened Libby's spine. She looked back across the tracks to the army depot. She'd approach it employing stealth, aid Lieutenant Danforth if possible, and if unable to accomplish that, at the very least record the event upon the note pad in her hand bag so that the miscreants—Sheriff Bainbridge in particular—might be brought to court and hanged for their villainy!

L.A. Barrett, ace reporter for the *Somerville Independent*, was on the case! Her exuberance faltered. She must proceed with caution, she warned herself, aware that she was feeling a bit more bravado than good, common sense ought to dictate.

Libby came about and practically plowed over the

man who stood quietly behind her. "Oh!" By time the impulse to flee reached her muscles, it was too late. He'd clasped her wrist in an iron grasp and laughed.

"What a pleasant surprise, Cupcake. I thought I saw someone snooping about out here. Should have guessed it would have been the pretty newspaper reporter."

"Dr. Bartlow. Release me." Libby wrenched her wrist. His grip tightened.

"Why would I want to do that? You eluded me once. Now that I have you again I'm thinking the lovebird gods have given me a gift. Wouldn't want to make the gods angry, would we?"

"I shall cry for help."

"To no avail. No one will hear you. And if you do I'll slap those pretty lips so hard your head will spin."

The thump of footsteps came from the corner of the station, behind them. Sheriff Bainbridge stepped out of the building's shadows into the brighter moonlight, stopped and leveled his revolver.

Libby gasped and tried to break free of Bartlow's grasp.

"Move aside, Davy."

"I don't like what I'm seeing in your eyes, Bainbridge."

"She knows. She'll talk. I've got plans for my life and I won't let her ruin them."

"I've got plans, too. None so grand as life-long. My plans are more immediate, and pleasurable, and she's part of those plans."

Libby attempted again to twist free with no better results than the last time she had tried. "He murdered Mr. Beltorie. In cold blood," she said, her scorn untempered. The name obviously meant nothing to Bartlow, and the deed even less. He may not have heard at all for his attention was focused on Sheriff Bainbridge and the gun pointed at them.

Bainbridge said, "That's another reason why she needs to be silenced."

"I'm sure we can come to some arrangement that will satisfy both our needs." Bartlow transferred Libby's wrist to his left hand, his right hand lowering near his revolver. "But for now she is coming with me. Later we'll talk about your concerns." His voice hardened, his words suddenly challenging. "Unless you want to try your hand here and now."

"Bold talk, Davy, considering the only thing between you and a bullet is a bit more pressure from my finger."

Bartlow's short laugh sounded like chuckling deep in his throat. "Think about it, old man." He emphasized the *old man* part. "Twenty feet between you and me. You're standing in the light and I'm in shadows. You best make your first shot count 'cause I promise you to the grave you won't get a second one, and I don't miss."

Not wanting to be anywhere near where bullets might fly, Libby struggled against his grip. Bartlow wrenched her arm sharp enough to almost put her on her knees. Keeping his eyes on Bainbridge, he growled, "Try that one more time, Cupcake, and I'll throw you to him."

She stopped struggling, her view frozen upon Bainbridge as he pondered the situation. Slowly, the muzzle of his gun lifted and the soft click of its hammer lowering came across the cold distance. He shoved the revolver into its holster and said, "We'll finish this later."

As if out of some macabre, topsy-turvy Poe-ish story, circumstances had taken a queer turn. Libby's captor had become her protector.

———

Libby scrambled to keep up with Bartlow and Bainbridge; a toe catching a tie, a heel skittering down a cinder ditch as Bartlow tugged her ruthlessly through the rail yard toward the army depot's single lighted window. She was furious at being manhandled across the dark tracks. Maintaining her balance was a challenge; she had no time to think of escape. Even if she could break free, where would she flee to? A railroad yard in the dark of night was not a forgiving location for sprinting. As a little girl Libby danced upon the shiny rails like a mountain goat bounding across an impossibly steep rocky cliff. But she had done none of that since putting away her little-girl skirts…much to Mother's delight.

They reached the depot where two men were hauling a strongbox out the door, lifting it over the side boards of a wagon. It thumped heavily to the floor. One of them was tall and burley, wearing a bowler hat…*the second stranger from the train*! The other was familiar, too, yet it took moment to place the face that presently was not framed by a pair of long, half-frozen braids.

"You! You're the dead Indian."

He smiled instantly at being recognized and gave Libby an exaggerated bow. "For sooth, could it be the beauteous newspaper lady with the face of an angel? You have no idea the joy your presence gave me as I lay upon the floor drawing my final breaths. I lingered between here and eternity simply to gaze into the deep blue pools of your concerned eyes." His eloquence took a more pragmatic tone. "And I almost ruined the scene, thanks to you."

"Well pardon me."

He laughed.

The stranger from the train said, "What's she doing here?" By his authoritative tone Libby took him to be the leaders of this band of hooligans.

Bartlow said, "She's my little reward, War. I've had an eye on this trinket from the moment we stepped off the train."

Past the open depot door Libby glimpsed two soldiers. One lay upon the floor, the second bent over him appearing to be applying pressure. To a wound? With a start, she realized the wounded one was... "Lieutenant Danforth!" she cried and moved toward the door. Bartlow snapped her back to his side nearly dislocating her shoulder.

The one called War said, "Don't be a fool, Davy. We can't take her with us. She'll only cause trouble."

You're darn right I will be trouble. Libby's scowl would have given Miss Penelope apoplexy.

Sheriff Bainbridge said, "He's not thinking, War. Davy's in rut. But I got a cure for trouble."

War appeared only then to become aware of Sheriff Bainbridge's presence. "You're not supposed to be here."

"Plans changed." His head hitched toward Libby. "She poked her nose about and got wise to what was goin' on." His voice lowered. "There was a shooting and Matthew got in front of a bullet."

"Cousin Matthew! Is he...?"

"I suspect so. No time to see to him. She and her friend hightailed it and I had to go after them."

War struggled with the news. "That was the shooting we heard?"

"I think I hit James but couldn't find him. Probably crawled off. If we're lucky he bled out. She's the only one left who can cause us the most trouble now that she's seen our faces."

The "dead" Indian climbed onto the wagon seat and gathered the reins. "The pen is indeed mightier than the sword," he said, the deep and sonorous sound that emerged from his scrawny throat surprising Libby.

Bartlow's defiant grin melted a little. Was that resignation Libby saw? Bartlow gave a quiet sigh and with it a weight of finality settled in Libby's stomach. Her protector was about to relent and cast her to the wolf! Bartlow shook his head and said, "What an awful waste of such fine female flesh," and cast her into Bainbridge's clutches.

"It'll all work out," Bainbridge said, his powerful fingers sending needles into Libby's arm. "I'll tie up the loose ends here and tell how by the time I come upon the scene you were already gone. I tried to save Miss Barrett but it was too late. A sad situation, and I'll surely gather a posse and track the scoundrels who did this to hell and back…just as soon as enough men wander back into town."

"It wasn't supposed to turn out this way." War looked grim and sounded deeply disappointed.

"Like I said, plans change."

Libby struggled to rein in the desperation that clouded her thinking. If appealing to his honor would not work, then an appeal to his lust just might! "Don't leave me here, David. I'll go with you. I'll do whatever you want. I won't make trouble." The plea sounded perfidious even to her own ear. Lying had never come easy to her, even now with the stakes so high. Never mind that. The point was to stall them as long as possible in the faint hope that somebody might come to investigate the gunshots. The chances of that seemed slim since so few men remained in town to do the investigating. How could so many level headed men and women have so easily fallen victim to Dr. Blinker's gold chip deceit! Were folks really so naive and easily led astray? It did seem so.

David Bartlow shook his head and said, "If I even half-way believed you, Cupcake, I'd take you up your offer."

Bainbridge said, "No more talk. Get moving. Leave our shares where we'd agreed on...all three of them."

War said, "They'll be there." He called to the depot. "Sal, time to get moving."

A man emerged from the depot, shoving a revolver into a holster under his coat, up high beneath his arm. He looked at Libby and grinned. "She's a pretty one, Davy. I do understand what all the fuss was about."

And yet another man came out of the shadows from the direction of the mule stables. *How many desperadoes were there?* As he stepped into the light Libby was surprised by lines of his face. He looked to be a carbon paper copy of the one called Sal.

This latest arrival said, "I thought I heard something moving around out behind the barn. I didn't find no one."

"Probably an animal," War said, "No matter, we're leaving now."

He spied Libby. "Who's this? She coming with?"

"She's staying," Bartlow said regretfully.

The miscreants started for the horses tied to the hitch rail. In another moment Libby would be alone and helpless against Bainbridge's murderous scheme. A tidal wave of hopelessness rose up and threatened to drag her out into a sea of despair. Libby refused to let it happen! Now more than ever she needed her wits about her. *Think, girl!* She was not well-versed on the peculiarities of the male half of the human specie. Hitherto, the power of her mind had been focused on the more practical aspects of life—her career—but she did possess a keen female perception, and perhaps, like the "dead" Indian, a smattering of the dramatic, which she sometimes employed in the newspaper articles she wrote when attempting to sway—no, *to point*—readers in a direction she wanted them to look. She'd used the skill to a fine touch in her epic *A Monument to the Future* appeal for the new school-house. Men...even scoundrel men...might from time to time display a chivalrous streak if unexpectedly stimulated.

"Please don't leave me," Libby implored, and then teetered. Giving forth a weak cry and with a fluttering of eyelashes, she flung a hand to her forehead and fainted straight away in a dramatic swoon that would have taken her all the way to the ground if not for Bainbridge's hold upon her arm, which he refused to release.

The performance elicited a startled response from the desperadoes who reversed their retreat and gathered around her. Through slit eyelids Libby spied David's face. Sal and his doppelgänger came into view. It had been a fairly convincing performance, Libby thought, but at best would provide a reprieve of only a few minutes. She was pretty certain Sheriff Bainbridge would not be so bold as to murder her right here in front of five suddenly *stimulated* men.

"She's fainted." That was War stating the obvious.

"What ought we do with her now?" a voice whom she could not connect to a face wondered.

Bainbridge gave her arm a couple tugs. When Libby failed to respond he said, "Get on your way and I'll see to her."

Libby pleaded silently, *Please don't leave now.*

"You just can't shoot her when she's down," another objected.

"I said I'll take care of it," Bainbridge barked. He retained a firm grip on her arm as if he suspected her ploy.

Reluctantly one or two drifted off toward their horses and then the others followed, and with them went all prospects of delaying. Plainly, succor was not coming.

But then from out of the dark a voice cried out and

rekindled the dying ember of hope within her breast. "Libby!" it wailed. "Unhand my daughter!"

Father? Libby's eyes sprang open as Father dashed from around the corner of the depot, his old army sword thrust out, its plunging point aimed straight for Bainbridge.

Bainbridge's gun hand shifted toward him.

"No!" Libby cried, giving a mighty pull that unbalanced Bainbridge the instant his revolver roared. Unharmed and unimpeded, Father rushed forward until one of the doppelgänger tackled him to the ground.

Bainbridge cast Libby aside and moved a step to get a clear shot at Father.

"Put up the gun, Walt," came the command from the shadows; strong, confident, and deadly, and it immediately froze everyone where they stood. Tall, broad, and shaggy like a tough old buffalo, Tom Gannon stepped into the light and stopped a dozen feet from Bainbridge. The butt of Tom's Winchester rested upon his hip, it's barrel tilted up, Tom's finger curling the trigger.

Bainbridge went rigid and half turned careful to keep his gun turned away, clearly not wanting to provoke Tom Gannon. He considered the rifle and the manner in which Tom held it. It's meaning was plain to even Libby, who had not known very many dangerous men. It bespoke a readiness to attack yet a willingness to talk. A rattlesnake coiled yet not drawn back to strike.

"We can work something out, Tom." Confidence had curiously vanished from Sheriff Bainbridge's voice. From where Libby lay upon the cold ground she sensed Bainbridge grow taut, a spring winding tight, calculating his chance against Tom Gannon. Libby guessed at the thoughts racing through the sheriff's head. Could he beat Tom's hand? Had it not been Bainbridge who once said

Tom Gannon was too ornery to die? And had not father confirmed it?

"Drop the gun, Walt."

"We can talk."

"I have all night. You can talk yourself hoarse if you want. Why don't you begin by telling me about the body in the train station, bound hand and foot and shot execution-like. But first I want to hear the sound of that revolver hitting the ground, and your friends can all do the same."

Libby pulled herself across the ground a little way, opening the distance between herself and the two men and what must surely come next. War was stealthily backing toward the wagon where the "dead" Indian sat staring, the reins clutched in his fingers. One of the doppelgänger reached slowly under his coat. The other pulled Father to his feet and shoved a gun into his side. She was sure he wouldn't hesitate to harm Father. And David Bartlow? Libby cast about. Where was Bartlow?

Bainbridge eased around to face Tom. "There's gold enough for all of us. Matthew's dead. You can have his share."

"You kill him?"

"Not intentional. He got in the way of a bullet meant for someone else."

"It was meant for me and Jimmy," Libby said.

Neither man looked at her. A moment of quiet stretched out. Tom said, "Last time, Walt. Drop the gun."

"Not gonna do it, Tom. You and me, we're too old to start over. I'm not gonna finish my days behind bars or at the end of a rope." The tight-wound spring let loose the same instant the rattlesnake struck. Gunfire blasted the night and the snake was faster by a heartbeat. Bainbridge spun and hit the ground in front of Libby, his eyes wide, staring, and dead, his revolver clattering to the ground next to him.

The night exploded, blasting guns spitting fire. Libby flung her arms about her head. Past them she saw Tom Gannon working the lever of his rifle, his hand a blur. Any moment Libby expected to feel the deadly impact of a bullet...and then it was over. The night was suddenly dark and silent except for the ringing chaos of gunfire still lingering in her ears.

Libby unfolded, aware of a muddled discord of voices warning her that the battle wasn't over yet. The man called War lay against the wagon wheel, an arm caught in a spoke where he fell. The "dead" Indian still sat upon the wagon seat, his head turtled down between his narrow shoulders, his arms stiff as whalebone stays thrust toward the stars. Her view traveled and stopped. In the pale shaft of light from the depot doorway lay one of the doppelgängers, violently spun about and slammed to the ground.

The muddled voices were becoming clearer now as the discord inside her head subsided. Mr. Gannon's was saying, "I make no deals with murderers and thieves."

"You'll deal with me or he ends up like Tony and War," Sal said, his voice rising with alarm.

"Don't wish for anyone else to die, but if any hurt comes to Mr. Barrett..." He left his clear meaning unspoken. "We're all one heartbeat from a grave, mister, don't let tonight be your last one."

Libby's breath stilled. Sal had Father in a neck hold, using him as a shield against Mr. Gannon's rifle.

"Listen. I didn't hurt nobody, okay? That man in there, that was Davy's doing, not me. All I'm askin' is to get on my horse and ride and no one will get hurt." The alarm in his voice was rapidly being shoved aside by desperation.

Mr. Gannon's voice remained even. "You're not listening. I'll say it again and that will be the last. I make no deals."

Libby wanted to leap to Father's side but dare not move. There could be no escape from Mr. Gannon now. The desperado must have known, too. The only question was, would he harm father in a hopeless attempt to flee?

"Yo-you think I'm bluffing, old man?" Sal's voice rose like a Sunday morning alto casting the notes through the church ceiling and up to heaven. The gun at Father's side began to tremble.

The old Indian fighter's eyes hitched briefly and then came back. Tom Gannon's mouth took a set half between a grin and a snarl. "Looks like you have outmaneuvered me, mister." His sudden change confused Libby. "There's your horse. Set Mr. Barrett aside and I won't stop you."

"Now you're talking sense, old man. First you drop that rifle."

"I said I won't stop you, but if it puts you at ease—" He leaned the rifle against the building and took a step away. "Now set Mr. Barrett aside."

"Soon as I'm in the saddle I'll—" His words halted with a gasp, his spine suddenly stiff.

Cochise's voice came from the dark. "Two barrels. Buck shot. Make big hole."

Sal's eyes grew white in the moonlight. He dropped his revolver and raised his hands.

Weak-kneed, Father slumped. Cochise caught him in his free hand and steadied him. Mr. Gannon strode over, nudged the body of Sal's look-alike, and getting no response, bent for the revolver and flung it into the dark. He was taking no chances. He showed the same precaution with the man named War, and then turned to the "dead" Indian, head still ducked, arms still reaching, looking like a scrawny meat fork.

"Get down off there," Mr. Gannon ordered.

"Yes sir, yes sir. I's got no dog in this hunt, mister. I's jest a poor actor hired to play a role," he moaned, altering his diction from Shakespeare stentorian to timid, deep-south plowboy.

Libby pushed herself off the ground into a sit as Tom escorted the actor to Sal and sat them both on the ground where Cochise's shotgun would keep them obediently in place. Father appeared to have recovered from the ordeal and levered himself away from the depot wall where he had sought temporary support. Libby rose to go to his side. As she gained her feet an arm snared her from behind and cold steel pressed hard against her temple.

Mr. Gannon wheeled. He glanced toward the rifle leaning against the wall a dozen paces out of reach.

David Bartlow said, "Go ahead try for it. Cupcake here will be the first to get it, and then you."

Mr. Gannon showed Bartlow his empty hands. "I won't try to stop you, but you're going to let Miss Libby go." It wasn't a request but a plain statement of fact. There was that same grim set of his lips Libby had seen before, that same quiet confidence that was both reassuring and terrifying…and impossible to understand.

"Pretty bold talk seeing as your gun's over there." He backed toward the wagon. "Cupcake and me, we're going to take a ride and if I catch even a whiff of being followed you will be burying her alongside Warley and Tony." He shoved Libby against the wagon. "Up on the seat, sweetheart."

Libby glanced across the killing ground. Three men dead and she felt nothing. Her heart had gone cold. With pleading eyes, Father advanced a step, halting near Cochise where he held the other two beneath the deadly bores of his shotgun. The Apache appeared unconcerned, his steadfast attention ignoring the drama between Tom

Gannon and David Bartlow—a deadly tragedy in which Libby, unfortunately, was playing a leading role.

"I said get up on that wagon seat," Bartlow growled, his eyes locked upon the big man in the shaggy buffalo coat.

Libby gathered her skirt, probed the dark for the iron stirrup, and hefted herself up onto the wagon. Upon the footboard lay the tangled lines to the horse. She grabbed them up.

"How far you figuring to get in that rig?"

"Far away from here, mister. Far as I need to get." He called to his friends. "Sal, Snake, get our horses."

Sal stared at the shotgun at his chest and said, "I don't think he's going to let that happen, Davy."

Bartlow's impatience flared. "Tell your friend to back off, mister!"

There was that odd grin again. "I don't tell Cochise what to do, and he's gentleman enough to return the favor."

"You want her dead?" Bartlow shrilled.

Libby quietly untangled the reins. Although Bartlow's gun was aimed at her, his attention remained upon Mr. Gannon. Libby bristled at the implication that a mere woman could pose no real threat to him! And then suddenly a small grin moved to her lips. Bartlow's arrogance was opening a path for Libby's queen to capture his unsuspecting king. Startled, she realized that the grin shaping her own lips was the same look of confidence she'd seen on Tom Gannon's face, and suddenly she understood.

"The way I see it," Mr. Gannon pointed out, "Miss Libby is the only reason you're still breathing."

Bartlow glanced at Mr. Gannon's Winchester, out of reach. The game board looked to be his to command. He had declared *check* and now would move to *checkmate* the

King. He stepped toward the wagon and said, "I believe we've talked too much. Time to put it to bed." Bartlow's words sounded bold but a slight waver in his voice telegraphed uncertainty. Was it that quiet boldness in the old warrior's eyes suddenly putting a big question mark atop Bartlow's next move?

As Bartlow moved closer to the wagon Libby played out a length of rein recalling a similar situation with a buggy whip yesterday. The gunman's attention was fixed upon the Mr. Gannon. He'd discounted her as a threat, and that's often the precise moment a pawn sneaks in to capture the knight.

She lashed out with a whipping strike to Bartlow's face and at the same time dove off the far side of the wagon. The desperado lurched at the slap of cold leather. Instinctively knowing where the real threat would be coming from, he fired at Mr. Gannon. Libby hit the ground in time to see Tom sweeping back the heavy buffalo coat. His gun leaped out and blasted. Bartlow fired again. Tom's gun kept talking as the big man strode forward, blasting the night with orange tongues of deadly fire. Bartlow jerked from the bullets ripping through him. He went to his knees. The gun dangled a moment from one finger, fell, and David Bartlow followed it to the ground.

Mr. Gannon came on another step and stood peering down at Bartlow. Then like an old winter tree in the wind, he swayed. His fingers clutched the shaggy coat and he, too, went to his knees, catching himself at the last moment before collapsing.

At the fall of Tom Gannon, Libby's world trembled.

DAY SIX
SATURDAY

In that hazy realm between sleep and wakefulness where dreams and reality merge, the impossible may appear normal, the inanimate sentient…and vengeful. The inanimate in this case is a chair with a wicked attitude and prodding cat claws. Libby shifted away from the sharp attack. The chair responded with lobster pincers to her neck. Another adjustment exposed a hip to which the chair immediately produced a hard lump upon its once smooth seat. Enough of this!

Giving a soft groan, Libby ran up the white flag casting aside the tattered vestiges of sleep. She straightened upon the chair, which innocently had become…a simple chair again. Her hip screamed; a reminder of the tumble she'd taken off the wagon last night.

The dawning sky past the windows was streaked soft, salmon pink while the world that pressed against the glass panes remained dark. Shadows gathered in the corners of the long room, beds and tables indistinct in the trembling glow of four wall lamps needing their wicks trimmed.

Memories roared back.

Mr. Wilson and Keavy had been the first to arrive, drawn to the army depot by the gunfire. Mr. Wilson sent Danny to rouse the town—what remained of it to rouse—while he, Father, and she began moving the wounded by means of battlefield stretchers into the nearby barrack where beds, and a reliable stove made tending them possible. Sometime later Dr. Brownlee arrived from McPherson. By then Jimmy and Dr. Blinker had been brought over. Dr. Brownlee had his hands full.

Libby looked at her watch. Five-ten. Out of routine she gave the stem a dozen winds and then rose from the chair and pressed a hand against the ache in her side. She rotated her tight neck. Four of the six army beds were occupied. Mrs. Winchell sat at the head of one of them. Libby went to her.

"How is Jimmy?" Libby asked. He looked wan in the poor light, eyes closed, head sunk deep in the pillow, but at least his breathing was regular.

Mrs. Winchell didn't look much better. She was exhausted having sat all night at her son's side holding his limp hand. She said, "Now that the bleeding has stopped, Doctor Brownlee thinks he's out of the woods but it will be a long recovery."

"I was so worried."

Mr. Suredor said, "So were we all, Miss Libby." She hadn't noticed him standing nearby. "Jimmy will be all right," the stableman said confidentially and placed a gentle hand upon Mrs. Winchell's shoulder. She gave it a brief squeeze and then resumed her grip on her son's hand.

Next bed over, Lieutenant Danforth slept. Well, he appeared to be asleep. Dr. Brownlee held his wrist counting pulses when Libby came alongside and inquired as to his condition. At the sound of her voice, Lieutenant Danforth's eyes opened and he grinned.

"Ah'm in tall cotton and sitting in the middle of a watermelon patch."

Libby laughed…and it felt good. "That is wonderful news, Lieutenant."

"And there is more. Received a letter yesterday informing me Ah am to be promoted to Captain and to be transferred to Fort Sheridan, in the town of Lake Forest, Illinois."

"That *is* good news. Bully for you, Lieutenant…I mean Captain."

He looked at her, a sudden, strange yearning in his bright blue eyes. "Is it?" he asked unenthusiastically. "Perhaps."

His reaction stirred an odd emotion inside her that she did not wish to examine too closely. She smiled, touched his arm, and turned to the next bed where a sheet covered a body head to toe.

Dr. Brownlee came alongside her. "I did what I could. He passed during the night."

"Poor Dr. Blinker." Libby's throat constricted, her eyes suddenly stinging. "I shall miss your quick smile and your tangled metaphors. I wish you happy adventures on whatever far off worlds you find yourself." For a quiet moment only the ticking of the wall clock intruded upon her sadness.

"He was lucid before he passed. It happens that way sometimes. He asked me to give you this." Dr. Brownlee's hand dipped into a pocket and came out holding Dr. Blinker's Waterman Ideal Fountain Pen. "He said you would appreciate it and have much better use for it than he will where he is going."

Choking back emotion, she said, "Thank you."

The final bed held Tom Gannon. The big man lay bare-chested and bandaged, his eyes shut.

Libby and Dr. Brownlee stood on either side of the

bed. She spoke not in words but gestures; a quiet gulp, a small sniff, a gentle hand upon the old man's sparse gray head.

Dr. Brownlee said, "He's a tough bird."

"His breathing is so shallow."

"That's the laudanum. I dosed both him and Mr. Winchell. Neither one are feeling pain…for the moment. I think he's going to pull through just fine. Mr. Gannon had an angel sitting on his shoulder last night."

Libby reviewed the scene still fresh in her memory. The rush to move the wounded upon battlefield stretchers, Dr. Brownlee's arrival. His assessment—Larrey's Triage, he'd called it—a new phrase to her. And then the surgery with Ava Pickering and Keavy Wilson assisting. The battle to save lives was waged long into the night. Father had remained there helping, too—at least until Libby had fallen asleep in the chair. Looking about now, she realized he had departed sometime during the night without waking her.

Dr. Brownlee reached for a tin cup on the bed table and plucked out a smashed chunk of lead. "Thirty-two caliber would be my guess. Hit the pocket of that buffalo coat he was wearing. It passed through two layers of buffalo hide and fur, a leather belt, and at least three inches of adipose." He grinned. "That's good, old fashioned fat to you. Kept the bullet from puncturing an intestine." The grin became a grimace. "Would have been a much different story if it had. We'd have lost Mr. Gannon, most likely."

That startled Libby, and the words she heard herself speaking came unexpected and unedited. "Lost him? Not Tom Gannon. Tom Gannon is too ornery to die. The Apaches tried. Rattlesnakes and General Grant tried. They all failed. What chance does a little thirty-two caliber bullet have?"

Her proclamation made Dr. Brownlee smile, then chuckle.

———

A buttery February sun in a bright columbine sky welcomed Libby when she finally emerged from the impromptu barrack infirmary and started home. The warmth upon her shoulders lifted her spirits and the terror of last night faded into the hopes of a new day. The road, she noted as she crossed over to the west side (for she still had one more task to tend to), was dry and finally free of snow. It had been less than a week ago that she'd battled the winter monster to the front door of Wilson's Barbershop where the strange journey of the gold chip had begun.

Coming up the street were Bo Huffman's wagons and kin. Plainly they had seen the folly in their hunt for the white buffalo. Bo gave a wave from the high seat as he passed on his way to his blacksmith's shop. She spied the Blatz brothers leading a mule along Lyman Street. People were beginning to straggle back into town. Libby had suspected it would not take many nights sleeping out in the cold before the folks of Somerville began to see the absurdity of their quest.

Libby turned into the sheriff's office. Two of the three jail cells along the wall were occupied...probably for the first time in many months. The Tappermountys looking gray and glum occupied one of them. Sal the doppel-gänger and Snake the "dead" Indian sat on the floor of the second cell. Heads lifted and eyes shifted when she entered and stopped to return their gazes. No words, just stares. The undertaker and his wife looked forsaken and desperate. Seeing them like that sent a sharp twinge into Libby's heart. She turned away.

Cochise had agreed to take on the job of temporary jailer until deputy Toby Snyder returned from his white buffalo hunt. Cochise sat at the desk and appeared to have comfortably taken possession of the office. He leaned back in the chair, his feet propped up upon the ink blotter exactly as Libby had observed Sheriff Bainbridge doing many times. She'd seen father do the same. It must be a man thing. Plainly they had not been schooled in proper office decorum by Miss Penelope.

The Apache grinned at her from around one of Sheriff Bainbridge's fat cigars. The desk humidor's lid stood open and half a dozen cigars bulged Cochise's shirt pocket.

Libby said, "I see that you have all well under control here."

Cochise plucked the cigar from between his lips. "No problem." He lifted the cigar. "Good smoke. You want?" He snatched one from the humidor and presented it to her.

Libby thanked him but demurred. He shrugged and jammed the cigar into his shirt pocket with all the others.

"I just stopped by to let you know that Dr. Brownlee expects Mr. Gannon to recover from his wound."

"Hmm." Cochise shifted his boots on the blotter and rotated the cigar between his lips apparently enjoying the tactile sensation. He inhaled and blew a spectacular smoke ring at the ceiling.

"Well, aren't you pleased to know Mr. Gannon is going to recover?"

"Am pleased, Miss Libby Barrett. Tom Gannon, him make good amigo, him make very bad ghost."

Libby didn't quite know what to make of that. She felt suddenly uneasy standing there, the focus of his inscrutable gaze. "Ahem. Well, I need to go home now to learn how Mother and Father have fared throughout last night's ordeal."

Cochise snatched another cigar from the humidor and extended it to her. "Give to father."

"Um. Okay. Thank you, Mr. Cochise. You are being quite generous with the sheriff's cigars."

Cochise grinned. "Sheriff no need 'em now."

———

The newspaper office had the disheveled look of a whirlwind having blown through. Mother was on her knees scrubbing at a dark stain when Libby came through the doorway. Mother sprang from her penitence and engulfed Libby in a suffocating hug. "I almost lost the both of you last night."

Stooped behind his desk gathering scattered papers, pencils, and books off the floor, Father said, "Dr. Brownlee claims we were surrounded by angels, Dorothy." Father had already told Libby all about Jimmy's bloody arrival as she and he had helped transport Jimmy to the army barrack.

Libby peered at the mess. "How can I help,"

"No need," Father said, depositing an armload of papers on the desk. He sighed and fell wearily into his chair. "Just got to put it all back in order." He sighed again. "I needed to sort though all this anyway. Circumstances have forced my hand."

Libby hung her coat and stepped to her desk avoiding the prominent bloodstain Mother had attempted to expunge. "Folks are coming home. I saw Bo Hoffman and his wagons this morning. The Blatz brothers, too."

"I suspect we're soon to experience a groundswell of disappointed treasure seekers. They'll be feeling foolish and want to know what happened." Father paused. "You will need to write the true account of The Gold Chip. The people need to know."

"I'll do my best." She lowered herself into the desk chair. "But first I must carry myself upstairs and put myself to bed." Her exhaustion suddenly became over-powering.

Toting the scrub bucket to the back room, Mother said, "We all need to sleep. This mess can wait. Hang the sign in the window, Harold."

"Yes, dear."

Libby heard Father's shuffling footsteps, her thoughts growing hazy, drifting toward dreams. She may have briefly fallen sound asleep when Father's voice startled her awake. "I discovered this letter beneath a stack of papers. It's addressed to you from the editor of the *Chicago Daily Tribune*. I wonder what it is about?"

Libby remembered receiving it from Jimmy at the post office. That seemed so long ago now. She slit the envelope with her opener and drew out a single sheet, typewritten, bearing the *Tribune's* letterhead. "It's from the editor, Mr. Medill! He says he read *A Monument to the Future* and was so inspired by my writing that he is inviting me to attend The Chicago Columbian Exposition this May…at the newspaper expense…and he hopes I will write a 'crackerjack'—that's his very word—a crackerjack series of articles for the Tribune like the ones I wrote for the *Independent*."

"Oh my, Elizabeth Ann. Does that mean you will be leaving Somerville for Chicago?"

"I…I don't know. I suspect it might."

Father did not look pleased. "Am I to be losing my Ace reporter?"

"It's such a grand opportunity, Harold. And there are so many young gentlemen in Chicago!"

"Will you accept his offer?" Father asked.

Libby reread the letter. "I shall have to consider it. As Mother says, it's such a wonderful opportunity."

"Yes it is, indeed," Father reluctantly agreed. "Chicago is a bustling town, a lot different from *Nowheresville*, Kansas."

Libby brightened. "Yes it certainly is."

"Hmm. Before you pack your suitcase and fly off to the big city, I expect you to a write *crackerjack* story about the Gold Chip for the *Somerville Independent*."

"Of course, Father. Oh, by the bye, do you happen to know where Lake Forest, Illinois is located?"

A LOOK AT: THE OUTCAST SERIES

FATE THREW THEM TOGETHER.

They are not wanted where they come from. They are not welcome anywhere. They are outcasts, rootless and friendless, until luck or destiny throw them together.

A former Apache scout shunned by his tribe, an ex-Union Army major, a former Confederate captain, and two army deserters, all forced to band together to stay alive.

Can they bury their anger and work together long enough to do what they have to do? It is no easy task, because even if they manage not to kill each other, there are plenty of others eager to do it for them.

"Fans of westerns should give this one a read — Hirt is a talented and exciting western author that shouldn't be missed."

The Outcast Series includes: Outcast Brigade, Black Justice, War Hatchet, and Pistols and Powder.

AVAILABLE NOW

ABOUT THE AUTHOR

Douglas Hirt was born in Illinois, but heeding Horace Greeley's admonition to "Go west, young man", he headed to New Mexico at eighteen where he earned a Bachelor's degree from the College of Santa Fe and a Masters of Science degree from Eastern New Mexico University. During this time he spent several summers living in a tent in the desert near Carlsbad, New Mexico, conducting biological baseline surveys for the Department of Energy.

Douglas Hirt drew heavily from this "desert life" when writing his first novel, DEVIL'S WIND. Doug's novel, A PASSAGE OF SEASONS, won the Colorado Authors' League 1991 TOP HAND AWARD. His 1998 book, BRANDISH, and 1999 DEADWOOD, were finalists for the SPUR award given by the Western Writers of America. Doug's 2015 novel, BONE DIGGER, won Western Fictioneers's PEACEMAKER AWARD for best novel.

The author of over forty novels, short stories and non fiction, Doug makes his home in Colorado Springs with his wife Kathy. They have two grown children, Rebecca and Derick. When not writing or traveling to research his novels, Douglas Hirt enjoys collecting and restoring old English sports cars.